STILETTO

Also by Billie Sue Mosiman

Widow
Night Cruise

STILETTO

Billie Sue Mosiman

HEADLINE
FEATURE

First published in Great Britain in 1995
by HEADLINE BOOK PUBLISHING

A HEADLINE FEATURE hardback

10 9 8 7 6 5 4 3 2 1

British Library Cataloguing in Publication Data

Mosiman, Billie Sue
Stiletto
I.Title
813.54 [F]

ISBN 0 7472 1361 5

Typeset by Avon Dataset Ltd, Bidford-on-Avon, B50 4JH

Printed and bound in Great Britain by
Mackays of Chatham PLC, Chatham, Kent

HEADLINE BOOK PUBLISHING
A division of Hodder Headline PLC
338 Euston Road
London NW1 3BH

Everybody's a mad scientist, and life is their lab. We're all trying to experiment to find a way to live, to solve problems, to fend off madness and chaos.

David Cronenberg, *Cronenberg on Cronenberg*

Change begets a change. Nothing propagates so fast. If a man habituated to a narrow circle of cares and pleasures, out of which he seldom travels, steps beyond it, though for never so brief a space, his departure from the monotonous scene on which he has been an actor of importance would seem to be the signal for instant confusion . . . The mine which Time has slowly dug beneath familiar objects is sprung in an instant; and what was rock before, becomes but sand and dust.

Charles Dickens, *Martin Chuzzlewit*

ACKNOWLEDGEMENTS

I would like to thank some special people for their help and advice, loan of reference books on organized crime, gentle encouragement, ideas and love.

Mr husband, Lyle
My brother, Brent
Richard Ferguson
Jodi Berls
And all the nice folks I know on the Genie Network.

1

Geneva, Texas

'We're not far outside of Dallas,' Jake Mace said to his father. Tony had called from Las Vegas. The cellular car phone had been his idea.

'Ask him if Hugh knows some babes,' Byron Epson said from the passenger seat.

'Byron wants to know if Hugh will get us dates in Houston.'

'*Babes*,' Byron repeated. 'We don't have time for *dates*.'

'He says Hugh will work something out,' Jake reported. He turned his gaze back to the highway. 'Okay, don't worry, we're fine, Dad. I'll talk to you tomorrow.'

When Jake disconnected, Byron let out a whoop and turned up the volume on the CD player. 'Babes!' he screamed at the windshield. 'Awwwwright! We're gonna lay some pipe in Texas tonight!'

Jake grinned at his friend's enthusiasm. Byron liked food and girls. Well, he liked girls best, of course, who the hell didn't, but food was a close front-runner. Between Byron's feet on the floorboard sat a white paper sack crammed with pastries, candy bars, and bags of potato chips. He ate something every hour of his waking life. Jake thought that might be why he was so tall. He stood at least six inches taller than Jake. Walking down a street, hands stuffed in his pants pockets, Byron reminded Jake of a big gawky crane.

The tranquil Texas summer day waned, light shifting to the west and dying through various luminous shades of rose and peach. Ahead, in the far distance down the straight highway, as if Jake stared into a tunnel across the flatland, the day dimmed from misty blue to a steadily darkening purple death just at the rim of the horizon.

They were on their way to New York City. The thought was like a candle flame burning in Jake's mind, constant and throwing all else in his life into unimportant shadow. He hadn't been back since he was twelve and the city at that time had dwarfed him. The streets had been filled with cars, trucks, and pedestrians jockeying for position. Hustle, bustle. Racket that made him breathe fast and pant and wake up in darkness longing to be out on the street, in the midst of the seething chaos.

Since that one visit, at night in his bed in the quiet residential neighborhood just outside Las Vegas, Jake imagined he could hear New York rumbling at the back of his head, like an old whore desperate and hungry and calling to him. Times Square, Fifth Avenue, Broadway, Greenwich Village, Central Park. These common tourist areas were all he knew. And all he ever cared to see again, he thought, though he admitted there were at least a million avenues and backwaters in the city he yet needed to explore.

For six years he had wanted to experience the city again; a dream come true. For his eighteenth birthday, Tony said he could drive there in the new car, the Dodge Viper, another fine present from the greatest dad in the world. His father's only warning was to watch his back. The road was dangerous.

It was Jake's idea they zip down to Houston for a visit with his Uncle Hugh, pick up some girls for the night, and then take Interstate 10 over to Florida and move up the seaboard to the city of his dreams.

It was a primo drive from Dallas to Houston anyway and Jake could make the low-slung Viper sing like a chariot on fire along the yardstick highway that lay bordered by flat fields and vast green pastures dotted with longhorns and creamy white Brahmas.

Byron had a CD by Nine Inch Nails with the volume loud as it would go without blowing the Bose speakers. The windows were down, the air smelled of new-mown hay, and Byron had a perpetual grin plastered on his face. Even with that big Jewish nose taking up too much air space, Byron looked handsome as hell when he grinned like that.

'How long we been gone?' Jake yelled. 'Four days or five? I'm losing count.'

2

Byron reluctantly turned down the stereo volume control. 'It matter? Four, five, it doesn't matter. We don't have to be back in Vegas any certain time, your dad said so, and hey, mine don't give a rat's fart how long *I'm* gone.'

'I was just wondering. Is this Tuesday or Wednesday?'

'What you got to know for? Won't Hugh be home when we get there?'

'Yeah, sure, but I was trying to figure what day we'd hit New York. I don't want to miss spending the weekend in the Big Apple.'

Byron thought it over, the trouble of calculation reflecting in a fierce concentrated stare at his right hand, held in front of his face. His fingers ticked off the days. 'We left Saturday. Sunday, I had porterhouse.'

Jake smiled. Food again. Meals served as a calendar. Jake figured his friend ate as much as two fat people, but where it went, unless it was into Bryon's long legs, who could guess.

'Monday I had that wild spicy Indian food, remember? It was so hot I had to have a pitcher of water to wash it down?'

Jake nodded, remembering Byron gulping glass after glass, ice and all, his knobby Adam's apple working double-time like some kind of mechanical gear and lever system.

'Tuesday I got barbecue ribs. Stack of them so big I could hardly finish. Great sauce.' He turned to Jake. 'You liked that sauce, didn't you? Wasn't it better than what we find in Vegas? Of course the Sahara has pretty good ribs . . .'

'Yeah, it was good.'

'Okay. Where was I? Oh yeah, Tuesday was ribs. So! That makes this Wednesday. Which reminds me. I'm hungry as hell, when are we gonna stop?'

The sun was at their backs so that the Viper raced its own elongated shadow. The digital clock read 5:28. Traffic had thinned the farther they drove from Dallas until now the highway belonged almost solely to them. Jake pushed the speedometer up to eighty, feeling an adrenaline rush with the accelerated speed. The power under the hood seemed to radiate through the steering column into the wheel, into his hands.

'I'll get off soon and find a restaurant. I'd like to be in Houston tonight sometime. We don't want to fuck around too much.'

Byron reached for the radio, but before turning up the music again he said, 'We leave Houston in the morning, you drive flat out, we could hit the east coast two more days. That would make it . . .' He paused, the calculating frown back between his eyes. ' . . . Saturday and then up to New York.'

'Shit,' they both chorused, then laughed.

Jake said, 'We're going to miss the weekend in the city. No way we can get there earlier. I make this baby fly and we still can't make it any faster.'

'Maybe Tony will tell you to stay the week.'

Jake knew his father would suggest it if the boys really wanted to. 'I could use a whole week there. That's what we'll do. We won't start back until the following Sunday. I can use the credit cards for more ready cash.'

The sun had died swiftly and dark dropped over the long empty fields on both sides of the freeway as if someone in the sky had pulled a switch. The automated headlights flicked on of their own accord, responding to the lack of sunlight. They cut through the dark like laser beams, paving the way.

'Let's take this exit,' Jake said, swinging into the exit lane. 'Geneva. Maybe they have a decent place to eat.'

'Awwwright!' The car surged with voice and music as Byron turned the volume to max. He got into Nine Inch Nails with his shoulders, jamming all the way down to his seatbelted waist. He looked like a long-necked goose with its feet caught in a trap.

Jake didn't know the cop was behind him until he was slowing for the stop sign and he saw the blue bubble lights washing over the interior of the Viper.

'You boys going to a fire?'

Jake hated that tone of voice. The Law. Man, they *always* used that voice. 'No sir,' he said, keeping his own voice steady. Trying to be polite. Trying to get out of this without stirring any shit.

'You were doing sixty-two in a forty-five. You know that? Got you on radar. What is this car, anyway, something new? I never saw one before.'

4

Jake said, more than a hint of pride in his tone, 'It's a Dodge Viper. They don't make too many of them. It's not an assembly line model.' He could have added: This car is worth more than you make in ten years, Troop.

'That so?' There was displeasure creeping into the cop's attitude. Jake saw it and wished that for this encounter he was driving a Camero or a Mustang, some kind of regular young-guy car, *anything* but the Viper.

Byron fiddled with the Nine Inch Nails compact disk he had ejected from the CD player. The luminous sides picked up blue light and spun it into silver. He kept his head down.

'How 'bout you boys getting outta your fancy vehicle?'

Jake swiveled his head to look up at the trooper. He saw the gut, the wide black belt cutting into it, the tan material stretched taut over the chest. Badge. Gun. Night stick. The guy was decked out like crazy. Loved his job. Probably spit-shined the brass on his belt buckle every single night while he watched *Cops* on television.

'You want us to get out?' he asked.

'Did I stutter?' The cop stepped back from the driver's side door. 'Keep your hands in sight and get out of the car. Both of you.'

He had Jake's Nevada driver's license, car registration, and insurance papers. Jake knew he suspected them of transporting drugs. Which pissed him off. He wouldn't touch that shit with *Byron's* fingers. And he *certainly* wouldn't have any in his Viper, and chance having the DEA confiscate such a rare and beautiful, not to mention costly, possession. This was no factory model Viper. It was special order – everything from the pearl white paint job to the cellular phone and computer road-mapping system. He wouldn't put this car in jeopardy for anything.

Jake opened the door and slid out of the perfectly molded driver's seat. Byron was out the other side, standing there, not knowing what to do with his hands. He still had the CD.

Trooper said, 'Walk to the front of the car and put your hands on the hood. You, too, sonny.' He pointed at Byron.

'We don't have anything,' Jake said.

'I say you had anything? I ask you to speak?'

Jake bit down on the tip of his tongue. Why did he have to get pulled over by a piss-ant two-bit cop with a hard-on for kids? Byron was next to him, hands out on the warm hood. Cars slowed, the passengers gawking at the two boys leaning forward over a super-radical, futuristic car for all the world to see. It was the six o'clock TV news happening right before their eyes. Cops busting kids. Old news, at that.

The trooper pushed Jake's legs apart roughly, almost causing him to lose his balance and fall on his ass. When the cop patted him down, he slapped just a little too hard on the inside of Jake's thighs so that his balls quivered and crawled up tight to hug his groin. What a bastard.

Byron groaned out loud when he was being searched, then fell silent. Jake heard the trooper step back, felt him eyeing them. 'What's in the car?' he asked.

'Nothing's in the car,' Jake said. 'Why can't you just give us our ticket and let us go?'

He knew he shouldn't say a word, shouldn't protest. He knew all about the law and how it worked, the type it attracted. But goddamnit, all he was doing was speeding a little coming off an exit ramp. This whole song and dance was outright harassment. Out-of-state plates. New car. Kids. It spelled out *illegal* to this rube and Jake knew he shouldn't open his mouth unless it was to draw a breath.

But he always did. It was like genetic or something, how he couldn't control his fucking mouth.

The trooper was at his ear, spearminty breath brushing against his hair. 'I'll give you the ticket when I get good and ready, son. Until then I suggest you don't give me a hard time, and I especially suggest you don't give me any lip. You think you can do that? Otherwise we got a judge here likes to see little rich boys go to jail when they're smartasses. He likes to keep them overnight in the cell and slap outrageous fines on them just out of general principle.'

Jake swallowed hard. Tasted blood. Held his breath so that the stench of the mint might go away.

'I'm going to search your car. You care if I search your car? Do I have permission to do that, you think?'

Jake nodded, giving in. He said anything else the night was going to turn to brown muddy puppy shit. He and Byron straightened from the hood of the car, their palms warm, their legs weak from holding them stiff and still. Jake shot Byron a look. *We don't mess with this one.*

Byron blinked, then for some reason put the CD he still held against his right cheek. Jake glanced at the trooper making his way through their front and back seats. He hoped like hell he wouldn't check under the dash just to the left of the steering wheel.

He watched him pop the trunk and focus the beam of his fat black flashlight. Finally he clanged the trunk lid down and came again to the front of the car where they waited. Behind him Jake saw the round, burnt-orange sun pretending to peek over the rim of the horizon.

'Okay, looks all right to me. I thought you boys might be hauling something down to Houston, but it looks like this time you're clean. Sign this ticket. It doesn't mean you agree that you're guilty, it just means you know I wrote this ticket for speeding. You can send in the fine. I don't wanna waste my time taking you in to the justice of the peace.'

Jake signed the paper with savage strokes of the pen the trooper offered him. He watched from beneath lowered brows as the officer tipped his hat and made for the car parked behind the Viper.

'Fuck,' Jake whispered, eyeing the patrol car. 'I could kill him for that. I thought he was going to grab my dick on the pat-down.'

Byron touched his arm, reminding Jake he was there. 'Let's go. It's over. It wasn't so bad.'

Jake sighed at how easily his friend accepted the unwarranted hassling. 'Bad? It was fucking *humiliating*.'

Byron shrugged. He moved to the passenger door and climbed into the car. Jake slid in next to him and turned the ignition key. He pumped the accelerator, making the engine roar like a beast. The trooper's car left, driving past them into the lowering night.

'Let's just go eat, Jake. Forget about it.'

'I didn't get a ticket all the way from Nevada to Texas and this purple chunk cunt has to stop me for a few miles over the limit. The radar detector didn't even give out a beep.'

'No big deal, Jake. He was just showing off. They all like to show off. You've heard about Texas cops.'

'He was a simple fuck with a gut the size of Dallas and Fort Worth combined. Somebody ought to shoot out his eyes. One at a time.'

'Oh, that's a tasty image to stick me with when I'm starving to death.'

Jake didn't want to hear jokes out of Byron. He dropped the transmission into drive and spun gravel from his back wheels pulling onto the road. He hung a left at the stop sign.

GENEVA, 2 MILES.

Before they reached the city limit he was talking to his father again. 'I got a ticket, Dad. Stupid asshole in some little hick place here where we wanted to stop to eat.'

Byron had not inserted the CD into the player again. He sat flipping it in his hands.

'What'd he say?' Byron asked when Jake hung up.

'He said to watch my speedometer.'

'He's not mad?'

'No, he just said to take it easy.'

'You don't sound like you're taking it easy.'

Byron knew all about Jake's famous temper. 'I'm trying,' Jake said from between gritted teeth. 'You can see me trying.'

It would have been all right if they had gotten back onto the main freeway for Houston, but Jake's anger kept spiraling as he tried to drive thirty miles an hour through the mid-size Texas town. Everything his gaze rested on for more than two seconds made him itch with suppressed rage. The closed store fronts on the main street made him want to break out windows. The cars rolling slowly by looked to be driven by people in a happy, ignorant daze. He wanted to run into them.

There was a turn sign for a university and he wondered what they taught there, how to dehydrate cow patties and use them for fuel in the cook stove? The lights from the big Walmart store illuminated a parking lot full of old, beat-up farm trucks and half-assed, rusted cars held together with baling wire. This was definitely a Ford and Chevy kind of town. The Viper stood out like a space rocket.

Jake knew he was feeling mean, that these were just people, just people he didn't know and wouldn't like if he did, people who had done nothing to him, but he hated them all the same, hated them for their small lives and large prejudices. Hated them for their cops and their judges who enjoyed handing out fines to 'little rich boys.'

In fact, he hated so much for one instant that when Byron exclaimed, 'Turn right, turn right, man, there's a Pizza Barn!' he jerked the wheel right with such force it took the Viper up and over the concrete curb with a leaping crash that jolted them out of their seats so that they hit their heads on the roof of the car. The bottom of the Viper squealed and whined with the grinding and rending of hard metals. He hit the brake, cursing loud enough to be heard outside the car. 'Goddamnit, shit, fuck, see what you made me do, you dick, you fuck!'

They were grounded. The Viper was tilted up off the right side, the front wheel hanging in the air four inches above the curb. The car *sat* on the curbside, caught like a big, snow-white fly on gray fly tape.

'Christ,' Byron said.

'What'd you tell me to turn like that for? I didn't know I was so close to the curb!'

'Let me get out, look at it.' Byron gingerly opened the door and climbed out like a man with legs too long to unbend quickly. 'Christ,' Jake heard him repeat. 'Oh shit, Jake.'

Jake turned off the ignition and hurried out of his seat. He slammed shut the door. Cars were slowing again, Geneva's dazed residents peering out windows at them.

'We're gonna need a wrecker,' Byron said.

Jake saw the way the front tire hung suspended above the gutter. 'Great. New car and I fuck it up already.'

'It's just a little . . .'

'Shut up! You know what this car cost.' Jake glared at his friend before stalking off down the sidewalk to find a pay phone with a phonebook attached. He had no idea who to call if he used the cellular. Geneva was turning into Helltown. It was costing him money he meant to spend on good times. And his car, his beautiful car! No telling what damage had been done to the undercarriage. Maybe five hundred Dodge Vipers like this one in the whole country, and the one he owned was already wrecked. No way could he tell his dad. Absolutely no way.

Jesus Christ on a stick.

* * *

The tow truck charged them one hundred and thirty-four dollars to haul the car off the curb and to the only open mechanic's shop in town. Jake ripped the bills out of his wallet, all the while putting on a snarl. The wrecker driver ignored the bad temper and said, 'What's this thing anyway, some kinda experimental race car?'

Jake sighed deeply. 'Dodge Viper. Few of them made, cost so much if you put one scratch in the paint job hauling it off, I'll get your paycheck for a month to repair it.'

'You don't have to be so snotty. I just asked.'

The grease monkey in the garage came out from under the lift and said, 'Don't look good. This car's built so low to the ground, the whole bottom of it kissed pavement.'

Jake glanced at Byron as if to say, *What can we expect, this guy's going to take us.*

'What's wrong with it?' he asked.

The mechanic gestured for Jake to take a look underneath the car while he pointed out the problem. 'Tore the hell out of your transmission's oil pan, mashed it into the filter, so the transmission couldn't get any oil pressure. See that there?'

Jake was smart and he was worldly wise for an eighteen-year-old, but he didn't know diddly about fixing cars. His father had a mechanic on call in Vegas, preferring someone he knew over the dealership techs.

Jake saw something that was crushed like a beer can, but it might have been a Roto-Rooter for all he knew. 'I don't know for sure.' Stalling might help.

'Well, *I* know, son, and that transmission is busted.'

'Can you fix it?'

'Can a few longneck Lone Stars give you bare-titty dreams?' He grinned at his witticism, revealing choppers too big for his mouth. When neither of the boys smiled, he said, 'Sure, I can fix it. Got to replace the oil pan and filter.' He wiped his hands on a red rag. 'Be expensive, too. This is one of those expensive kinda cars, looks to me.'

'Just about what I figured. How long will it take you?'

'Two-three days.'

'*What*? We don't have two or three days! We have to be in Houston tonight.'

The mechanic shrugged. He kept his silence, wiping and wiping his hands on a red rag long after any of the grease might have been rubbed off his fingers.

'How much this going to cost?' Jake asked.

'Two hundred, two-fifty.'

'If I give you five hundred dollars can you fix it tonight?'

Byron whistled.

Jake turned around and walked off to the open end of the garage. Byron followed. 'We got to fix it, Byron.'

'I know. But shouldn't we call Tony first?'

Jake gave him a look like he had 'stupid' written across his face. 'I can't tell him about this after I just called about the ticket. Get real. We don't have any choice. I've got enough money, I just wanted it for . . . other things.'

'Well . . . ?'

Jake returned to the mechanic. 'It's seven. Try to have it finished by eleven. We have to get to Houston tonight. Here's half the money now . . .' He brought out his wallet and handed over two hundred dollar bills and a fifty. 'The rest when we come back to pick it up.'

'Seems reasonable to me. I better get to work. My ole lady's gonna fry me for missing supper.' The mechanic ducked under the Viper and to the other side where his tool cart stood. He chose a tool and disappeared beneath the car.

Jake took Byron by the arm and propelled him out onto the sidewalk.

'What are we going to do for four or five hours?' Byron asked. 'Besides eat, that is. I'm getting a belly cramp.'

'We'll just hang out. Let's go see what this burg offers.'

Geneva offered very little. The Walmart was the big center of commercial activity and it closed down at nine p.m. Besides the mechanic's shop, a few service stations and convenience stores, the whole place folded its wings and went to sleep. There wasn't a restaurant in town open within walking distance that served beer except the Pizza Barn. That's where Jake and Byron were forced to hang.

From ten o'clock onwards the two boys were the only customers. They had ordered and devoured three super-large supreme pizzas, or rather Byron had devoured most of them. Jake was too frazzled and on edge to eat more than a few bites. They'd had salad from the salad bar, cinnamon buns running with melted butter, and three pitchers of draft beer.

They had played a half dozen games of Donkey Kong on an old, scarred, coffee-table type machine, two dozen games of Star Wars pinball on a machine that kept eating every other quarter, and had kept the juke box thumping with music. Byron complained about the out-of-date games. Didn't they ever upgrade this stuff, he wondered aloud? He hadn't played Donkey Kong since he was a little kid.

They sat now, tired, dispirited, sick to the stomach from too much food and an overabundance of stimulating noise.

The manager grew more surly as the night deepened. He refused to run a tab, making Jake pay for each new order with cash – *that* after taking his time memorizing their IDs to be sure they were of legal age. Every time he brought a pitcher of beer he managed to set it down hard enough to slop some over onto the red-and-white checkered plastic tablecloth. Then he would ceremoniously lift a dish towel from where he kept it draped over one shoulder and wipe the spill.

Bored out of their skulls, Jake and Byron began telling the dirtiest jokes they'd ever heard. Byron kept falling over in the bench seat of the booth laughing like a hyena, his long legs lifted high into the air. He'd repeat the punch line, laugh some more, and this amused Jake so much, he told even raunchier jokes, throwing in obscene gestures as he did so. For the first time in several hours they transcended their surroundings and were once again two boys on a holiday, having a little fun.

At ten-thirty the last of the waitresses folded her apron and left through the side door. At ten-forty-five the manager, a young man not much older than Jake and Byron, came over to their table.

Jake sobered. He didn't like the guy for shit. He looked almost exactly like a younger version of a chemistry teacher he'd once had, a guy who'd given him an 'F' for a project, then called it 'the most amateurish scientific approach I've ever seen from a student.' Scientific, my ass, Jake thought now, glaring at the approach of the other man.

The manager nervously coughed and then said in a voice a little too loud, 'You boys are getting rowdy. And . . . uh . . . we don't allow loitering in the restaurant.'

Byron's mouth fell open. Jake raised his head and stared at the man. His white, short-sleeved shirt had a pocket and on the pocket was a red name tag that read: Walter, Service Manager.

'Well, Walter,' Jake said, just as sarcastically as he could manage, 'I don't see anyone loitering here, do you? As for *rowdy*, I don't see any other customers in here we could be offending, or am I blind?'

'I'm just telling you the rules. My boss says a party stays longer than two hours, I ask them to leave.'

'Even though that *party* just dropped close to forty or fifty dollars in this joint, including all the beer and the games and the songs on the juke?'

The manager was now more nervous than ever. There was a tic developing on one side of his mouth, pulling up his top lip every few seconds. Jake thought again of how much he had despised his chemistry teacher. He'd barely passed the course, one he needed for being admitted to college.

'You're making my assistant manager nervous,' Walter said, hooking a thumb over his shoulder.

Jake looked past Walter to the counter at the back of the room. He saw a teen girl with her hair in a pony tail trying to look busy wiping down the tile counter. No one would mistake her for pretty, that was a certainty. Her head looked like a box sitting on top of her thick neck, and her eyes were placed too close together, giving her a myopic appearance.

He turned his attention back to the manager. 'I guess we don't make *you* nervous, though, do we, Walter? You got a big job. You run this place and keep it clean and make the pizzas. You even get to ask customers to leave. Duties like that could make a man strong or break him, but you don't break, do you, Walter? You're competent and courageous. Nothing bothers you. Being rude doesn't bother you. Acting like an asshole doesn't bother you. *Getting in my face* doesn't bother you!' By his last sentence Jake had risen from the booth and was facing Walter.

Byron tried to make his way out from where he'd been lounging with his back against the wall. He tipped the table when bearing down on it for leverage and had to grab for the nearly empty pitcher to keep it from dropping to the floor.

'I'd just rather you leave,' Walter said, sticking to his guns, refusing to be intimidated. 'If you don't want to, I could always call . . .' He let the threat go unfinished.

Jake stared, the irises of his eyes darkening perceptively from brown to black. He didn't make a move. Didn't say a word. Without turning his head he looked over at Byron and back to Walter.

'We're on the way out the door,' Jake said.

Byron was on his feet. Walter moved out of the way. He watched the two out-of-town boys leave and then he sighed. A big deep sigh that swelled then emptied his chest.

Outside the Pizza Barn Jake turned to Byron. 'That's it,' he said. 'That's the last straw that broke this fucking camel's back.'

'He's just a country boy,' Byron said, fumbling in his shirt pocket for another cigarette. 'Don't take him seriously.'

'I'm taking this whole damn town serious. They give me a ticket, they screw me out of money repairing my car, they take my money and then ask me to leave a place where *I'm not doing nothing wrong*!'

'C'mon, keep it down, they're going to hear you.'

Jake walked off and Byron had to catch him. 'I'm coming back soon as we get the car.'

'What would you want to do that for?'

'I'm just going to put a scare into that Walter and his stupid, ugly *assistant*.'

'Aw, Jake, we don't want to mess with these people. They aren't worth this kind of thing. Look, let's call Tony and . . .'

Jake halted and spun on his heels. Byron almost collided with him head on. 'I ain't calling my dad on this, get that through your head. And scaring them is worth it to me. You understand that? My grandfather practically owns Las Vegas. My father is going to be the next in line to inherit the running of every operation we have a hand in. If I'm any kind of man at all, I'll be my father's successor. You think I'm going to let some backwater hick asshole push me around? You think my grandfather would have let him do it? My father? You think either of them wouldn't have handled a pretentious little shit like *Walter* in a minute? I don't have to call home to find that out. That's something I *know*.'

'The family would frown on this, Jake, I really think they would. They'd tell you he's a nobody, don't bother yourself.'

Jake wasn't listening. Blood boiled, turning the tips of his ears red, his stomach churned and his heart swelled with pints of new bitter black hatred. He couldn't talk back to a cop. He couldn't fix his own car. But by God, he could talk and fix Walter until he was blue in the face. He could scare him so bad he'd shit bricks and call it sugar cake.

Which is just what Walter deserved. Just one good Halloween fright night pow-wow. And then they'd hit Houston.

The Viper ran like new, although it got under Jake's skin that his car would never really be original or perfect again. He parked it at the back of the Pizza Barn parking lot next to two old cars, an eleven-year-old Chevy and a broken-springed Toyota truck. Walter's truck. The girl's car. Or vice versa, whatever. If he had to lay a bet, though, he figured the truck for Walter.

Jake took the gun from a special holder beneath the dash and checked to be sure it was loaded. It wasn't a big gun or a great gun, just a typical Saturday Night Special .38. But Jake knew how to use it, though he never had, not for scaring or hurting anyone. With a target set up at the end of a practice range, he could hit the shadow man wherever he aimed, chest or head. Even some of his father's bodyguards weren't as good with handguns as Jake.

'What are you going to do?'

Jake thought it over a few seconds. 'We'll take them out in the woods around this burg and put a scare into them.'

'I wish you wouldn't, Jake.'

'Wish on the moon, do you more good. I'm doing it. No more static from you about this thing. I've taken all I'm going to take in Geneva Fucking Texas.'

Jacob Macedonia had witnessed his father brow-beating a man and undermining his self-esteem when he was three. Jake never knew who the man was, but he had been in his father's office, and understood in some way the victim had bungled an important job his father had asked him to perform.

When he was five Jake had walked out into the front yard with his grandfather on the way to a family wedding and a car had driven by with a man hanging out the back window. The shots had rung out like popping firecrackers and his grandfather had thrown him to the ground, then covered his body with his own.

When Jake was ten he had gone to three funerals in one year. Two uncles and a cousin. Separate murders, unsolved. Unsolved only to the police. Jake's grandfather knew the killers and had them put away. For good.

Between the ages of twelve and eighteen Jake had seen very few strong-arm tactics and knew of no murders remotely related to the family. The business was changing, had to change, and these days strings were pulled, people in high places came often to visit to talk over lucrative deals, and the family diversified their interests. Jake was slowly brought into the business. He learned about all the ways to make money, some illegal, most legal and covered by a bevy of lawyers working for the Macedonia family.

At fourteen, Jake's father had provided to him, as a present, his first woman. Given them a suite on a top floor of the Regale Casino Hotel, one of the operations the family had an interest in.

Jake was going places. Going far and high. He had just graduated from the best private school in Las Vegas. In September he had been accepted as a student at UCLA. Upon graduation with an MBA degree in business he would return to become his father's heir.

But Jake had always been admonished about his temper. Tony said, 'Son, you're a smart boy, bright, intelligent, good-looking. You have a real future, an important future where a lot of people will depend on you, but there's one thing you've got to overcome first and it's that quick tongue and bad temper. You don't always think before you act, and that's going to get you killed or thrown in prison.'

A martial arts instructor had been called in to try to channel Jake's boyish rage. It helped none at all. He just kept hurting the competitors. Hurting them bad.

He'd been tutored after school by a philosophy professor who was

16

of no other use to the family except for training boys like Jake, boys who tended to spin out of control. He had failed to get through to Tony's growing, obstinate son. Jake had ridiculed him and called him a fruit, causing him to ask Tony if he could be excused from any further teaching duties.

Jake was remarkably like a poisonous snake. He felt threatened, he uncurled and attacked. Provoked, he struck. Spoken down to, as he had been at the Pizza Barn, he required revenge. The thing inside him that ate like acid couldn't be abated without heated and immediate action.

The yellow lights ringing the Pizza Barn roof fizzed and blinked off. At that signal, Jake opened the Viper's door.

Byron tried one last time to restore order and sanity. 'Jake, Hugh's waiting for us. Let's go get some girls at his house, okay? What about New York? We're wasting time here.'

Jake shut the car door and circled to the back bumper. He kept the gun out of sight behind his back. He could smell the tar cooling off from long hours of hot summer sun. He smelled pizza and smoke. Flowers and grass. He looked once at the stars overhead, astounded there were so many and that the sky was so wide and open. You never saw the sky in Vegas. The neon lights illuminated that twenty-four-hour world, turning it into a rainbow-hued day.

Walter and the girl both came from the same side exit the waitresses had taken when they left. They were talking, chattering brightly about something that caused the girl to giggle. Her pony tail jiggled and swung as if chasing off night bugs.

They were nearly to their vehicles before noticing they weren't alone. And then they stopped in their tracks and fell silent.

'Want to take a little ride?' Jake asked.

'Betty, go back in and call the police,' Walter said.

The girl stood there, frozen.

'Betty, did you hear me? Go back in and . . .'

Jake crossed to where they stood together, bringing the gun forth as he did so. He pointed it at Walter. 'We are going for a ride.'

'What do you want?'

'Get in my car and shut up. Or I blow *her* fucking head off.' Jake re-aimed the barrel of the .38 at Betty.

Walter took her arm and walked in front of Jake to the Viper.
'Get in the back. Hurry up.'

They did as they were told. The girl cried softly. Walter shushed her, not so softly.

The Viper bumped and lurched over a dirt road that led deep into East Texas pine woods. Without Geneva's street lights, the night descended around the car like the thick shadow thrown beneath great, wide wings.

Jake stopped the car and ordered the two people in the back seat to step out. He walked them in front of the car so they stood speared in the headlights. The girl shielded her eyes with one hand. Walter stood rigidly, arms hanging at his side. If he was afraid, he didn't show it. There was one small splash of scarlet pizza sauce on his white shirt, positioned like a red blossom over the button near the shirt's neck opening.

'I want an apology,' Jake said. 'Heartfelt. Sincere.'

When Walter did not speak the girl glanced over at him in fear and began speaking rapidly in a choked voice. 'Walter's real sorry. I'm sorry, too. We were just doing what the boss told us to do. Lots of kids from the university come in there and stay until we close. They make a lot of noise, drinking too much, and they leave messes so we have to run them off.'

'I'm not one of your locals,' Jake said ominously. 'I spent a frigging pile of money to be able to sit in that dumpy place you work and I don't appreciate being treated like scum.' He paused and leaned a bit toward Byron who stood next to him. He poked him slightly with his elbow to alert him the game was underfoot. He waved the gun at Walter, 'What about you, faggot? You got an apology for me?'

'This is kidnapping,' Walter said, stretching his neck and head upwards. 'You can go to jail for this.'

Jake moved into the headlights so they could clearly see the gun. He was not more than six feet away from the young couple. 'And *this* is a fucking .38 Special, asshole. Now APOLOGIZE!'

Walter, out of nervous energy he had kept under restraint until then or because he wanted to prove something to Betty, stepped forward two, three, four, five steps, each step seeming to take an

18

eternity. His eyes squinted against the glaring light. The tic at his mouth had pulled half his upper lip up so that shiny saliva reflected from his square white teeth. He halted, set back his shoulders, and said evenly, 'I wouldn't apologize to you if you were God Almighty threatening to send me to Hell.'

Jake didn't know he was going to do it, didn't even know how it happened. It was as if his finger on the trigger squeezed down tight due to pure hate translated from his heart to the gun and his hand was just a conduit taking lightning from the storm of his brain to blast it out into the world. Walter's head snapped back as if he'd been hit in the face with a roundhouse fist. He fell straight backwards to the ground and lay there unmoving.

Betty screamed and screamed. She fell to her knees, hands over her mouth, screaming. Byron rushed into the headlight glare and knelt next to Walter's body. He saw the hole in the young man's head. He shut his eyes, so scared his teeth chattered unaccountably. He whispered, 'Jake, Jake, oh God, Jake, no . . .'

Jake stood a moment, gathering himself.

So that's what it feels like. Like being shoved over a cliff. Like falling out of bed. Like dreaming of dropping from an airplane to earth. Oh man.

Byron was at his side, talking so fast he tripped over the words. Jake caught just a few of them.

' . . . killed . . . dead . . . caught . . . Tony won't like it . . . out of here . . . what about her . . . ?'

Her.

What was he going to do with the girl now? She knew what they looked like, the car they drove, a highly distinctive car. She had witnessed murder.

She could not live to tell.

Jake skirted the body on the ground, feeling nothing for it except exasperation that it had cost him so much trouble. He approached the weeping, hysterical girl. He stood over her, thinking what a pity it had turned out this way, but then it wasn't so bad, it wasn't a big deal, he knew men in Vegas who used to do this for a living, and a few still did, didn't bother them in the least. Should it bother him, the son and heir?

He aimed the .38's barrel at the top of her head. She wouldn't even know it was coming. She had her head down, face in her hands. She'd never know what hit her.

He pulled the trigger, this time in full control of his actions and thoughts.

Falling off a cliff. Plummeting in a free fall from a high place, flying high on the air . . .

2

Geneva, Texas
1995

Jake was dead.

District Attorney Elizabeth Kapon, the woman who had stood in court making an emotional plea for the jury to hand down the harshest possible punishment to Jacob Mace, the woman who demanded the death sentence despite the boy's young age, took a back exit to avoid the crowd waiting for her in front of the prison grounds.

She had not been witness to the boy's execution – it was an act she could not quite bring herself to view – but she felt she should be present in the building when it happened. It was, after all, due to her efforts that the case had been brought down to this.

Beth Kapon might be one of the few attorneys in all the state of Texas who was ambivalent about capital punishment. On the one hand, she contended that one act of murder did not constitute the right to commit another act of murder. Whether it was the state or an individual extracting life, it was still a barbaric practice. The United States was one of the last civilized nations in the world practicing capital punishment.

Then there was the problem of executing, by accident, an innocent man.

On the other hand, there were some criminals that no justice system in the world could punish enough. Beth put habitual rapists, child mutilators, and repeat murderers in this class. She hadn't any doubt whatsoever that's the class Jake Mace belonged to.

Beth knew Jake was guilty. The boy, barely eighteen when the

21

crime occurred, twenty-two tonight when he died after four years of court appeals, had been found guilty by a jury, and the evidence was incontrovertible. Jake had abducted and then murdered in cold blood the young manager and assistant manager of Geneva's Pizza Barn. They had the gun and his fingerprints on that gun. They had him in town near the time of the murders and witnesses who remembered him and his companion as customers at the Pizza Barn. They had mud in his tire treads that matched the mud where the bodies were found.

If the crime had not been so unfeeling, if the victims had had some kind of chance to escape, or if Jake had offered an emotional or even semi-understandable reason for committing his crime, Beth wouldn't have pushed for the death penalty. In killing Walter Green there was a shadow of a doubt about Jake's state of mind. It could have been an accident. Tragic, horrible, but an accident resulting from uncontrollable passion. But the death of the girl, minutes later, was an execution. And the boy revealed no remorse for his crimes. He was cocky and arrogant and he certainly had the best defense that could be found in the state of Texas. He had had his chance. Four years of chances through appeals. Money seemed to be no object to his family.

Beth thought the boy was a horror and his crime so heinous the death penalty was the only punishment that fit it.

Why, what if a killer had taken her own young daughter from a place of work and murdered her so dispassionately? Betty Levy was brutally slain for having done nothing beyond being at the wrong place at the wrong time. Beth wanted this kind of killer stopped forever. Not rehabilitated or set free in a few years the way he would have been if he'd been given a life sentence, but taken out of society for all time.

Beth glanced back at the imposing walls of Huntsville Correctional Unit as she made for the employee parking lot. She knew the majority of inmates were hardened, violent, habitual criminals. Many of them lost what humanity they possessed once housed inside those walls.

She sat in her Cherokee Jeep and leaned her forehead against her hands bunched on the wheel. It was getting to be too much. She had spent fifteen years of her life working as a county prosecutor, but this case had been the limit. The big city scuz crime that used to stay confined in Houston one hundred miles southeast of Geneva had inexorably crawled out of the urban nightmare until it contaminated small-town life. For years crime had slithered like a multi-tentacled monster toward the rural quiet of the mid-size university town of Geneva.

Today there were youthful offenders who would cut off your head so much as look at you. Jake Mace had been one of those. What was she to do but persevere? Who would if she didn't? If young men had to be put to death to stop the madness, then she must accept it.

What was next, she wondered? Already police officers were forced to draw down on fourteen-year-olds. Was it going to come to bloody massacres between veteran cops and teenagers? For it was evident all across the land that crime was rising at a startling rate, and the criminals these days were kids, some of whom couldn't even shave yet. There were metal detectors employed in some of the Houston schools to find the kids carrying guns. Drug-sniffing dogs patrolled empty school corridors. Gangs of teen thugs and race-hating groups were on a startling rise all over the state.

It's miserable and we're all stuck in it together, she thought sadly.

She saw a clever reporter come around the corner of the building, her camera crew trailing behind. She moved in a determined tornado spin toward the Jeep.

Beth turned the key in the ignition, pulled on the headlights, and drove from her parking spot with a sharp squeal of tires.

She drove around the prison and passed by the two dozen sign-waving capital punishment protesters, the parked television vans, and the crowd of reporters.

How does it feel to see a boy you put behind bars die by lethal injection?

That's what they all wanted to know.

And she couldn't tell them the truth.

That it felt like hell.

It felt like Holy Goddamn Hell.

It was a sixty-mile trip from the prison to Geneva. It had to be after one in the morning, she thought, as she let herself into the house and found her daughter, Melanie, waiting for her. The girl stood in the

23

living room with a mug in her hands. Her blue eyes looked tired and too old for someone eighteen.

'Is he dead?'

Beth nodded, dropping her purse and keys on an end table. She slumped onto the sofa and kicked off the low heels that cramped her feet.

'Did you watch?' Melanie asked.

'No, I didn't watch.'

'The television news said there were protesters. They showed them with their candle procession in front of the prison.'

'I know. The place was swarming with news crews.'

'Did you talk to them?'

'Melanie!' Beth hated exploding that way, and this time it surprised her. She was more tense than she thought. 'Melanie,' she said, using a softer note. 'I really don't feel like talking about this. It's been hanging over me for four years. I didn't talk to the reporters. I don't *want* to talk to anyone about it. Not right now, all right?'

'They've been calling.' Melanie, once scolded, rarely gave up. It was a war mothers and daughters down through the centuries had battled. When a girl reached a certain age where she felt she was an adult, she did not take kindly to a mother's rebukes. 'I told them you weren't here, but they didn't believe me.'

'We may have to take the phone off the hook.'

The phone rang shrilly, causing them both to jump. 'I'll take care of them.' Beth pushed wearily to her feet and moved to the coffee-table extension. She saw Melanie head for the kitchen. 'Hello?'

'You got your wish,' a voice stated.

'What? Who is this?'

'He's dead because of you.'

'*Who* is this?'

'I was hoping for your sake they would grant him a reprieve, and then I prayed for a stay of execution. But it was a lost cause from the day you were handed the case.'

'Mr Mace?' Beth's voice was shaky. She hadn't talked to Jake's father in several years, not since the trial. 'Your son . . .'

'Don't speak to me of my son again. Never again. He's dead. I'll bury him now. I just wanted you to know he won't be forgotten.

24

Nothing you can do will ever rob me of his memory.'

The phone line clicked and then buzzed at Beth's ear with the dial tone.

Beth set down the receiver slowly into its cradle. She stared into the middle of the room, her eyes unfocused.

Melanie materialized at her side and placed a hand on her shoulder. 'Mom?'

Beth was not sorry she had done her job, not sorry Jake Mace had been executed for his crimes, but she was, in her mother's heart, sorry for Jake's father, sorry for all fathers and all mothers who lose their children too early to the grave. She reached up and wiped a single tear from her eyes.

'Mom, you did what you knew was right. That boy was a monster.'

Was he? Beth wondered. Was he so monstrous he should not live?

She had grappled with all these questions four years ago when she called for the death penalty. One phone call should not force her into rehashing the whole question of morality and ethics all over again. It was done. Fini. She *wanted* it this way.

'I'll be fine,' she said. 'I think I'll get dressed for bed. It's late.'

She stumbled getting to her feet and Melanie steadied her. She impulsively reached out and drew her daughter into her arms briefly. 'Go to bed,' she said. 'You have classes tomorrow.'

'I love you, Mom.'

'I know, honey. And I love you too. Don't worry about this. It'll all blow over.' *Will it*, she wondered? Would Jake Mace's father call her again?

In the dark bedroom she had shared with Melanie's father before his untimely death, Beth wrapped the sheet around herself mummy-fashion against the cold blast of air-conditioned air from an overhead vent. She drew the pillow from beneath her head and put it over her face to ward off the pictures tripping through her mind. She didn't want to remember Jake Mace at the defense table, turning in slow motion to her when she sat down after asking for his death. She didn't want to imagine the lethal injection, the boy's terror at fast-approaching death. She would not picture those scenes, painted so vividly by experts, of the recreated crime taking place in the woods outside of Geneva.

Evil had been eradicated from her life with Jake Mace's death. She had been instrumental in removing it, and that was not a bad thing, was it?

A vague memory of the father's face loomed before her closed eyes. No. She did not want to see the face of Jake's father, full of recrimination and loathing as she walked out of the courtroom to be greeted in the county courthouse hallway by media hounds. She firmly pushed away her mind's image. *Go away*, she thought. *It's over. Go away now.*

Fatigue and the late hour conspired to drop her into sleep. There she did not dream, there were no pictures or images, or if there were, she would not remember them when morning dawned.

After Tony Mace put the call through to Elizabeth Kapon, he carefully put away the car phone in the limo that would whisk him to Houston's Intercontinental Airport. He carried with him Jake's manila envelope of personal effects. These he now pulled onto his lap to hold tightly with both hands. Tomorrow the arrangements for Jake's body to be flown to Vegas for burial would begin.

After the funeral, the weeping, the sorrow, the dry-eyed stare into the earth, Tony sat at his desk at home. Still in mourning. He would always mourn.

He picked up the telephone receiver. He dialed a number. Let it ring three times, hung up, redialed.

Chase Garduci's voice answered at the other end of the line. 'Tony?'

'Are you still loyal to me?' Tony asked. 'Answer me cautiously.'

A slight pause. Intake of breath. Tony could almost see the tumblers in Chase's mind clicking over, trying to find a connection to lock into place. Truth? Untruth? Which would he choose?

'Yes,' Chase said finally. 'I'm your man.'

'That's good. That's excellent. Now, tonight I'm going to see Dalta. I'm going to ask a favor of him. When I leave his house, he'll call you to do the work.'

'Yes.'

'No matter what he tells you to do, I want you to increase it by a hundredfold. Do you understand? You don't tell Dalta this; he'll find out after the fact, and it won't matter by then.'

26

'Could you gimmee a clue what I'm going to be doing? And who I'll be doing it to?'

'My son's killer. That's who you'll go after. I want her smashed. I want her crippled in every sense of the word.'

'Dead? You want her dead?'

'No. Worse than that. I want her wishing she were dead. Use your arsenal, invent new tortures she could never even imagine. And by the way . . .'

'Yes?'

'She has a daughter.'

Another small pause and intake of breath before Chase said, 'I'm your man.'

Tony smiled ruefully. 'I know. I wouldn't have called you otherwise.'

Around ten p.m. Tony told his housekeeper he was going out. He waved off his personal guards once they arrived at his destination. 'Wait in the car. I don't need you here.'

Inside, ensconced in a leather wing-back chair sipping whiskey neat, Tony felt in control for the first time in days. Relaxed and lounging across from him, Jeff Dalta took his whiskey over ice. He now swirled the ice cubes in the crystal highball glass and said, 'Why don't you do it yourself?'

'If I have a hand in it, and something goes wrong, or she tries to press charges, they'll trace it back to me.'

Jeffrey Dalta was Tony's truest enemy, a man jealous of Tony's position and power, a man who might have been nursed on envy rather than mother's milk from the time he was born. He was the perfect candidate to handle the job. You ask your enemy to work for you, you are in his debt. You force him to have a close relationship, a tie that binds.

'You don't like me, Tony. I don't understand this favor you're asking and why you've chosen to ask it of me.'

Tony crossed his legs and saw the pleat down the center of his slacks fall off to the side of his leg the way it should. He approved of Dalta's home, the marble entrance, the quiet luxury and old-time charm of the library where they now sat with their libations, the beautiful mahogany shelves with row upon row of limited editions.

Jeff had taste. He was a learned man, a Harvard graduate, and he would have been a real asset to the Macedonia family except for his unhealthy and ultimately disloyal ambition to run a family of his own. He would never be happy as a captain under anyone else.

He was young yet, trim, looking even younger than his years, but a hot-head, and thoroughly evil, an attribute Tony depended upon to get what he wanted from him.

Not everyone Tony had to deal with exhibited such decorum in his surroundings, however. In fact most of them had rather shoddy, yet extravagant tastes, all plastic and glitz and cold ugly chrome. His own father, though he did not go in for modern decor, had succumbed to his fourth wife's demands that she be given a free hand redecorating and had turned what had been, under Tony's mother's care, a lovely, staid mansion into a gaudy replica of some Arab sheik's estate. Plaster statues peeing water and velvet furniture in the most violent colors imaginable.

The house where his mother had lived now looked like something out of the movie, *Scarface*. The dumb bitch had made his father's home into a stereotypical palace of an organized crime boss. It was a travesty. Why couldn't *she* be knocking on death's door instead of his father? He hoped she inherited the monstrosity of a house, it suited her so well.

'I ask this favor because I know you can do it, and since I ask it, you'll protect me from any ramifications.' Tony knew he would not be refused. It was unthinkable.

Dalta sighed and put his whiskey on the coffee table between them. 'How far do you want me to go?'

'For killing my only son?'

Dalta held out his hands. 'I can have her killed.' There was question in the statement.

Tony shook his head, but not without a certain hesitation. 'I don't want her dead. I want to hurt her, but not physically.'

'Do you have specific requests?'

'I want you to call our man in the Senate in Texas. He can contact the judge and the judge can have the county attorney's office turn up something to get her disbarred. I want her out of work. Permanently. In the law field, anyway.'

'Disbarment. We'll need an airtight frame.'

'You can't do it?' Tony raised one eyebrow.

'Consider it done. Since our senator was not much of a help with the governor granting a reprieve, I expect he will be happy to do this to redeem himself.' Dalta sat back and spread his arms along the sofa back, at ease again.

Tony saw his nails glinting in the soft light. Buffed. A small vanity, and one he realized that he approved of. If Dalta had slightly less prominent cheekbones and a softer jaw, he could be called something other than handsome. Perfect was the word that came to mind. A Hollywood kind of perfection that dazzled, that would captivate millions if shown in close-up on a panoramic theater screen.

Tony recalled what he had come for and said, 'That's all.'

'Is that enough?'

'I think it is.'

'Are you sure? You're being easy on her, if you want my opinion.'

Tony almost smiled. He counted on Dalta thinking he was being too easy. On everyone. 'It's enough. She won't have a way to make a living. She will suffer hugely. My portfolio says she came from a medium-income family and worked her way through law school. Losing this is losing something it took half her life to accomplish. If she's disbarred, the university will reconsider keeping her on the faculty. She'll go down to nothing.'

'I'll take care of it.'

Tony stood, signaling the pact was made, the discussion at an end. His host stood with him. He reached out to shake Dalta's hand. 'If you ever need anything, you only have to ask.'

Dalta lowered his head just the tiniest fraction to indicate respect for Don Macedonia's son.

As Dalta stood in the doorway watching Tony leave, he wondered why the man just didn't set out a contract on Elizabeth Kapon. After all, she had pressed for Jake's death. She had killed him as much as the state and the lethal injection. If Jake had been given life, Tony could have paid off enough people to get him out after a while. But you didn't get a kid out of hell. The door was closed to that place for all eternity.

This would take deep thought. Why did he feel he had just been handed a gold-plated opportunity? If he played it right, if he was clever enough, he could snare the woman and Tony Mace at the same time. He could shackle them together in a dance of death. Once and for all rid himself of the man who ruled the perpetual nights of Las Vegas. Create a vacuum that must be filled by the best available man in the family. And who else qualified except himself?

He closed the door and returned to the library for his whiskey. The fire crackled in the fireplace, casting shadows over that end of the room. He turned on another table lamp to dispel the gloom. He loved the smell of wood burning. He took the whiskey glass and brought it to his face to breathe in its aged, pungent scent. He felt like Arthur Conan Doyle, hidden away in London, contemplating how to maneuver Sherlock into desperate intrigue.

In the morning he'd call the senator. And by morning he would know – it would come to him – what it was he should plan for the woman's future after the phone call that ruined her legal career for all time.

If he did enough irreparable harm in her life, she would eventually seek out her tormentor. And he must make sure the path led directly to Tony Mace. Either she would try to ruin him or kill him. Then Tony would be forced to stop her whether he wanted to or not. Permanently. Either way suited Jeff's needs just fine.

Denise's voice intruded on his reverie. 'Jeff, is Tony gone?'

'Yes, he left.'

'Is it anything you can tell me about?'

He had not told Denise the truth about much of anything in probably five years. It was a boring marriage, his liaisons with dance girls the single relief. He would have divorced her if she didn't have so much money. And if he didn't love his daughter with all his heart.

'It was nothing very interesting.'

Denise came into the room, causing it to shrink and feel suffocatingly close just by her presence. The walls moved in. The floor rose up. The ceiling descended. Jeff drew in his breath, trying to get enough oxygen before it fled at her advance.

She took her place next to him, careful not to sit too close on the sofa. She stared at the fire, mesmerized. 'Will you go with me tomorrow morning to talk to Lydia's physical education teacher? It may involve the principal, too.'

Lydia in a gym suit presented a grotesque image in Jeff's mind. His daughter would look like a troll in green shorts. She was not only fat, a genetic affliction passed down from Denise it now seemed, but she was also awkward, clumsy, and suffered from a heart murmur. She wanted out of her phys-ed classes. Denise wanted her exempt, too. Jeff thought she needed all the exercise she could get. He never seemed to agree with the women in his family. Or women in general, come to that.

'I'm afraid I'm busy in the morning,' he said. 'Sorry.'

'I'll handle it alone then.' Denise rose, her long, powder-blue, satin dressing gown trailing behind her as she moved, stately as a great ocean liner, from the room.

The floor-length garments Denise wore these days helped disguise some of her blocky heaviness, but the massive hips could hardly be hidden. He turned his eyes from her departure, unhappy about his thoughts of her. Once she had been the most beautiful woman in the world in his eyes. She had weighed no more than a hundred-twenty. The way she arched one brow when she spoke, the way she rounded her vowels, the stir she could create entering a room – these things had once convinced him she was a good partner, a steadying force for him. But the weight gain started with her pregnancy, and it never stopped. Gradually, over ten years, the fat swarmed her exquisite frame until it totally engulfed the young woman he had married. His ardor cooled. These days he could hardly look on her without embarrassment, and he thought she had guessed his feelings. How could she not, she wasn't stupid. That's why she never pushed him to deal with Lydia or anything else that involved them working together intimately. She didn't really want the naked truth to come out, be exposed for her to do something about.

Was the old Denise locked in there, imprisoned by layers of flesh? Did he care anymore?

How things change, he thought.

He sipped the whiskey. Watched the fire. Thought about the woman in Texas, wondering how much she weighed and if she were pretty. He smiled to think he might destroy another pretty woman, the way time, and possibly discontent, had destroyed his wife's beauty.

Things changed, they did, they most certainly did. But sometimes wasn't that lucky?

His gaze trailed from the fireplace to the shelved books. He stood, crossed the room, took down a volume of Emily Dickinson's poetry, remembering something about beauty she had written. Seated again, he leafed through the gilt-edged pages until he found the poem, 'I Died for Beauty.' He savored the words of two corpses in adjoining tomb rooms discussing their deaths. One died for beauty, the other for truth. The one who died for truth confessed they were one, brethren. And so they talked until the moss reached their lips, covering their names.

Jeff let his eyelids lower to shut out the room, the book fell closed in his lap, one of his hands resting on top the leather binding. If truth truly were beauty, and they were interchangeable, then he had lost the truth, Denise had let it slip away from her, and she had not even replaced it when giving him a child. It was like a punishment to watch Lydia struggle against the whale blubber that she had inherited. It was a crime to be born without any choice but to lumber through life while people stared or turned aside their eyes, disgusted.

To be without truth in a life, without beauty, the days were hardly worth living, were they? Wasn't that why he fell for the showgirls, taking them one after the other, just to be reminded of the presence of resplendence in the world?

He opened his eyes and put away the book on the end table near his drink. He had to shake himself from this ridiculous sentimental melancholy. Emily's poetry always did that to him. He shouldn't allow it, shouldn't indulge that slow ponderous train of thought she ignited when he read her work.

He must go to his room, having moved out of Denise's bed so long ago he could not even remember when the decision was made, and get some sleep so his mind would be clear come morning.

There was a woman halfway across the country he must find a way to deal with. And use to his own ends. He saw her as a stepping stone, perhaps even a catapult to what he most desired. Place. Position. Power. All of it handed over to him by Tony Mace, the unknowing son of a bitch. If he thought honor would prevail here, he was far less astute than anyone had previously surmised. Screw that Sicilian bullshit. It hadn't been working as a code of behavior for twenty years now.

Elizabeth Kapon. Nice name. He hoped she was as devastatingly beautiful as a sunrise over a silent sea. If she was fat like Denise, it would not be nearly as much of a challenge.

Lydia's voice surprised him from the doorway where she stood in her pajamas and terry housecoat, her feet encased in pink slippers shaped like pigs. What could her mother be thinking, buying those slippers?

'Daddy? You can't go to school with me tomorrow?'

He stood and went to her. He put an arm around her wide, padded shoulders and pulled her against him. She buried her face into the lower part of his shirtfront. 'Baby, I told your mother I had something to do. I'm really sorry. If I can help later this week . . . ?'

She shook her head. Sighed. Pulled free of his embrace. 'It's all right. Mom will talk to them. She said it would be all right.'

'I'm sure it will. If there's any trouble, I'll handle those officious types for you. That is, if you're sure you don't think you can do the exercises and the sports . . .'

She spoke against his belly, her breath hot and heating his skin there. 'I hate it, Daddy. They make fun of me because I'm so . . . so slow. And I get pains in my chest.'

'Then we'll make sure you're taken out of the class. Stop this worrying. Now off to bed. Scoot.'

She did not wait for him to kiss her for he had stopped that, couldn't help himself, couldn't bear to put his lips against her chubby rose cheeks without breaking down altogether, falling into a rage he would take out on her mother in private.

She paused in the hallway, turned and waved, as if she were embarking on a long journey. He gave her a sad smile and watched until she reached the stairs before he felt impelled to turn from her so as not to see the square heaviness of her shoulders slumping as she took the steps, doggedly, breathlessly. She must now weigh a hundred-fifty, he thought for the millionth time, and only ten! Only ten years old! My God.

He wished, clenching his hands, that he knew how to kill and that he had a convenient victim standing before him.

He rushed to the end table, grabbed up the glass of whiskey and downed it in a gulp. Maybe one more would help him sleep. At the very least it would help him survive until the black thoughts released him.

3

Chase Garduci stared at the phone for long minutes after hanging up with Tony Mace. At last a job with some teeth. They had been treating him like an old, worn-out hitman for too long. He was not, by God, going to take much more of it. If Tony hadn't told him to get 'inventive' on this job, he would have screamed curses at him and told him to go fuck himself. 'Fuck yourself!' That's what he would have said, even to Tony. He was sick and tired, sick, sick, sick to death of tailing asshole capos to see if they were trying to start up trouble, sick as a dog with a bellyful of tainted bologna of lying around on his backside scanning photos in girlie magazines and never being asked to do something chewy.

So he was old, big fucking deal. Fifty-two. Old. At least for his line of work he was thought ancient and that's how the family's other hitmen were winding up lately. Sitting on their asses waiting for something to do that would require their genius. 'We don't *do* that anymore,' the bosses whined at them. 'You're out of sync with the modern world,' they said.

In other words, we don't need you goons these days so get fucking lost, pal.

Until now.

Tony had said he could get nasty, get *inventive*, and, goddamn, it felt good to have the chains off him. You don't take a fucking pit bull and try to make him into a hand-licking blind man's dog. You don't put him in a cage and let him go wild-fucking-insane-crazy from lack of a fight. You *use* him. You put him to work doing what he does best. Chewing off ears and taking bloody bites out of necks, that's what you had to do. Else kill off the old guard. And just let them try coming after Chase Garduci! Be the sorriest day of their lives.

He stood and rubbed the front of his faded jeans. Damn thing was hard. Thinking of being set free made him want to fuck something – celebrate. Right now he could fuck anything, a hole in a wall, a whore with syphilis, any goddamn thing.

He frowned. Lately the only thing he'd wanted to fuck was Tony's wife, Connie. Oh man, oh holy man of Jerusalem. Good thing Tony didn't know about that. He'd let loose ten other goons to put him away.

Connie was like a disease with him. It had only started a couple months ago. Before then he scooped the female Lost and Found characters off Vegas streets and did them. Whether they offered it or not. He did them with their hands tied behind their backs and their legs lifted up over his shoulders. Who were they gonna tell? Fuck, most of them were whores anyway, what did they care he took it a little roughly? They peddled their asses, they ought not complain somebody like Chase happened along. Teach the cockteasers.

Then for some reason he was at a family function, somebody or other's wedding, he remembered, and there was Connie Mace. He'd seen her at a distance before, never up close. This time he was no more than two feet from her, Tony introducing him, and something went POW in his head, like a vein busted or something, and his dick swelled to twice its normal size. Right there. Two feet from her, her husband saying, 'This is my wife, Connie. Chase here used to work with my father a few years ago.'

Chase couldn't catch a good goddamn breath. He had to hurry and turn away before either Tony or Connie saw his hard-on. He excused himself, pretended someone across the room was looking for him, and he fairly ran from the house.

After that he got into the habit of sneaking over to the Mace's house at night, avoiding the electronic cameras – no step for a Stepper – and peeking in their bedroom window, snatching illicit glimpses of Connie asleep in bed, half nude most nights.

Hell, he'd never get near her. It was all a goddamn fantasy that drove him into nervous fits. Made him go out on the street hunting some young meat he could stick it to, her screaming, maybe having to be shut up permanently. It was a fucking mess.

If he went off to Texas to do a job for Tony, though it was Dalta who would actually send him, at least he'd be away from Connie and his obsession with her.

The woman in Texas had a daughter, too. Tony at least knew his tastes. The younger the goddamn better. Except for Connie . . .

Fuck it, this would do him good. Get him out of town, keep him out of trouble. He ever made a move on Tony's wife, it was all over for him. Blackout. Say your prayers, eat your last meal, get down on your knees and hope it's quick. Tony was no guy to fuck with. Dalta might be tough and mean, but anyone mistaking him for an equal of Tony's, he had to have his head up his ass. Way far.

Chase hurried to the closet and snagged a jacket. He had cruising to do on Las Vegas Boulevard. He wanted a woman so bad he thought he'd choke.

He sort of hoped he didn't have to kill the piece he picked up tonight.

He needed to save all that for Texas. Not that he'd kill anyone. Tony said no, don't do that, do worse.

So he'd do worse. Goddamn guarantee it.

4

Phan Lieu had been in America ten years and spoke elegant English with only a slight accent. Yet he had not forgotten his native tongue so that on this day as he sat secluded in a brocade-covered booth in one of Houston's finest restaurants and he heard a couple speaking in Vietnamese in the next booth over, he understood every word.

'May I take your order or would you like a cocktail?' the waiter inquired, standing over Phan and waiting.

Phan glanced up and said, 'I'll have a companion for dinner. I'll take hot tea now, thank you.'

'Certainly, sir.'

Phan leaned his head back to listen a bit more to the conversation taking place at his back. It was not about their home country or anything of import, really, but the swoop and rhythm of the language smoothly moving back and forth between the couple caused Phan to slip effortlessly from the present in the restaurant and return to the thoughts of his first days arriving in America.

The US Immigration Service would not allow the poor broken vessel to land. The boat people, including Phan, were near starvation, sick with various viruses from lengthy exposure to the elements. There had been arguments and several fights. One child no older than a year sickened and died in his mother's arms and had to be sewn into a shroud and lowered into the sea. An old woman's heart failed her from the difficulties encountered on the trip and she too died and was sent to a watery grave. The boat had been blown off course and that course rectified. They had survived gales and storms that soaked them and made them fear for their lives. But once the shoreline came into sight the Vietnamese refugees rallied. They had made it to the promised land. They would be free now and earn livings for their families; they would be able to make money and save a portion of it to send for other family members and friends.

Now they sat bewildered that they must wait longer out in the dead calm of the sea while authorities discussed what was to be done with them. Some of the men debated hotly the idea they might not even be allowed to enter the United States despite having come so far and endured so much to reach it.

A helicopter circled and periodically hovered above the boat. Counting them? Trying to discern their status and desirability as new citizens? A Coast Guard cutter sat white and huge as a giant bird of prey, all its brass twinkling in the sunlight. They remained just astern of the small boat, waiting, the Vietnamese thought, for instructions. A Navy ship lay on the water a little distant, its great hull so tall it dwarfed the small craft they sat in.

Phan took in this stalemate and wondered too if they would be allowed into the country. Unbeknownst to him, some boat people were being turned away now and sent to other countries. There had been an overflow of Vietnamese. The US government was not so lenient in taking in refugees these days.

Though Phan did not know the politics of the situation, his instinct for survival kicked into alarm mode and he pushed his way through the crowd to the captain. 'Move the boat closer to shore. Just a little closer.'

The captain argued that he should not do this. 'They have their policemen here,' he warned, pointing to the Coast Guard. 'They might fire on us.'

'Don't be ridiculous,' Phan said, taking the wheel from the captain's hands. 'Get out of the way. I'm starting the engines.'

And he did. He saw the helicopter swoop down menacingly and ignored it. He heard American voices over bullhorns and shut his ears to them. The Coast Guard cutter went into gear and surged forward to trail them. But Phan was not going to be stopped. They might kill him, if they wished, but he would not be denied his day on this new land, not after such a hazardous journey, not after he knew there was no other place on earth to go where he might be truly safe.

A clamor rose from his kinsmen and after a few moments underway, three of them joined the captain and threw Phan aside from the wheel housing.

That was all right. They were closer now. The land was far away, but not so far he couldn't make it. Only the strong ever sought for and gained freedom and if he was not strong enough, he would at least die trying. Why risk so much to come this far and not risk it all?

He shouted, poised near the side of the boat, 'Who would come with me? We can swim to the shore now! Come! The Americans can't stop you now. Come with me!'

A riot ensued and cries filled the air. Phan climbed onto the railing and dove into the blue, cold waters. He struck out for land. All behind him he heard splashes of others following. A whole contingent of the strongest men and women leapt from the boat and headed inland.

'Your tea, sir.'

Phan blinked, then nodded his thanks to the waiter. He had been in the water again, swimming for shore. He felt his lungs bellow and his arms ache from the tremendous effort of pushing his way through the deep, gently-rolling waves toward the beach.

They had finally let the ones who swam ashore remain, processing them through detainment centers and later yet they told the captain to bring in the boat. Phan didn't know if his action and that of the other swimmers caused that softening of the American rules and orders or not, he only knew they were permitted into the country and that was what mattered. For all he cared they could have killed him. He would rather have died than be sent out again into that perilous ocean to make yet another desperate journey.

He had arrived. And it was hell again, though of a different sort than the one he'd escaped in Haiphong.

After being processed and set loose from the detainment center, Phan faced many of the same hardships he had encountered on the streets of his own native city. Houston was not a friendly place for foreigners broke and unable to speak English. He found his way to the Vietnamese section of the city and lounged around the shops trying to decipher how to make his way in this new land. He asked for work everywhere, but of course the shopkeepers were thrifty and already had all the help they needed. They could not provide jobs for all the refugees who had come over on the boats for these past few years.

Still, they understood him when he spoke and he began, slowly, to pick up a few English words and phrases. When he had to steal to find clothes and food, he left the Vietnamese enclave and stole from American shopkeepers. He was too good at theft to be caught by them and, in fact, thought Americans singularly sanguine in their shoplifting prevention. Once he understood surveillance cameras and had noticed in some stores, the presence of undercover detectives dressed as civilian shoppers, it was no trouble at all for him to lift what he desired and make it away without discovery.

It was after several months of living beneath freeway overpasses and from inside cardboard boxes that he happened upon someone who would raise him from this torturous borderline existence into the world where people owned possessions, had their own places to live, and money to burn.

He had been rifling through a garbage dumpster at the back of a Vietnamese restaurant in the Vietnamese quarter when the cook came out to empty a pail. Phan knew the cook by now and passed pleasantries with him and then was able to pick from the pail what he wanted to eat before it was dumped and made dirty in the dumpster. When the cook returned to the kitchen, he accidentally left the door open and Phan was standing near it when a conversation began inside at a table set near the back of the restaurant and near the kitchen and the outside door.

It was two men talking about murder. About hiring a killer.

They didn't know who to turn to, evidently not having made contract killing part of their lifestyle before this instance, and Phan took this opportunity for what it was. An excellent stroke of good fortune. He pushed open the door wider and stepped into the shadowed, air-conditioned restaurant. The two men immediately fell silent, scrutinizing him in his soiled, ragged clothes and tattered, leather-thong sandals.

He asked politely, 'May I join you? I know that I look like a street rat and that is what I am, but in Haiphong I was a respected man with many talents, some of which you might wish to take advantage of.'

The two men looked at one another and blanched, realizing their conversation had been overheard.

Phan smiled. He pulled out a chair and seated himself across from them. 'You need not fear I'd reveal your plans to anyone. I've come here to offer myself for your use. If we can have an agreement of terms and compensation, I will do the job you wish done and do it so no one will ever know you were involved. I have *never* been caught. I am Phan Lieu and I was trained by a member of *Pinus Khasya* in Haiphong. I will not let you down.'

These men had knowledge of the dreaded assassins who called themselves *Pinus Khasya*. That they sat now at a table in Houston, Texas with one of those men caused them to tremble and bite their lips. It took two more meetings with them at the same restaurant before Phan was able to convince them of his availability, his skills, and his loyalty.

He performed the assigned murder. He collected his money. With that money he rented a room in a Vietnamese boarding house and paid a tutor to teach him English. The two men recommended his services to others and soon Phan had all the work he could handle and all the money he had ever hoped for. He learned to speak the new language. He bought better suits and shoes, rented an apartment, put a down-payment on a car.

Within two years he was enrolled in night classes at a community college learning about United States history and culture.

And now, ten years later, he was at another restaurant, one frequented more by whites than Asians, and he was waiting once again for a client who would detail to him a job. There would be a file for him to study and plans for him to make. He had moved beyond hits for the Asian community and now took care of any job for anyone. He had worked for many people of varying colors and nationalities in the city of Houston, his fame spreading by word of mouth, his clientele growing yearly. He had flown on jets to other parts of the country to assassinate victims. He had killed fifteen people in those ten years and not one of the murders was ever traced back to him or his clients.

But one thing he had not yet done and that was to find his father.

43

Everywhere he went he asked how to go about it and had already tried several tactics suggested to him. So far he had come up empty on his father's whereabouts (or his death; he might be dead for all Phan knew), but one day he would meet someone who had the power to pull the strings that would help him. And when he did, he knew that day would be one that changed his life forever.

'Phan?'

He looked up from his hands lying on the tablecloth and only his lips smiled at the woman who stood before him. In his eyes were calculation and cunning, the attributes that set him apart from the normal man. 'Yes, sit down, please,' he said, scooting over to make room for her on the bench seat of the booth.

'I was afraid to come here,' she said. 'It's so public. Aren't you afraid of being overheard?'

Phan kept the smile in place. 'We'll go to my place later and discuss the technical minutiae. Unless, of course, you are afraid to be alone with me?' He tried not to make his statements end in a query, but it was a habit from the past he could not quite shake.

He watched her arch her brows and think what he might be saying before she replied, 'I'm not afraid. If I were afraid I never would have found a way to get in touch with you in the first place.'

Phan gently laid his hand over hers on the seat between them. Her nails were manicured and she wore a diamond tennis bracelet on her right wrist. She wore a perfume made from the magnolia blossom, a heady, heavy, sexual scent that stirred him to licentious thoughts. 'You're a beautiful woman. I will enjoy our time together.'

She was too experienced to blush or turn aside his compliment. She was too cold-hearted to let it sway her either.

When Phan and the Texas senator's executive assistant left the restaurant after their meal, heads turned to watch them and conversations dwindled to sighs.

The tall, curly-headed, handsome Asian and the expensively coifed and stylishly dressed business woman at his side made such a striking couple.

5

Two weeks after Jake Mace was put to death, he still haunted Beth. She couldn't shake thoughts of him no matter how hard she tried.

Never before, except once in a nightmare, had she seen true evil. She'd always suspected evil to be a real force. She thought most people who came from a certain religious unbringing believed there was evil in the world. Evidence of evil was everywhere. But she believed its face and the opportunity to see that face were rare.

Many years before prosecuting Jake, she had had the dream that showed her Evil's reality. She was a young law student then, studying for the bar. Her life hung in the balance between success and failure. Yes, she could take the bar exam over again if she failed it, but in every young attorney's mind was the fear that he or she might not pass the bar *at all*. That fear drove the majority of them to wring their minds to the breaking point in order to succeed and pass the test. No matter how many times it took.

She had worked all night studying her law books. If preparedness will take me to victory, she thought, then I'm ready.

At four-thirty in the morning she fell exhausted into bed and was swept immediately into deep slumber.

That's when the dream came. The dream-that-was-as-real-as-life. Everyone has them. It was the kind where the victim does not know she sleeps and dreams, where she misinterprets her state of being or is so stressed or fatigued she believes the dreamworld to be the waking world.

45

In the dream Beth found herself with a madman. He was human enough. A killer. Perhaps she had studied too many cases of criminal law, perhaps she feared heavily the failure of the bar exam; no matter what triggered the nightmare, it had found her and had her in its thrall.

In the dream, besides herself and the killer who possessed the face of evil, were two other people. One was her young husband; they had been married a year. The other was a stranger to her, but she sensed in the dream he was someone they knew, a friend of her husband's, maybe. Had they been to dinner together? It seemed they had spent the evening sharing some entertainment.

It lasted no more than two minutes, the nightmare. The madman burst onto the scene, coming from the thick dark while the three of them headed, laughing, toward their parked car. It was night, but Beth didn't know where she was. The killer had a gun. He hit the stranger with them in the face with the gun's butt and knocked him sprawling over the hood of a car. He then pushed her up against a car opposite and told her to shut up and be still. Only then did she realize she had made any sound at all. She was on the verge of terrified keening. Already she whimpered low in her throat, an animal trapped.

The killer then turned her husband to face the car where the stranger lay on the hood, perfectly still. It appeared the explanation for this event was robbery. The man wanted what they had and was willing to do whatever was necessary to take it.

Beth must have made sounds. She didn't know what caused the killer to turn to her a second time unless that was it. She had lost all control over her physical being by then and could not have kept quiet no matter what threat he made to her.

And that is when she saw evil. Real and horrifying evil. There was not a vestige of humanity in it. It was an alien thing in the man's eyes, something that froze her heart instantly. She was sure they would all die for having seen it. *Sure of it.*

The madman turned to her and said something about how he had *told* her to shut up and then he shot her three times in the chest. Just like that. He shot her rapidly, bang, bang, bang and she fell, collapsing immediately to the ground. She knew death hovered and swooped and would take her now. She felt a soft peace descending to snatch her away, but she felt an urgent need to say one thing before she died. Her love stood just above her and he still had to endure the coming of his own demise. She had to let him know he was not alone, would never be alone, even in death.

She turned her head toward her husband standing beside the car, his terror and alarm a palpable thing linking them, and she said, 'I'll meet you.'

She meant she would meet him on the other side. In death. She knew he would understand.

She thought she would die then, suddenly, for having voiced her last message, but life clung to her body. She saw the killer thrust his gun into her husband's back and she knew he too was going to be shot and killed.

It was all horror. It was so intense that just the experience might have killed her had not the killer shot her three times.

But as bad as dying was, as frightening as it might be to face oblivion, it was worse to live and be in the presence of that true evil she had glimpsed in her murderer. Looking upon it in that moment before he shot her, she had wanted to die to escape it.

The gunshots blasted again and her husband slid toward the tarmac of the parking lot. Evil was having a field day.

She woke then from the nightmare, bathed in sweat, heart hammering madly, her mouth hanging slack as it might be in death. She could not believe what she'd just experienced was nightmare and this waking, this trembling and beating of her wild heart was the true life.

She threw back the covers and sat up in bed knowing for the first time in her days on earth that there was something verifiably called evil. It wasn't like anything she imagined it would be from thinking about it at church as a child. It was nothing like the evil portrayed in Hollywood films – actors had not even come close to capturing its glittering implacable face. It was not like anything she had read about in religious texts, in mythology, or in fiction.

It was the scariest thing in the world – much worse than dying could be – and it came to her that people who died violently of murder were the only ones, besides those like herself who happened for one odd reason or another to dream it, who had ever seen true evil. Evil had a face. It did not care what it did, how unjust it was, how cruel. It did not bother for one moment with reason, empathy, or care for humankind. It was a thing separate from the killer himself, a mantle over him that protected him from conscience. It was something without mother or father, without hope or light. In that way it was supernatural. She knew some way, having seen it if only in nightmare, that it was not an *entity*, a demon, a devil overtaking a human being. It was of and from the soul of that human who called it forth from the dungeon of darkness.

So when she saw it again that day in the courtroom in the young Jake Mace, she knew she must call for the death sentence and try with all her might to have him erased from the earth. It was one more glimpse into the abyss when that day she glanced to the defending attorney's desk and happened to lock gazes with Jake. It lasted but a second or two. No one else had time to catch it unless he had been staring directly into Jake's eyes the way she had been. She recognized the raw battering soulessness of it and shuddered where she stood with her hands full of papers. The courtroom dimmed and the background faded and she was in the nightmare again, choosing death over knowing this terrible face.

How could she forget someone like that so easily just because now he was gone? First she had seen evil in dream and now after many years she had seen it in a real person.

It shook her to her core to think she had to move through a world where evil resided. She feared more for her daughter than she ever had before. She pitied and mourned Jake's two victims, knowing what they saw as the last thing on earth. They had looked upon the same thing she saw in the dream, the same thing that reached out and turned her heart to ice in the courtroom that day when he let her see it for herself.

She now walked uneasily in the world. Thinking you know what evil is and really coming up against it are vastly different affairs.

She never spoke of it. Her colleagues and friends would not understand what had come over her if she'd tried to explain. Evil to most people was a theory, an intellectual exercise to be debated. It might be thought psychological or part of the great archetypes Jung had explored. It might be called myth or religious brainwashing. But

Beth knew differently. Though she could not speak of it or warn others of how real was its essence, she could put it down when she encountered it, as she had in Jake Mace. She could do whatever was in her power to eradicate the infected carriers of evil. It was part, now, of her job, to notice and observe, so as not to miss the criminal who kept it hidden inside.

Not all lawbreakers, she realized, were evil. Some were misguided, impulsive, or psychologically damaged. She still believed true evil was rare and that was a fortunate thing.

She sat over her coffee at the breakfast alcove thinking about her nightmare and of Jake Mace when her daughter bounded through the kitchen, hair flying, in a hurry to be on her way to her first college class of the day.

'Hey, Mom, why the long face? You get your period?'

Beth frowned slightly. She was not sure she approved of the open way her daughter talked about private and personal things. 'No,' she said. 'I was just thinking.'

'Still got that kid on your mind, huh?'

'Kid?'

'Jake Mace. Look, I'm going to be late. I have to make my nine o'clock. I'll see you this afternoon.'

Then she was gone, the kitchen and alcove resounding with her footsteps. It was a little brighter where Beth sat for the passing through of her daughter's energy and intuitiveness.

Beth smiled a little as she brought the mug of coffee to her lips. She was not the *only* perceptive person in the house.

She must soon go to the bedroom and dress for the day. She had her own class to attend. She taught undergraduate law at Geneva University where her daughter studied arts and the humanities. After her class, she must return to the office and her duties as the elected district attorney for the County of Harlan, Texas. This afternoon she had criminal charges on a suspect to present to the grand jury.

Perhaps she'd stay so busy she'd be able to forget, at least for a little time, Jake Mace, and the ominous call made to her by Jake's father.

6

Jeff Dalta hung up with the Mace family's friend in the Texas Senate. The man had given him a difficult time, but finally was persuaded around to the right way of thinking. Did he want his holdings in various Texas oil wells and pipe lines yanked from his grasp? Did he want leaks to the local news media that they should investigate more closely his ties with a certain shady bank president?

It was finally decided the senator would bear down on his contacts in Harlan County where Elizabeth Kapon practiced as county prosecutor. Setting her up for cocaine possession and use was the best way to go, the senator said. 'If we find a way to get her caught with coke on her person and then have a known dealer confess to being her supply, then the ABA will suspend her from practicing law until after she has a trial finding her guilty or innocent. Actually, bribing a witness in a trial would be better, but it's too tricky. Drug possession is a lot better.'

'It's not necessary she go to jail, Senator. I just want her unable to make a living.'

'There's not much we can do about keeping her from jail. If she's indicted on a trumped up felony charge, she'll face prison time unless the judge she draws goes easy and gives probation. And it has to be a felony crime or she won't get disbarred. But she won't face jail immediately. First she'll lose her ability to practice and then the trial process will take quite a bit of time. She'll no doubt get continuances in order to investigate on her own how she wound up charged.'

'You know she'll try to find out who did this, don't you?'

'Yes, I know that. Let me handle whatever problems that entails. Your people can come up with a dealer who can be bought? And you can make sure drugs are planted on her?'

'Mr Dalta, if anyone can do it, I can.'

The senator owed many favors and this was the second time he'd been called to return one. He'd been ineffectual with his pleas to the governor to give Jake a stay of execution. He knew this time he had to come through. To fail to give *two* favors was out of the question if he wanted to keep *himself* out of jail.

Technically, the senator was under the watchful eye of Chuck Corsina, the family don in Chicago who had, under other names, given heavy money to the senator's re-election campaign. But Corsina graciously gave Dalta his blessings to call in a favor on his behalf.

Dalta sat toying over the breakfast leavings the maid had not yet cleared from the table. He had fulfilled his bargain with Tony. The woman would be disbarred. She'd probably lose her teaching position with the university. She'd go broke in a short amount of time and eventually be in court facing a punishable offense as a felon.

Tony expected Dalta to stop here. With this arrangement.

Dalta would not stop. He'd hound Elizabeth Kapon into the ground. He'd burn her so bad, she'd come looking for the enemy who had destroyed her life.

Dalta would begin right now the next stage of his plan to bring first Kapon, and then Tony, down. As a group leader beneath Tony (though by all rights he should have been Tony's second in command), he could plot his boss' downfall while keeping a semblance of alliance with him. It had been done before. Many times. Luciano was father until the mid-thirties, replaced by Frank Costello, who in turn was replaced by the 'boss of all bosses,' Vito Genovese, in nineteen fifty-five. In fifty-one Anastasia replaced Mangano, and later Carlo Gambino replaced Anastasia.

The whole hierarchy was like the child's game of musical chairs, but deadly dangerous to play. Only the brave and smart lived through it.

Dalta needed his most trusted man to initiate the next stage of harassment against Kapon. That would be Chase Garduci, his cool, utterly unemotional, right-hand man. Together the two of them could turn Kapon's world into hell and guide her to Tony as the culprit, once she had had enough.

He couldn't wait for time to pass. He was enjoying this too much to stand for very many intervals where he had to wait for the outcome.

He stood from the breakfast table and went to his study, closing himself in. He dialed a number, let it ring four times, hung up. He redialed.

'Jeff?'

'Yeah, Chase, it's me. I need you for something,' Dalta said.

'What's that? Bailing one of the boys out of a gambling debt?'

'No, something more serious than that.'

'Yes.'

'Can you come over? Say within the hour?'

'I'll be there, boss.'

'And Chase?'

'Yeah?'

'Don't talk to anyone before you get over here, okay?'

'You think I'd consult with anyone when you wanted me?'

'I'm just saying.'

'Hey, Jeff, I'm your man.'

Tony sat at his dying father's bedside. Jill, his father's latest wife, bustled in and out of the sickroom like a bad wind blowing through the open windows, ruffling everything in its wake.

'Can't you ask her to stay out for a bit?' Tony asked his father. 'She makes me nervous. She does this every single day I visit. In and out. In and out.'

'She's only trying to help.'

'Her kind of help you don't need.'

The next time Jill rushed into the room, carrying a new pitcher of lemonade for their refreshment, Tony's father waved her out again with his right hand, the one that bore the tiger's eye pinkie ring he had worn since he was a young street punk in Los Angeles.

'Let me just sit this on the . . .' She took a few more steps toward the bed then halted when he waved again. 'All right,' she said, giving Tony a glare before turning. 'All right, dear.'

'Shut the door, Jill. And ask Marco in the hallway to see that no one disturbs us.'

'Thank you, Father. I don't know how you put up with her. She's . . .'

'Don't speak against my wife.'

Tony held back his criticisms. His father did not need to be told again how much his son disliked his choice in women these days. The old man was on the wane, his strength deserting him as fast as air from a balloon. Yesterday he had seemed stronger than today. Each passing hour leached life from him. Tony thought if he watched his father closely enough, observed him without any lapse of concentration, he could actually see life leaving him by slow, methodical increments.

He wanted Tony at his side as often as possible. It was a passing of the torch, Tony assumed, and a time of remembrance, of memoirs. His father talked about nothing but the old days.

'I'm sorry,' Tony said, genuinely meaning it. 'I've been on edge since Jake's death.'

The old man winced and his freshly shaved jowls quivered as he turned aside his head on the pillow. Warm desert air washed through the room, bringing with it the welcoming scent of roses. Tony loved his father's roses and always had. He'd had contractors create a rose garden behind his home so that he could enjoy the same scent and beauty he had been used to as a child in his father's house.

'I loved Jake,' Don Macedonia said. 'If it had not been for his sudden angers . . .'

Tony looked to the window. He couldn't see beyond the sill to the garden, but he could smell the flower-blossom scent on the wind. He wondered if the hybrid tea roses were in bud yet. His own were just leafing out nicely this year.

'There was a place for men like our Jake in the old days,' Tony's father continued. 'He would have made Luciano or Costello or Capone a good capo. But today, everything's changed.'

It was his father's litany, Tony thought. Things changed. They never stayed as they were. The old men deplored it and the young men rushed forward with zeal. It was always this way in any community of men.

'My biggest job has been peace keeping. I've been like Bonanno and Joe Profaci in that way.'

Tony nodded. 'I know, Father.'

'Jake didn't understand peace. Peace was not a word in his vocabulary. He would not have made a good leader, Tony.'

It was Tony's turn to wince, though he tried not to let his face show his pain. How would they know if Jake might have made a good leader or not? He had not lived long enough for them to find out. He had made one stupid momentous mistake and it had killed him.

He'd get that goddamn bitch for that. He would.

'The new Commissions – they believe that the business of America is business. They forget the old teachings. That the business of America should have been respect, they don't remember.'

Tony settled deeper into his chair and narrowed his eyes so that from the slits he could see just the edge of the brocaded bedspread. It was not that he did not wish to hear his father explain again, for the thousandth time, the differences between the Sicilian Mafia and the New Order. The sadness for him was that his father was right, but it didn't matter any longer who was right or who was wrong. The Families had taken a fork in the road and they now trod down that direction. They could not turn back, no matter what. Complaining and not accepting the new direction only held a leader back. And it sometimes killed him. Moving forward was the only alternative. You could still kill, mutilate, ruin, but you had to do it with more finesse. His father didn't understand that.

Everyone was waiting for his father to die so that Tony could take the reins and move ahead. They knew he would, despite the respect he had for his father's ways. If he didn't, the entire Family threatened to disintegrate. One of Tony's rivals would take control.

Tony could not allow that to happen. His father had spent his life making it what it was. It would not die out because of a conservative approach. Already New York and Chicago had long since given up the old way. All eyes were on him, Tony, to prove that he could join them. What the others didn't have to know was that he *liked* murder. He positively relished it. So the others were moving away from it. So fucking what? They hadn't the insight Tony Mace had. They didn't know the Family was built on blood and would die on it.

Perhaps his son had been a mirror reflection of his father. The only difference was poor Jake hadn't been old enough to handle affairs. Tony could. And would. He'd spill some blood before this was over. Lots of blood.

'My boys forced me into the prostitution, you know that, Tony. *E una sporca macchia sul' onore di Macedonia.*'

It's a dirty spot on the honor of Macedonia. Ah, now his father wanted forgiveness for what Tony thought needed none. He'd supply it, he supposed, to make him happy.

'It was unavoidable,' he said, opening his eyes wide to find his father staring at him sternly.

'A woman should not be used for profit, not by men of honor,' he said.

'Unavoidable,' Tony repeated. If the Family hadn't taken over, the gangs would have, he might have argued, but not to a man on his deathbed.

'Did you know that Capone gave me five thousand dollars as a gift at my wedding to your mother?'

His father had changed subjects. He did that often in these last days. It was as if his memory slipped from one spot to another in his past and he never noticed.

'That was a fortune then,' Tony admitted.

'It was as much as he gave to Joe Bonanno. We had a lavish wedding. From the money gifts I was able to buy partnerships in two casinos and one laundry, Franco's down on Washington Avenue.'

Tony smiled. Now his father owned a piece of nearly every casino in Vegas, half of the laundries supplying linen to the casinos, several all-night cafés, four mini-warehouses for furniture storage, a moving-van company, and various construction outfits. He had come a tremendous distance over the long years from one of the 'boys' to the Father of his Family. Had he not come from Sicily and been steeped in the old ways of doing things – no finesse, no quality control – he might even have profited more. Much more.

'Franco's is nothing anymore compared to the franchises, Father.'

The old man waved his hand in the air, frustrated. 'But then, in the forties, Franco turned a tidy profit for your mother and me. Capone's generous gift bought it for us,' he added.

Tony sat and waited, smelling the roses. He might have liked to have known Al Capone. Everyone said he was a crazy man, lived crazy, died crazy. There was purity in being crazy, doing crazy things. No one expected it. It was unpredictable. Al Capone was Tony's idol. He tried, whenever possible, to imitate him.

Every day Tony came here to listen to his father, to watch him slowly repeat his life aloud before he let it go. He would not have wanted to be anywhere else. Except perhaps next to his son, Jake, on a day trip into the desert in that little white Dodge Viper he had loved so much . . .

'I hear you make plans to revenge yourself on the lawyer in Texas,' his father said, apropos of nothing.

Tony, startled that his father knew of this, blinked slowly. 'And should I not?'

'I would think it through carefully first, Tony. You have a personal sense of justice and that is what men of honor must have, it is something I hope I've taught you, but the lawyer, she is female. I was told she had a child of her own and that her husband is dead.'

'I'm supposed to go easy on the person who took my only son? My *son* is dead.' Tony marveled now at his father, fearful he would be against him on this. It still mattered to him what his father thought.

'If anyone took Jake from us, it was a state law that allowed him to face a death sentence. You cannot fight a state.'

Tony shook his head. He could feel his heart beating faster as anger grew like a wild stallion locked in his chest. The scent of the roses in the garden now felt cloying and intrusive. He would rather at this moment have smelled the sewer or the open grave, something appropriate to his feelings of black suppressed rage. 'The woman lawyer called for death, Father. She didn't have to do that. She convinced the jury in the punishment phase to take his life. I can never forgive her for it. For that she will have to pay.'

'If you make her your enemy, every member of the Family is obligated to harm her.'

'I held a meeting. You were too ill to attend. I assured everyone this was my business alone, that they were not involved in my battle. There were protests, but everyone is busy anyway so I think they were relieved.'

'So you went to Dalta. I have never truly trusted him, how can you trust an Irishman? His recruitment, it seemed to me, was our worst mistake in twenty years. I never liked his father, either. Nor trusted him.'

'I have my reasons.'

'And I think I know what they are,' his father replied. 'But you run a great risk, Tony. You have indebted a snake to you. Given a chance, he will turn and bite. I may not be around to give you fair warning when he unsheathes his fangs.'

Tony glanced down at his right hand and the ring there. It was a gift from a friend in Sicily and it had a wide gold band with a rounded top imprinted with the opened, fanged mouth of a viper. He'd worn the ring since he was sixteen years old. It reminded him there were always enemies, deadly, belly-crawling enemies who came slinking through the dark with poison dripping from their teeth. It kept him wary. The ring's seal was one of the reasons he'd approved of buying Jake the Dodge Viper. He thought – mistakenly – the car's name would protect his son on the cross country trip the way his ring had protected him from all harm. 'I have it under control, Father. Don't worry. These are things you no longer have to contend with. Let me do it.'

His father stared at him a few seconds longer and then he turned onto his side and shut his eyes. Just before drifting into sleep he mumbled, 'We don't have the feasts we used to have in the old days . . .'

Tony calmed, sat back, opened his mind to the garden beyond the window again. No, they did not have the old feasts on important days any more. They didn't carry machine guns, either, or dress like gangsters in zoot suits, spats, and watch chains that hung to their knees. They didn't have the control over their men they once had or gain as much public notoriety for their exploits.

They were in business, the business of America, that dull boring corporate beast with all its far-reaching tentacles.

But they still had their snakes, their revenge when necessary, and their honor to protect. At least *he* did.

Just like the old days.

7

Beth closed the textbook on criminology and began gathering her things into her briefcase. Noise filled the room. Chairs scraped, desks were bumped, footsteps shuffled, students laughed and talked.

She did not know someone stood near her desk until he spoke.

'Has there ever been a case where someone involved in the law – besides Ted Bundy, that is – committed awesome criminal offenses?'

The young man who stood to her side with his books held to his chest made her uneasy. He had been in two of her classes so far and his questions were always troublesome. His sense of morality, she suspected, lay somewhere between normal American values and the deep blue sea of violent anarchy.

He did not look strange. He appeared to be a bookish creature, his dim gray eyes hiding behind amber-rimmed spectacles, his jaw soft, with a deeply cleft chin. He couldn't have weighed more than a hundred twenty although he was of average height for a twenty-year-old. He invariably wore black jeans and T-shirts with an oversized flannel shirt, the sleeves rolled to the elbow. As he walked the shirt hung open and flapped behind him.

'I'm not sure I recall anyone else,' she said, snapping shut the briefcase and hefting it off the desk in preparation to split the classroom and this obnoxious boy.

'You don't think the criminal mind is smart enough to enter the law?'

'That's not what I said.' She made peevish hand motions at the air to chase away the misconception. 'I have to hurry, I have a court case pending. If you'll excuse me . . .' She moved around him, heading for the door. The classroom was empty now. She was in too much of a hurry to be waylaid.

'Well, I think there are more crooks working within the judicial system than outside of it.'

Without turning she said, 'You have a right to your opinion, as wrong-headed as it might be.'

'You don't think so?'

She turned at the door. 'Paul, what is the point of this line of questioning?'

He shrugged and his narrow shoulders squeezed in toward the cache of books he still clutched tightly. 'I'm just curious, that's all. No one ever admits to how bad things really are.'

'Of course there are shyster lawyers and crooked judges and unfair jurors. Is that what you want to hear me say? That doesn't mean we need to completely overhaul the system, if that's what you're getting at. The American Bar adopted high ethical standards for a comprehensive code of professional responsibility in 1969. The majority of attorneys live by that code. There are fewer rogues inside the system than you might imagine.'

Paul came toward her, ready to argue, she could tell by the set of his grim mouth. 'I think there are murderers getting away with murder,' he said solemnly, his eyes twinkling grotesquely behind the lenses of his glasses. 'I think the law looks the other way when it feels like it. Consider Senator Kennedy and Chappaquiddick. I think . . .'

'I have to go. Maybe we can discuss this later.' She turned and moved into the throng of students who filled the hall. She knew Paul was at her back, marching right along to her steps. He was not someone to be deterred by rude and sudden departures.

'I'd like that,' he said. 'I'd like to hear your take on the subject.'

Beth neglected to answer him, but immediately felt guilty for behaving so badly. He was just a kid. She should show more patience. If only she had the time!

She rushed down the steps to the outside doors and down more steps to the walkway. A spring breeze ruffled the leaves of the water oaks that bordered the walk. She would not turn back to see if her student followed. After years of teaching she knew there would be an odd student like Paul nearly once every semester. They might not be the *same* as him, but incomprehensible on some level she could never reach.

There had been students who argued with her, students who fell in love with her, or so they thought, students who wanted to become a part of her life, adopted in some way so they could be near her. Yet it was the ones like Paul who asked the chilling questions who confused her the most.

What was a pre-law student doing interested in the darker side of the law? What was it about corruption that lured his interest away from the brighter aspects of justice? There seemed to be more and more of a counterculture attitude invading the new generation of law students. They came into her classes weaned from *Tales of the Crypt* and the cheap detective and law thrillers put out by Hollywood. These young people had been dubbed 'the X-Generation.'

She had tried to make some sense of what the X-Generation meant. Some of the kids told her the X stood for 'nothing,' they were the Nothing Generation or the Unknown Generation. Some said they were not boomers or children of boomers, so they had an unnamed generation. One clove-smoking young girl told her the title came from an old punk rock band headed by Billy Idol, but another claimed it came from a young author she called 'General X-er' who had written a book using the phrase.

All these explanations left Beth more muddled than she had been before. All she knew was that some of the pessimistic strain of their belief systems jarred against her like sandpaper against the jaw bone.

She needed a cup of coffee. Quick. She'd stop by the Sigmore station and run in for a large cup to take with her to the courthouse.

She drove past the pump island and parked at the end of the building, the last remaining parking spot at the convenience store. She reached into her bulging leather purse and grabbed her wallet. Hurrying from the Jeep, forgetting to lock the doors, Beth made for the glass door. There was a kitten, a stray one, it appeared to her, pale yellow fur matted with grease, huddled against the brick wall. She halted and picked it up. She whispered close to its face, 'What happened to you? Did someone drop you off to starve?'

The kitten purred and rubbed its head beneath her chin.

'All right. If no one claims you, I'll pick you up on the way out of the store. Wanna go home with me? Huh? Want some warm milk?'

She set the kitten down again and rushed forward. When in a rush she looked like a whirlwind, spinning along the walk, arms swinging, legs pumping, gaze straight ahead.

The coffee was old and nearly gone. She lifted the glass pot from the Bunn warmer and let out an exasperated sigh.

'Can you make fresh coffee?' she called to Joe, the day clerk.

'Sure thing, Ms Kapon, won't take a minute.'

'Listen, there's a little kitty outside hanging around. Is it yours?'

'Not mine, Ms Kapon. I don't have cats.'

'You don't know who it belongs to?'

'No, ma'am. Probably a stray.'

Not any longer, Beth thought. I guess I've been adopted. Now I will be owned by a cat.

She smiled, waiting for the coffee to drip.

Jazzy Deaver figured it wouldn't take a minute. He had followed Elizabeth Kapon's car from the university campus. After a week of tailing her, he noticed something she did that would allow him near her purse without the danger involved of having her catch sight of him. She was often in a hurry and left her car unlocked. Lot of people in this town did that. They didn't believe their vehicles vulnerable to theft the way they were in nearby Houston. They believed wrong, of course, but who was he to educate the fools?

More importantly concerning Kapon, however, was the habit she had of stopping off for gas or coffee at the Sigmore, something she did at least once a day, and how she usually ran inside with just her wallet and keys in her hand, leaving her purse on the car seat.

For a week Jazzy had been carrying around the baggie of coke. It made him sweat bullets to drive through Geneva with it on him, but those were the chances he was prepared to take to get his lover out of Huntsville prison.

He parked his old, rust-red truck behind a car filling up on gas, jumped down to the ground, and walked casually over to the Jeep at the end of the parking area out of sight of the entrance to the Sigmore. He opened the door, leaned over and at the same time slipped his hand into his shirt front, pulling out the bag. He stuffed it down into her purse, closed the leather flap, and got the hell away from the Jeep.

Back in his truck, he turned the ignition, backed up, and drove from the lot into traffic down Main Street. He wiped sweat from his face with a hand towel he carried on the seat beside him. Now all he had left to do was get another baggie smuggled into her house, into her bedroom. No big deal, that trick, not nearly as difficult as getting it on her person. He was on the way to unload the shit right now.

Soon he would go to prison on a charge of being Elizabeth Kapon's dealer. It wouldn't be for long. He'd been promised that. And about the time he'd get out, Juan would get out too. They'd be paroled together.

He couldn't wait for the time to fly.

Today everything conspired to make her run late. Paul asking his disturbing questions, the old coffee at the Sigmore station, the kitten that she'd put in her car, borrowing a box from the Sigmore attendant to keep the little ball of fluff safe until she got it home. And now the guards at the metal detector in the court house were waving her over to go through to be checked. She didn't recognize either of them. Maybe the city had made some new hirings she didn't know about. Usually she was waved on past because, after all, she was the district attorney, the guards knew who the hell she was, she didn't have to show her pass.

She frowned and walked over reluctantly. Where was her ID pass card? She kept it on her, of course, but it might be anywhere at the bottom of her purse.

'May we see your pass, please, Miss?'

'Sure, hold on . . .' She had her head down while rummaging in the big purse. The flap was back and stuff surged up from the bottom of the purse as she felt around, her fingers searching blindly for the hard plastic ID card with the little metal clip on the corner. She felt something soft and squishy encased in plastic and her fingers halted. A look of surprise transformed her face.

'Is something the matter?' the taller of the two guards asked.

'No . . . I . . . it's here somewhere. I'm Beth Kapon, county . . .'

She hauled up the squishy thing, thinking Melanie had slipped some kind of snack into her purse, wondering what in the world . . . ? and suddenly the guards had her by the arms, one on each side, and the tall one with the fierce look in his eyes was taking the baggie from her hand. 'Oh, what's this?' he said. 'Bringing an illegal substance right into the court house, ma'am? Lady, you got the balls of a brass monkey.'

Beth's mouth hung open, but she couldn't speak. Drugs? In her purse? But how? Who?

'Wait,' she said, trying to pull free. 'There's a mistake, this is stupid . . .'

'That's what they all say, ma'am, and frankly, the only mistake here is that you got out of bed this morning and we *know* who the stupid one is.'

Beth was held in questioning for two hours before she discovered the immediate warrant that had been issued for her house uncovered a second bag of coke hidden in a hat box in her bedroom clothes closet. It was claimed they also found a vanity mirror on her dresser with residue on it and a few sprinklings of cocaine in the carpet at the foot of that dresser.

There was no point at all in protesting the ridiculousness of these charges. She knew seconds after being hustled into custody by the guards at the metal detector that she had been had. The only thing she did not know was why and by whom. The fact of the set-up was hard to swallow only because it was so unexpected. She realized early into the interrogation that someone must have slipped the baggie into her purse at the Sigmore while she waited for fresh coffee to be brewed. She told the detective that, but he dismissed it out of hand.

Who and why? She had lots of friends in the court house. She had cop friends, judge friends, attorney friends. Even the law secretaries and county clerks liked her. What enemy could she have who would go to these lengths to involve her in a serious felony?

Nevertheless, someone had come gunning for her and the situation looked bleak. It looked so bleak she kept having to rub at her throat to loosen the constriction there that signaled she might break down and cry. She'd, by God, not weep like a weak female. She was trapped and she didn't know why, but she wouldn't find her way out by letting the tears flow.

She could be hard and unrelenting when necessary – that's how she had racked up a good record of convictions. So now she must be hard, not soft; most particularly, she must be cool. Surely everyone could see this was a frame? It was just too ridiculous to think she was into nose candy. All right, so last year a prominent contract real estate lawyer in town had been found to be an addict, and the corruption and ease of acquiring drugs tempted some cops, judges, and attorneys, but not her. *Not her.*

She called in an old trusted friend, Attorney Everett Shaw, to post bond. They sat in his car in the late hour just before sundown. The front of the court house was in deep shadow, the green lawn before it dappled with gold splotches leaking through the tree cover.

'This is serious,' Everett said. 'How did this happen, Beth?'

She hung her head and closed her eyes. She had been talking for hours, talking until she thought she couldn't talk again. 'Someone wants me bad,' she said. 'Do you know anything about it? Have you heard any rumors?'

He shook his head. 'Not a word. Why would someone plant drugs on you?'

'You're not implying I really do cocaine, are you, Everett?'

'I simply asked a question, Beth. Look, I know you're tired and this is a terrible blow, but you're going to have to trust somebody. If you don't trust me, you'd better call in someone else right now.'

She stared into his eyes. He was a man of character with a face that reflected the years it had taken to form that character. He had been the family lawyer before her father died. She had never had any reason to think him other than loyal and competent. But then she had never had any reason to believe she'd wind up needing legal counsel to get out of a mess like this either. People sometimes changed or were bribed or were threatened to act other than they should.

Nevertheless, Everett was right. She had to trust someone. If he was in on the frame, God help her because she really had no one else to turn to.

'I trust you,' she said. 'I just thought I heard a scold in your tone of voice. It's true I was stupid leaving my purse in the car the way I did. I started doing that the last couple of years because I carry so much . . . junk . . . in my purse. I just take in my wallet and keys when I run in for coffee or a quart of milk. How was I supposed to know someone meant to stash several grams of coke in my purse while I was gone? What we have to do now is find out how to get me out of this.'

'Getting you out of it is going to be hell.' He took off his glasses and pressed the flesh over the bridge of his nose, massaging it with his eyes closed. 'They have the dealer.'

'What dealer?'

'Purportedly *your* dealer. Your supplier.'

'It's worse than I thought.' The lump was back in her throat and she had to swallow around it.

He nodded and put on his glasses. He started the car and looked over his shoulder before pulling from the curbside. 'You're going to get suspended while this thing is worked out,' he said.

She hadn't even thought of her job and her license to practice, there had been too many charges and questions in the last few hours. 'But no one's found me guilty!' As soon as she said it, she knew it didn't matter. A charge as serious as this got an attorney suspended.

He gave her a long sad look. 'If they find you guilty, you're going to get disbarred, Beth. Since your past is squeaky clean and your record as prosecutor so good, there's every chance we can get you out of doing any time for this. But right now the Board of Bar Overseers will be forced to suspend you. These serious charges can't be overlooked. Life is not going to continue for you the way it has.'

She wanted to say, no joke, or, what a surprise, or, hell, I knew that as soon as I was grabbed, but the sarcastic replies merely burbled in her throat and issued forth as a groaning sound.

'Who's the dealer?' she asked.

'Jazzy Deaver. John, Johnny, Jazzy, take your pick. He's been operating around Geneva for a while and never been busted although he's been picked up before, but they had to let him go, no real hard evidence on him to get a conviction.'

'Oh great.'

'Want me to drive you home?'

'Sure. I have to get something out of my car first.'

'What's that?'

'It's a kitten I rescued from the Sigmore earlier today. It's probably starving.'

Everett just smiled at her, indulgent.

During the trip home Beth was silent. She knew about Jazzy, or rather about his reputation. A gay man, refugee from Houston, who had taken up and taken over the lucrative drug trade in Geneva.

'If I'm the prosecutor and I'm out of the scene, will they make Harry take over? Will Harry have to prosecute me, his old boss?' She had the kitten in her lap, stroking its fur. It was too skinny. She needed to get it checked at the vet.

'It looks that way, Beth.'

Harry wasn't going to want to do that. He was her assistant DA and whenever they worked together on a case, he spent too much time mooning around and asking her out for spaghetti or bingo down at the local VFW hall or for a drink at the Geneva Inn. It was the worst case of puppy love she had ever seen and she hadn't been able to dissuade him for two years now. He was ten years her junior, engaged finally to a sweet girl about to graduate from the university, but he just never gave up on her. She thought his attraction to her had more to do with fannish worship than with a physical magnetism.

Now he would be standing up before a grand jury asking for her indictment on charges of buying and using cocaine.

The whole thing was a farce! Harry knew her stand on drugs. He knew her worries about Melanie falling in with the wrong crowd. Yet because of trumped up evidence and a lying scumbag dealer, Harry was going to have to try to pin her to the jailhouse wall.

If it wasn't so crazy, so desperate, it could make her laugh.

As she got out of Everett's car in her driveway she said to him, 'How long can we hold off action on this?'

He shrugged. 'I don't know for sure, why?'

'I don't think Harry will push it and I sure don't think Harry's part of this. If we can hold off, we need to do it. I have to find out who's behind it.'

'And if you don't?'

Her mouth turned down and her gaze drifted to the front door of her house. 'If I don't, my goose is cooked. Someone will have me for dinner with the apple sauce.'

Everett reached over and squeezed her hand before she left the car. She waved at him as he pulled into the street. He wasn't part of it either, she was pretty sure of that. The fewer involved in a conspiracy, the better. Whoever had done this to her knew that. Jazzy was the stooge. The guards at the court house who took her into custody, she suspected they were in on it. And who else? The narcotics detective, J.T. Marchberry, who questioned her today might be, she couldn't tell just by looking at him or listening to him. He seemed only to be doing his job and sorry at that, knowing who she was. Although that could have been an act. It was going to be increasingly difficult to tell the good guys from the bad guys in this confusing affair.

She turned up the walk to her front door just as the sun disappeared.

Melanie would be home soon. She wasn't going to understand any of this. Inside the front door, Beth stopped and surveyed the damage. The police had not been kind. Cushions were off the sofa, things were moved and dumped and prodded. In the kitchen drawers stood open or emptied onto the counter.

She had the kitten in her arms, mewling its head off. She took milk from the fridge and heated it slightly in the microwave oven. She left the kitten happily slurping up milk while she checked out the rest of the house.

In her bedroom the bedcovers were ripped off and lying on the carpet, the mattress was askew on the box spring, and the drawers to her chest had been riffled through. The top of her dresser was chaotic and the small vanity mirror where she kept bottles of perfume was missing, taken in to be tagged and used against her as evidence of drug use.

The closet door stood open. She walked to it and stood looking into the dim recesses there. They had taken the empty shoe box with the contents they found in it. It was probably the box from Mervyn's that held her black pumps. She had kept the box in case the shoes didn't fit and she had to take them back.

Would a district attorney keep her private stash in a shoe box?

She laughed and the abrupt sound in the otherwise quiet house

68

caused her to flinch and shudder and wrap her arms around herself.

She sat down on the corner of the bare mattress and covered her face with her hands.

Now she could cry.

'I have bad news,' Beth said as Melanie came in the door.

It was seven-fifteen and Beth had made herself a cup of coffee. She sat on the living room sofa with the television off, one lamp burning, and her stomach roiling with acid. The new kitten, replete and sleepy, lay purring in her lap.

She had put the house back into order, but it still didn't seem right. Melanie's high school graduation photo was not in the proper spot on the television. The crystal apple on the coffee table should have been put back on the mantel.

Melanie dropped her book bag on the carpet and sank into the chair across from her mother. 'What is it? You look terrible, Mom. And where'd you get that kitten? Can I see it?'

'I found it at the Sigmore station. I think it was abandoned there.' She handed over the limp sleeping animal. 'Melanie, sit down. There's been an accusation against me. It seems they . . . it's been suggested that . . .'

'What? What's going on?' She had the kitten up against her cheek, her nose buried in its fur. The kitten woke, stretched.

'I was nabbed going into the court house around noon today with a bag of coke in my purse. Then they got a search warrant and found more of it here in the house.'

Melanie laughed then caught herself. 'Is this a joke? You know, I meant to apologize for all those times when I was a kid and played jokes on you, Mom. Maybe now's as good a time as any . . .'

'It's not a joke. Someone framed me. Everett had to post bail to get me home tonight.'

'Oh, Mom, that's the dumbest thing I ever heard. It's crazy.'

'It's not true. It's patently not true.'

'Someone's set you up?'

Beth looked around the walls of the living room, searching for a way out of her confusion so she could even talk about it with any semblance of intelligence. 'It's all I can think. I don't know why. What reason would someone have to do this to me?'

'Someone who wants revenge? What about some of the jerks you sent to jail? There's been a lot of them.'

'I suppose so. It has to be someone with enough power to get to people. But you know what this means, Melanie? It's my whole livelihood up for grabs. If I don't get off on this, I could be disbarred.'

'But you're an attorney, why would anyone believe you'd have drugs? How'd it get in your purse?'

Beth explained how she had run into the store for coffee on the way to the court house. How someone must have planted it then.

Beth rubbed her forehead hard as if to get the thought to stick. 'If it holds up, I could be ... I could be indicted myself. I could ... they could take away my license ... even send me to jail.'

'Shit!'

Beth looked at her daughter. 'You're so right,' she said. 'I'm in it up to my neck, sweetheart.'

'What will happen to us?'

Beth stood, the coffee mug shaking in her hand. She tried to control herself. She must think it all through, without emotion. Her intellect had saved her all her life. She must depend now on using it without getting so infuriated or worried that she missed the warning signs and pitfalls ahead. 'Nothing's going to happen,' she said, afraid not to believe her own optimistic words. 'I did nothing wrong. It will all come out in court and this will be thrown out.'

'Sure it will, Mom.' Melanie came to her. 'You can prove the stuff wasn't yours. Can't you?'

She didn't know if she could or not. She had become a master at undermining the defense and getting juries to believe their clients were guilty beyond a reasonable doubt. She wasn't so sure about defending herself since she'd never been called upon to do it before. Now she was on the other side of the table, the rules had all changed.

'I have a lot of work to do,' Beth said, patting her daughter absent-mindedly on the shoulder as she passed her. 'I need another pot of coffee. Think you can keep the kitty with you for a while?'

'Can I name it?'

'Sure. Everyone needs a name.'

'Can I call it Pope?'

'Pope?'

'Like in Alexander? Alexander Pope? I like his poems. You know . . . it's just . . . well, I just like them, that's all.'

'Sure. Take Pope and try to put all this out of your mind so you can get your schoolwork done.'

The house stayed quiet that night. Melanie didn't play her CD player in her bedroom and Beth didn't turn on the television, her usual form of relaxation, to watch old movies on the American Movie Channel. Instead, Melanie camped out in her room studying for a test in English the next day while Beth took notes on a legal pad at the kitchen table, trying to find a way out of a vast deep hole *someone* had dug for her.

'The wheels are turning,' Dalta said to Tony over the telephone. 'It won't be long now.'

'I appreciate that news.' Tony's eyes strayed to the French doors that led outside to the patio and beyond to the roses. The Parma-violet variety, a *reine des violettes* he had ordered specially last year, was finally sending out buds. It was an old-fashioned thornless cane, fragrant against gray-green foliage. If it bloomed this week, he'd cut a bouquet for his desk. He had a weakness for strange colored roses. He even had a black one, although so far it had not done well. Too much acidity in the soil.

'Do you want regular reports on her?' Dalta asked.

'I'd like that. Keep me informed.' Tony set down the receiver slowly, smiling. He had heard Dalta put out a call for Chase to come see him. It was all going along well. Just as planned.

Goddamn Dalta anyway. If the man was not so coldly ambitious, he would have been a wonderful asset to Tony. He once thought of making him consigliere. Until he knew him for what he was, that is. And until Tony's father pointed out Dalta's fault lines. He was riddled with them, like the San Andreas, ready to quake and crumble into disaster at any moment.

Picking up the gardening basket that held a hand trowel, a digger, scissors, and soft leather gloves, Tony opened the French doors and walked into the falling dusk. Soon the sprinkler system would come on so he must hurry. His roses needed trimming, the old blooms taken off so new ones could form.

71

He thought of his father, dying in his bed, and mentally walled off those thoughts into a room of his mind. He did not want to think of death just now. Jake was gone. His father was almost gone.

The world was shrinking to a smaller, colder place, and but for the roses, the freedom of money, and the hope of revenge, Tony might embrace a real despair that would break his heart and kill him.

Settling the basket at the foot of a glorious five-foot bush of Reine Victoria, Tony took out the gardening shears and began to clip the browning, warm, rose-pink blossoms and gently laid them into a heap for his regular gardener to pick up for the trash in the morning.

Even beautiful things died; that's what the rose garden taught him. Like Jake, the roses had a short span of life, and then they were gone forever, not even their scent left behind for remembrance.

8

The same week Beth found herself framed for the possession of cocaine, Phan Lieu made a quality buy of two grams for his own personal use. He rarely drank alcohol and he had never experimented with other drugs, but during the last year he had fallen hard for the improved sense of well-being cocaine provided him. He had tried it by accident at a friend's party. He knew it was dangerous for a man in his line of work to dabble in drugs, knew that addictions could ruin him, but the feeling he got when he first tried coke could not be duplicated in other ways. He felt invincible, energetic, swift and sure.

Always, while on a contract to kill someone, he knew in the back of his mind that he might forfeit his own life in the course of taking another's. He took only risks he had to in order to reach his victim, but some of those risks bordered on the suicidal. He had run through heavy traffic, walked a ledge on the fifteenth floor of a condominium, immersed himself for hours in swampy waters full of venomous snakes, and taken all manner of other possibly deadly actions.

After years of this, it began to wear on his nerves, even give him night sweats and wake him in terror. Unlike the joy of control he experienced as a child assassin in Vietnam, his adult years brought with them dread knowledge of all the possible events that might go wrong when trying to take someone's life. Once he began using coke, those risks frightened him less and his worries had been set free, floating in a balloon high into the sky.

It might not be smart to feel so invincible now, but if it calmed him, that mattered; it was what he needed. He took no *greater* risks under the influence. He just felt up to the tasks he set himself. His energy was boundless. His optimistic outlook restored.

Standing in a closed stall in the men's bathroom, he took the small vial now from his pocket and had a couple of toots. He wiped his nose and put his head back, looking up at the ceiling. He could almost time the exact moment when the drug hit his bloodstream, releasing that feeling of health and bright silvery intelligence he had come to rely on.

It was after eight at night, the St Louis train depot half-full of ticketed passengers waiting for the arrival of Amtrak's Superliner from Dallas/Fort Worth. From St Louis it would take them up the midwest corridor through Springfield and Bloomington to Chicago. Judging from their faces, not many of them seemed to be excited about the prospect. Many were probably business people, rather than vacationers, shuttling between St Louis and Chicago.

To spend the empty time Phan had on his hands he played a game where he guessed who was traveling for business, who for pleasure. The elderly woman with the thick spectacles and paisley traveling bag was pleasure. Three young males were dressed in sweatshirts with college emblems. They shared a single Sony CD player, passing it between them every few minutes. Easy to guess they weren't business or vacation, either, but students returning to a university. The dowdy middle-aged couple were on a second honeymoon, Phan imagined, seeing how they held hands and kept sneaking smiles at one another.

The rest of the people in the small station room were traveling for business, briefcases and overnight bags stacked next to their legs or lying in their laps. They all had a weary, overworked look about them, resigned to the fate of several hours on the tracks before they could get to their hotel rooms for the night.

Phan stepped outside the station room into the fluorescent-flooded night to wait impatiently for the same train. It was due in thirty minutes. On it was a passenger getting off at the station to catch another train heading west to Kansas City. This man was his target. One of Texas' most influential and powerful senators had hired Phan, through his beautiful – and sexually expert – executive assistant, to take the target out of circulation. Phan knew his name, had studied a photograph of him so he'd recognize the man, and understood that he was a blackmailer. He had harassed the senator for six months and was now demanding a million dollars to keep his mouth shut. His damaging evidence of corrupt financial dealings with certain state banking systems could unseat the senator from office and muddy his reputation so that he would not be able to hold office again in his life.

The senator thought paying Phan a quarter of a million to shut the blackmailer up permanently was vastly more economical and afforded him much more peace of mind. The blackmailer might change his mind later and talk. Or come back for more money. You couldn't deal with these sorts any more than you could bargain with terrorists.

A teen girl came through the exit door from the station. Phan glanced at her. She kept her distance as she shook out a Carlton and lit it, dragging in deeply. He watched the expelled smoke spiral up past the overhead station lights and disappear beyond into the darkness. That one pedestrian event caused Phan to daydream, his mind slipping skyward with the gray smoke.

He turned his body to the side so that she wouldn't be tempted to start a conversation. He hadn't any time for kids, for complications. No time, no time for daydreaming! His attention must be completely focused on his job, seeing it through to conclusion.

The Amtrak station abutted the train tracks and behind it lay a shadowy parking lot. Through that lot and around a fence was a street that led up to Union Station, the old train station that had been refurbished and changed into a giant shopping mall. Phan fully expected his man to leave the small station and walk toward the brightly lit Union Station.

According to the schedules the train leaving for Kansas City and points beyond would not arrive for his transfer until eleven p.m. No one sat in the tiny, boring track-side station for that many hours. You couldn't even get a decent cup of coffee as there was no café, just a vending machine with vile black fluid in it labeled coffee and costing too much.

Where Phan meant to make his move was on the dimly-lit street leading to Union Station. A building, a huge red-brick church, was being renovated on the right side of the street and had a fence barricade to keep out the riffraff. This insured there would be no witnesses from that direction at this time of night who might see the murder take place. To the left of the street and down a small slope, sprawled Union Station's great open parking area. Phan would watch for people going to or from their cars and time his approach when the lot was empty.

The rattle-roar of an approaching train from the south brought Phan from contemplation of his plans. He noticed the teen girl had moved to the far end of the railing and she was still smoking a cigarette. The door behind him opened and eager passengers spilled from inside the station, down the ramp, and to the gravel lining the side of the tracks. Phan followed at a leisurely pace, but hung back to the rear, waiting for the train to halt and unload the transferring passengers and the people whose trips ended in St Louis.

The potential victim was a straggler. He came out with some of the last passengers, his arms loaded with three medium-sized bags. Phan stood quietly, his blood singing merrily through his veins with songs of victory. He was so glad his man had not been delayed or put onto another train or decided to take a later one. It cut down on all the hassle tremendously to have them show up when first expected.

As the shift took place, passengers departing for those going aboard, Phan went up the ramp again, walked purposely through the station, noting his mark stood at the bank of lockers stuffing bags into two of them, one he held open precariously with his knee. Phan went out the other side of the station, exiting onto a similar ramp. He strode down it and across the parking lot, never looking behind him . When he reached the street, he took the right sidewalk, the one his victim logically would *not* take, and finding a crêpe myrtle, lounged with his back to the church construction fence without touching it. He wouldn't even be seen here unless someone looked right at him. He fancied himself a shadow, darker than midnight, the kind of shadow the Angel of Death might throw if he visited Earth.

Give his man ten minutes and he would be along. Unless he stayed in the Amtrak station, which Phan hoped would not happen. It would ruin the entire plan and make him recruit a new one.

Less than five minutes passed and a figure moved beyond the fenced lot of the Amtrak station and into the street. Phan smiled. The figure was a man alone. It was him, the one, the dead man.

Phan watched him angle across the street to the left sidewalk, just as he was supposed to do. When he had gotten halfway up the block and no one else came from the station, Phan stepped out into the street and crossed it. He took great strides, but stealthy ones. He fingered the stiletto in his inside jacket pocket. When he reached his victim, he saw the other man's shoulders tense as if just hearing or sensing someone behind him, saw him slowly pivot his torso to look back, and then Phan had him around the neck, the stiletto out and buried next to his sternum, piercing his heart. One swift move and a powerful thrust was all it took. Phan knew where the bones were located, how to miss them, how to plunge the knife-tip straight down between the ribs and into the core of the pumping heart.

The victim let out a partial scream that Phan immediately stifled with his hand, moving it up from the man's neck to his lips. He pulled out the knife and lowered the falling body gently to the sidewalk, still warm from a day's sun.

Phan looked around quickly to be sure there were no witnesses and, satisfied there were none, reached inside the man's vest pocket and withdrew his wallet. He slipped it into his own coat, wiped the knife blade on the victim's shirt front to clean it, returned it to his own pocket and, swiveling, left the scene for his car parked in the Amtrak lot.

The deed was done. Contract fulfilled. It would appear to the police to be a mugging, the missing wallet proof that some vagrant thief had killed the man for his money.

And someone had.

Phan was a quarter million richer tonight and the senator was safe.

On the long drive back to Texas the highway sometimes paralleled the railroad tracks and twice throughout the remainder of the night Phan saw trains roll past, their wheels thumpety-thumping so loud he could feel it through the floorboard of his car. When the train whistle blew at crossings, he tried not to let the sound depress him, but the cocaine had worn off now and he did not feel so lordly and impervious. In fact, he caught himself checking the rearview mirror for police car lights and slowing down automatically, not wishing to be stopped for going a few miles over the speed limit.

He switched on the radio and listened to DJs playing soulful country tunes for lonely truckers. He frowned. Hated that crying-eye stuff. Hit the scan button and found talk shows and oldies' stations and all-news stations. Nothing suited him so he turned the power off on the radio and listened to the hypnotic hum of tires over blacktop.

He wondered idly if the senator might do him a favor now? If he had a way of checking military records from the Vietnam war? He would have to call him when he was home again and make the request.

Phan's father had to be somewhere. Anyone could be tracked. If the senator couldn't help, Phan had enough money now to hire his own private investigators.

The old scene of what he would do when he did find his father played through his mind. He had written and rewritten this scene countless times. He might stand in front of him and say, 'I'm Phan Lieu, your firstborn.' Or he might say, 'I'm the son you left behind to die in Vietnam.' Or, 'I'm the product of your callous disregard for my mother in Vietnam. I was born in 1968 and you are my father.' He had about six stock scenarios he played over and over, everything from how he stood to what he wore to what he wanted to see in his father's face when he told him the news.

Phan hated him. More than anyone in his life. It was not until he was grown and a US citizen that the hatred grew so large inside him it felt as if he carried around an old, rotting iron paperweight in his gut. The weight of it nagged at him, the rust ate through his intestines like a cancer and turned out bile into his blood. He never would have suffered in his life if his father had taken his mother to live with him. He would not have had to join with other beggers and outcasts to become a killer to make his way in the world. He would not have been cheated, molested, spat upon, left homeless, and called wretched names.

Any father who had caused such shame, disgrace, and pain to befall a son was not a man, but a worm.

Phan savagely rolled down the car window and thrust his head out into the rushing night air. He had gotten himself so worked up he had grown hot all over, his skin prickling with pinpoints of heat.

Maybe he should find a room for the night and try to sleep. He could drive into Texas in the morning when he was refreshed. The senator could wait to hear the good news.

He brought his head back inside the car and began to watch for exits citing lodging ahead.

It was nearly midnight and a kill always left him worn out these days. At twenty-seven he wondered if he was becoming an old man. He laughed a disgusted laugh while reaching for the coke vial for the second time that night. He thought he needed something to take away his dark mood and the drug was all he could think that might do it. Just living life in the raw certainly couldn't.

9

Chase Garduci flew into Houston Intercontinental Airport on a Friday evening and rented a Ford Taurus. It took an hour and a half to drive to Geneva, Texas, so that by the time he entered town it was night and the streets bustled with activity.

It was a real paycheck kind of town, he thought, smiling pleasantly at the pedestrians. He knew there was a state-supported university here, but you wouldn't know it from how the natives were dressed. The majority of people he saw consisted of stringy-haired women in tight shorts that showed off their hips to disadvantage, and sloppily dressed men, goddamn *cowboys*, Chase assumed, in denim jeans and rawhide belts.

He observed the thirty mile an hour speed zone and kept an eye peeled for patrol cars. His identification gave a false name and address, but he still didn't like to mess with the cops. Especially Texas cops. They were part of the problem leading Jake Mace to extract revenge in this town years ago. In a roundabout way, the cops were responsible for everything that had happened since and the reason Chase himself was here to make merry mischief. If that highway patrolman hadn't busted Jake for speeding, Dalta wouldn't have sent for him with instructions to make life miserable for a certain female district attorney in this backwater hick town.

Chase turned into the Geneva Inn and secured a room. Tomorrow he would find a house or an apartment to rent, but for tonight the little inn would do fine. In the attached motel restaurant he ordered the meatloaf dinner and decided Texans didn't know how to cook. It was a shame and disgrace how someone could ruin a recipe so simple as meatloaf.

It was going to be a long and unhappy visit, he could tell that right now. He certainly was not going to cook for himself when he got a place to stay. And if he had to keep eating this shit, he might wind up losing some weight.

He glanced at himself in the dark plate-glass lining the booth. He couldn't afford weight loss. He already looked like Harry Dean Stanton, the movie actor with the stick body and concave cheeks. Though he was handsomer than Harry Dean, he thought. Had better hair and fewer pockmarks. But he didn't weigh an ounce more, or stand an inch taller, he'd bet.

The waitress refilled his glass of iced tea and took away the half-finished meal.

Chase glanced over at a cherry pie protected beneath a clear cake plate cover. He'd have some of that, with vanilla ice cream. Sweets might keep him from turning to sinew over bone.

While nibbling at the pie, scooping the red cherries from inside the gooey crust, Chase gazed at a photo of Elizabeth Kapon he kept cupped in his left hand. She was a looker. A smaller, softer version of Kathleen Turner. But a bushy-headed blonde like Turner, with the tipped nose and the full lips. There was a wariness in Kapon's eyes that even an actress couldn't disguise, but that didn't worry Chase. He had spent his lifetime harassing much harder cases than her. She was a real step down for him, considering his former assignments. He wouldn't have come all the way to Buttfuck, Texas, to waste time on her if given his druthers.

Of course he didn't need her photo anymore. Before ever reaching Geneva, Texas, he had studied the photograph the way a student crams for a particularly important exam. Now he carried her face – every plane and curve, every quirk and glint of eye – on the rim of his mind like the memory of a lost love. She clung to his thoughts tenaciously as a willow growing from the side of a steep mossy bank beside a rushing river. By the time he drove into town, he was obsessed with getting a look at her in the flesh.

She looked nothing like Connie Mace. He groaned inwardly at the thought of not seeing Connie for a while. He looked back at the photo. This woman possessed the same indefinable quality he had always hoped to find in a woman of his own. Naturally the idea he could interest a woman like Beth or Connie was out of the question. He hadn't a thing in common with them or anything to offer a woman of their class. He was not fool enough to think otherwise. The only way he had discovered he might get close to these kind of women was to stalk them on the sly or find them alone and take them by surprise. It wasn't the most desirable conditions for telling a woman he loved her. Hostage situations didn't lend themselves to romance. Nevertheless, it was what he was reduced to and he had long since accepted the difficulties.

Jeff wanted him to scare the Kapon woman. Scare her good. Tony wanted him to make her wish she were dead.

There was no question of not following orders. If he did a good job, maybe Tony would reward him. He'd never get Connie, hell no, but Tony might give him Kapon's daughter for a plaything. He was so weary of getting off on street sluts or having to scorch his imagination with bare-breasted, rope-and-throat-collar scenes while he masturbated. You'd think once in his life he'd get what he truly goddamn wanted.

He paused with the fork halfway to his mouth. Cherry filling dripped from the tines into the saucer.

Morbid thoughts from the past were intruding again. He set the fork in the plate and let them come. Guys being buried in concrete foundations of buildings and parking lots, dropped off mountain sides into ravines, dumped into lakes and the sea. No shit, those were good times. Chase was one of those people who did those types of low profile jobs because . . . well, because he was good at it. He was the best, by God.

He was not too old to prove how good he still was. Short of taking Kapon's life, he could do whatever the hell he wanted with her. It was . . . it was going to be a *party*.

'Hey, baby,' Chase called to the passing waitress. He used his best Texas drawl. He sounded like John Wayne in a shitkicker western. 'I'll take that check now, if you got the time.'

While he waited for her to bring it to him, he wondered if that gleam he'd seen flash in her eye meant anything suggestive. She looked a little like Melanie Griffith with bigger teeth and a murkier complexion. And maybe a harder jaw. Still, not too bad.

He wouldn't kick her out of bed. He wasn't dead like Gene Autry.

But she'd have nothing to do with him. Even waitresses were out of his class. On some gut level they knew that and avoided him. The gleam he'd seen in her eye had probably been native fear. She knew something wasn't quite right about him. He had searched in mirrors for hours trying to guess what it was women saw in him, feared in him. Hell, he wasn't so handsome, but that wasn't it. He wasn't ugly. Maybe they saw what he really wanted from them. In his eyes or something.

You couldn't fool women.

As he left the restaurant and drove the small-town streets to familiarize himself with his surroundings, he had Beth's face in the forefront of his mind. Would her daughter look like her, only younger? Would she look better?

This trip was ripe with possibility. He had never stuck his tongue into the warm salty crevices of both a mother and daughter before. It sounded pretty perverted. And appealing. Goddamn if it didn't.

He began humming along with a song on the radio, 'When Doves Cry' by Prince. It was a good day to be alive. And Geneva, Texas, country-western sappy as it appeared, was as good a place as any for the kind of happy-time business he always enjoyed the most.

Beth admitted to herself one night during the showing on American Film Classics of an old Frank Sinatra movie that she missed teaching her classes at the university more than she missed prosecuting cases for the county.

Which was just as well. She'd never be elected again. Having to step down once she was suspended hit the daily paper with bold headlines. Everyone in the district knew about the drug charges. Geneva was so conservative they were the kind of people who wrote in Ronald Reagan on the presidential ticket years after he was ineligible to run and believed every over-zealous word the whacked-out, conservative radio talk-show hosts uttered.

The bank account dwindled over the weeks following her arrest.

Without a regular income, she and Melanie had to live on savings and the small checks from the university. Beth expected to be ousted from her professorial position sooner than she had been. But she knew the minute she was summoned to the dean's office, her job was gone.

'You understand our position, Beth,' he had said to her in his normal brisk and officious manner. 'What would it look like if we kept you on while there are suspicions of misconduct hanging over your head? Now when this is all cleared up, as I am certain it will be, your schedule will be reinstated. However, until then we have to protect the University's standing in the community . . .'

Driving home she beat the steering wheel and found that her cheeks were wet with tears of frustration. What was she going to do? At odd moments she would find herself standing rigid, feeling as if she'd been kicked in the gut. Everything had happened so suddenly she couldn't get used to the idea all she'd worked for was about to be stolen from her. She had gone through the indictment and arraignment processes. She had gotten the trial postponed, hoping to clear herself, but all she had accomplished was more trouble. She couldn't get a line on who might have done this despicable thing to her and she had grown to fear she never would. He or she or they seemed so cleverly concealed, she might never uncover the truth.

Melanie continued her classes without any break, but the tuition, book costs, and lab fees were escalating and draining the funds.

Beth's account at the bank dropped lower and lower.

Everett finally came to her and suggested she quickly invest in something before all the money was gone and she was destitute. He didn't care about his bill, he said, defending her was his pleasure. She could pay him back at some later date when she'd been cleared of all charges, but she couldn't just sit in her house every day and write out checks. If she didn't make what money she had left work for her, her daughter would have to drop out of college, and she might even lose the mortgage on her house.

The next day Beth called a friend she had in real estate and put her home on the market. She hated doing it, but Everett was right. She couldn't stew in her own juices while her whole world fell apart. There was Melanie to think about.

Beth was no stranger to working things out. She had worked her way through law school and was thrifty once she had a position with the county. Sure, it had taken a few thousand in publicity to get herself elected as DA but once she'd succeeded, she had felt secure for the first time since her husband died.

Now she was on the ropes again and if she didn't bounce back quickly, she was down for the count.

She smiled at Frank Sinatra, imagining herself Mohammed Ali, staggering around under too much weight and too many years, going down, smacking the mat. But he went out a champ and so would she.

Some way.

Pope jumped to the sofa, clawing his way up to her. She picked up the kitten and set it in her lap. Melanie had taken it to a vet for a check up and inoculations.

'Poor little kitty,' she cooed, stroking the cat gently. 'Poor lost little kitty.'

Her real estate agent friend had a buyer in the wings and the house sold before it was even advertized. 'I tell you what you ought to do with the profit,' Marge said, over the signing of contracts.

'What's that?'

'There's a nice three-story apartment house for sale that turns a good monthly income. You could pick it up, live in one of the units with Melanie, and not have to worry about making a living right now. It's an older building, but in good shape. New roof, newly painted outside.'

Beth went to see it. She expected the house to be full of college students living off campus and was surprised to find it inhabited by the elderly. She turned to Marge. 'You didn't tell me . . .'

'What's the difference? You think the college kids pay on time better than the retired?' She shook her head. 'This is a good investment, Beth. Keep your mind open about it.'

Beth talked it over with Melanie. Her daughter sulked more often lately and they had had arguments. She had been raised in the house Beth was forced to sell and she blamed her mother for losing it.

'I don't want to live with a bunch of old people,' she had said, grimacing as if she smelled something bad in the air.

'What do you have against old people? It seems impossible now, but one day you'll be old, too. I'm not happy about this attitude you've adopted lately, Melanie. You act like a spoiled brat. You think any of this is easy for *me*? You think I like sitting at home watching television and worrying myself to death? I'm the one facing all this loss. You'll finish college one day and leave me to live your own life. What if I get disbarred? What if I'm found guilty *and* get disbarred? Don't you ever think about anyone but yourself?'

Beth hadn't meant to browbeat her daughter so thoroughly, but Melanie's personality changes, though they might be normal for a young woman beginning her life, rubbed Beth all wrong. When Melanie was a child she was the most respectful, cheerful little girl anyone knew. Nowadays she moped around, nursed deep silences, and was super-critical of not only her mother, but of others as well. She wore disdain like a scarf around her neck.

'I just don't see why you have to buy apartments. We never lived in an apartment before. What will my friends think when they see a bunch of old folks tottering around the place?'

Beth sighed and sat down at the kitchen table. 'If you care so much what your friends think I suppose you can go find yourself a job, quit school, and support yourself. You can live wherever you want then.'

'I can't make any money in this town!'

'That's what I've been trying to point out to you. I can't make any either, not without practicing law. It's either invest in the apartment house or move to Houston and work as a secretary or go on the dole. Which one do you prefer I do?'

Oh, she could be sarcastic, yes, she most certainly could, and she wasn't particularly proud of her sharp tongue, but there appeared to be no other way of dealing with headstrong children intent on having their way.

Melanie sighed dramatically and said, 'Okay, it's your money. If you want the apartment house, I'll try not to say anything else about it.'

'Thank you.'

'But I can't promise I'll sit and read books to the old people or run errands for them. I don't have time for that kind of stuff.'

'I doubt they'll ask you to do anything, Melanie. We may never even see them that often.'

Melanie gave her a look, shrugged, and left the house. She had a date with the son of a chemistry professor. He had the cutest buns and eyes like starlight, she said.

Beth sat watching Frank on the small TV screen and wondered when women of her generation had stopped looking at men's 'buns.' And she was sure she had never seen eyes like starlight. It smacked of poetry to her and judging by the turns her life had taken recently, she wouldn't think very poetically about anyone or anything for a very long time to come.

She hugged Pope close and dreamed of easier days ahead. She believed in optimism. Everything would work out just fine. It had to, really.

10

The funeral for Don Alberto Macedonia brought so many attendees who had come to pay their last respects that Our Lady of Angels Catholic church was filled to capacity and a crowd overflowed outside to stand in reverent silence in the hot, bright sunshine of a perfect Vegas morning.

Tony went to his father's coffin, a perfect white long-stemmed John F. Kennedy rose from his garden in his hand, and placed it on his father's chest. He leaned down then and kissed each side of his father's cold face. 'Goodbye,' he whispered. 'Take care of Jake until I see him again.'

Tony turned, a military flourish, for he felt stiff, his limbs difficult to maneuver, and walked to the front of the church to lead the procession to the cemetery. His wife joined him, linking her arm through his, and he leaned on her a little, unsure of his own strength.

Later, at the large, subdued reception held in his home, Tony was approached by Jeff Dalta who bowed his head and said, 'Even though we knew he was going, this is a profound shock. I'm very sorry, Tony.'

Tony said nothing. He shook Dalta's hand and let him pass through the reception line into the room where there were refreshments. From the corner of his eye he watched for Dalta's man, Chase, and never saw him. It was not an insult, but there were a few who wondered why Chase had not attended the funeral of the man who headed the Mace family in Vegas.

Tony knew where Chase was heading so he was not surprised the man did not make the funeral. Nothing surprised him anymore really. He did not live to be forty-seven years old by remaining uninformed of all the moves his boys made.

Jamie Molissa, Tony's second, stood next to him. He leaned over now and said in a low voice, 'I don't like that look on Jeff. He's up to no good.'

Tony walked toward his office and Jamie followed. On the way, once they were out of earshot of the others, Tony said, 'Keep your eye on him. He's making a move without my say-so.'

Jamie stiffened. 'I could deal with him now if you want me to.'

'No, no, I don't want you to interfere. Give him rope and he'll dangle. I just want a very quiet watch put on him. Under no circumstances do you let him find out.'

'He's a fucking troublemaker, Tony.'

'He has never been other than that,' Tony said, opening the door to his office and going to the bar to pour them drinks. 'My father told me long ago it was a mistake to trust him.'

Jamie, forgetting himself, shook out a Lucky Strike from the pack in his coat pocket and struck a match. Tony turned from the bar, frowning. Jamie glanced up, remembered where he was and blew out the match. He put the cigarette back into the pack. 'I'm sorry,' he said. 'I've been nervous.'

'It suffocates my roses,' Tony said, turning his back. 'And those things will kill you.' If someone or something doesn't do it first, he thought. There was always intrigue and the time after a leader's death was the most dangerous time. With Tony as the new Don, his second was in just as much uneasy jeopardy as anyone. Not that he worried about Dalta doing anything directly to replace him in the seat of power. That wasn't Dalta's way, nor was it the way Tony had things planned to happen.

So far Dalta had acted just as Tony had expected him to. If he continued along the path he now followed, it would all work out just fine.

Although it did no harm to alert Jamie and place him in the watchdog position. Sometimes plans fell apart, causing serious repercussions. It was only proper insurance to have one's guard up just in case.

* * *

Jeff Dalta stayed as far away from his wife and child as possible while in Tony's house. When he caught Denise's eye, he smiled and moved farther into the crowd to pump hands, pat backs, and say hello. What would they all think if he appeared devoted to such a fat woman? Although family was sacrosanct with the Italians in the room, he still believed they took pity on him and whispered behind his back that once his wife had been a beautiful woman and now look at her, a whale of a woman in an ankle-length black shift with a sprig of lavender pinned in her hair as if she were still a girl, fresh and coquettish enough for the adornment of flowers.

The funeral was an important time to renew old friendships and establish new ones with some of the group leaders outside the city of Vegas who had flown in to pay their respects to the old man – and the new man who took his place. Dalta made the rounds, responded with proper regard for the fallen Father by recalling whatever kind, quirky, or humorous event Don Macedonia had been involved in, the deals he had made, the cohesiveness in the family he had inspired.

Not that he meant a word of this false praise. Alberto Macedonia had been a tired, mean, unlettered old man who had never liked him from the first. He wouldn't be surprised if he hadn't told Tony early on that they should shove him outside the city limits, his bags packed and his walking shoes on. Dalta was glad he was dead. He had lived far too long as it was. His ideas were outdated and his rule shaky. It had been ten years since he could remember all the names of his boys, much less what they might be up to.

It was good he was gone so it was difficult for Dalta to keep his smile fleeting and sad when he talked of him. Now and again he could feel his lips betraying him so that he had to turn from the conversation and reach for a drink or a sweet from a sideboard so others could not see the truth written in his eyes.

One of these times that he turned to protect himself, he turned back again to find Tony standing in the circle, staring at him with a coldness that sent a shock through Dalta's spine. Dalta nodded his head and popped a butter mint into his mouth.

After a couple of minutes accepting condolences, Tony wandered away to another gathering, but the suddenness of his appearance and the look on his face left Dalta feeling cold and empty inside. Tony couldn't know, could he? About Chase? It was ridiculous. How could he? The funeral had Dalta on edge, that's all, seeing suspicion where there was none, catching ghosts from the corner of his eye.

Dalta excused himself and went in search of Denise. He wanted to go home now. Maybe he'd drop off his family and head down to the Strip where he could find a pretty woman to spend some time with him, cheer him up. He'd want to be discreet. How would it look if it was mentioned he was seen out carousing with the dancers the night Don Macedonia was laid to rest? He'd have Tony breathing down his neck for sure then.

Nevertheless, he had heard there was a new line of dancers at the Four Kings. The rumor definitely needed checking into.

Dalta rarely moved in public with bodyguards or boys from his group. For one thing it made him look too conspicuous. He sure as hell didn't like being taken for a wiseguy. That was for the idiots who didn't have the brains God gave a chicken. And for another thing, he was a lone operator when it came to women.

There was an early show on at the Four Kings and he sat at a dark back table drinking good brandy. He watched the dancers, singling out those he wanted to know more intimately. This was worlds better than milling around with mourners, half of whom couldn't give a shit one way or the other about the deceased.

An hour into the show and Dalta called over his waiter and sent a note to a girl who would be going off stage in the next five minutes.

Twenty minutes and another brandy later the girl appeared at his table, dressed for the evening in a strapless little red number that made his heart skip a beat. Rattatat, rattatat.

'Hello there,' he said. 'Have a seat, baby.'

'Am I supposed to know you?'

He allowed a small frown to slip close around his eyes. Perhaps he had made a mistake choosing her. Obviously she had not consulted any of the other girls or the stage manager about him or she would know who she was dealing with. 'My name's Jeff,' he said, regaining his good humor. She really was a knockout in the red dress. 'Why don't you sit down and we'll get better acquainted.'

'Don't mind if I do. My feet hurt anyway.'

He thought she'd be brainless. Most of them were. Many of the dancers were scouted from clubs all over the country and offered high weekly pay in Vegas to strut their stuff. Half of them didn't last a month, but there was rarely one among them with enough sense to have saved enough for the bus ticket back to Podunk, Midwest America. He wasn't sure yet about this girl, but he had a feeling she wasn't as stupid as most of the girls in the business.

'What's your name? I notice you didn't much care for me calling you "baby." '

'No, I don't like that. My name's Jordan. You can call me Jordie.'

'What would you like to drink, Jordie?'

'Water with a slice of lemon?'

She answered with a question the way he had heard some of the Southern girls talk, although her accent was bland, not regional. 'Let me guess where you're from,' he said.

'You can try.'

'Nashville, Tennessee.'

Her blue eyes widened. 'Close. Gatlinburg. How'd you know?'

'It was the way you asked for the water.'

She shrugged. 'I've been working on getting rid of the accent. I thought I was doing pretty good.'

'Oh you are,' he lied, 'I've just met a lot of people.'

The waiter brought her spring water with lemon. While squeezing the slice into the water, making it cloudy, she said, 'The other girls tell me if I'm friendly with the customers they might take me out to the tables and let me bet with their chips.'

He laughed. 'They told you that, huh?'

'I don't think it's funny, especially. Are you going to take me out to the tables? I hear a girl can supplement her income by several hundred a week if the customer she's with has the knack.'

'For winning, you mean?'

'Sure, for winning. Do you win?'

When she asked him these questions she stared straight into his eyes, a challenge to lie to her. She was not brainless. Naive and too honest for her own good, too honest for the hustle, that was for sure, but not brainless. 'I've been known to win sometimes.' When he smiled she dipped her shoulders a little and his gaze drifted down to the tops of her breasts. She was probably a true blonde and her nipples pale pink . . .

'I believe you,' she said. 'So when are we going to make some money?'

'Jordie, anyone ever tell you you can be a little pushy?'

'All the time,' she said, not smiling even a little. 'So when are we going?'

He laughed again because he liked her and he wanted to fuck her and the only way he was going to get what he wanted was to play the game according to her rules. She was going to be costly. And worth it, he suspected.

Two hours later he had enjoyed a run of mild good luck at the craps table that netted Jordie almost as much as she was paid to dance for the Four Kings. When he led her from the table hugging the tray of chips she said, 'Hey, thanks, this is the biggest haul I've had since I've been in town.'

'How long would that be?' She amused him so much he had even been able to put off the thought of taking her to bed while playing the dice.

'Forty-one days come midnight.'

'You count the days?' He touched her elbow and aimed her to one of the cash-out windows. As they moved through people he saw how they gave her a second look. Any one of the men in the room would have been flattered to front her some gambling money.

'I keep a calendar. When I've been here three hundred and sixty-five days I hope to have enough saved to buy a Mercedes Sports Coupe. Silver,' she added.

'I wouldn't doubt you'll reach your goal.'

Once she had her cash tucked into a little red sequined bag, he stood facing her, serious now. 'Yes?' she asked, and the Southern lilt had slipped back into her voice so that the word came out 'Yeh-ess?'

'I have a suite upstairs. Will you join me there?'

She arched one eyebrow and he resisted a crazy urge to lean over and kiss it. Natural beauty in a woman could make him lose his senses. 'A strictly business proposition? I don't mean pay me for going upstairs with you, I mean will you come back some night and let me gamble again?' she asked.

'Absolutely. I'd have it no other way.'

She took his arm and turned to the elevators. 'You've come to the right girl,' she said.

He thought so too. Did he know how to pick them or what?

11

The movers had finished packing Beth's house and were shifting the cartons into a waiting semi-truck parked at the curb. Beth sat outside beneath an oak on a garden bench she had placed there when Melanie was a baby. It was a place she could retire to on busy days, a place to catch her breath and commune with nature.

Now as she sat in the shade, watching the movers, she felt as alone as never before except during the first black months after her husband's death. When he died of a heart attack while at work one day, gone from her before she ever had the time to reach him to say goodbye, she had been lost, adrift for almost a year before she realized there was nothing to do but go forward. There was never a way to go back, to right things, to save yourself from disaster.

So it was now, with the inexplicable changes setting her loose in a calamitous sea, called upon again to steer her craft forward through the rising waves.

Melanie was away from the house. Beth couldn't remember if she had a class or if she had said she would be visiting with friends. A lot of details came up missing these days. She couldn't remember bits of conversation, people she was supposed to call, items she had meant to pick up at the grocery. It had given her a start when she woke to the sound of the moving truck parking in front of the house. What could that godawful noise be, she wondered? Until she scrambled from bed and pulled back the curtains from the front window. Then at the sight of the big, yellow truck she remembered today was moving

97

day and she had meant to be up earlier to be ready for them.

She realized part of her confusion had to do with how rapidly her life had changed. It was as if a magic wand had been waved, upsetting every single solid aspect of her life. She didn't know how to keep up.

She sat now watching the four heavily muscled males hefting the pieces of her life through the door, onto the walkway, and to the curb and the open ramp leading into the dark maw of the truck. Had she told Melanie they were coming today? Surely she had. She couldn't be *that* disorganized.

A breeze rattled the leaves overhead and she looked away from the truck straight up into the tree. She would miss the oak. The street. Her home. What would happen to all her memories of cradling Melanie in her arms while sitting beneath this oak? She guessed they would be put away, stored, the way some of her other memories of the past were stored and rarely retrieved.

'Ma'am, there's a cat in here screaming its head off. We're afraid we might step on it.' It was one of the moving men, calling from the front walk.

Beth stood. 'I'll get it.' She hurried inside, found Pope, and scooped him up. 'Moving day,' she said to him quietly, cradling him in her arms as she went outdoors again to be out of the way.

The kitten cried a little then settled down in her lap, tail swishing. 'You don't like this much, do you?' Beth asked. 'Well, you aren't alone. It's not my idea of a good time either. I'd take a swift beating any day over moving.'

She yawned and cupped a hand over her mouth. She had been staying up nights, getting headaches going over her old cases trying to find someone she had put away who might have threatened her.

There were more than she'd ever thought. In one way or the other more than six defendants in the past ten years had made veiled or open threats to her person. She had always dismissed them as angry words, meaningless, all froth and no bite. Before her world crumbled she had mistakenly thought her life invulnerable to any more terrible change; could a person be marked or was there no order in chaos, did it just set up camp anywhere it wished, in whatever house it happened past? Now she had to decide which of the threats made over the years might have been real threats.

After her move into the apartment house, she needed to go back to her office at the court house and do some calling around. She would do it tomorrow. She must know how many defendants she'd picked out as being possibly responsible for her predicament had been released from prison. How many might have access to someone on the outside to set her up even though they were still incarcerated? How many could she find and get to so she could question them? It was obvious she was going to be railroaded if she didn't do something fast. She *would not* allow her career to go down the drain because of lies.

This dependence on the apartment rents was just a temporary solution. She and Melanie would buy another house soon, one of their own again, just for the two of them.

Within an hour the moving men were ready to go. They were quiet, efficient men. It was amazing how quickly one's possessions could be boxed and loaded. It took a lifetime to accumulate things, but mere hours to get them ready to move from one place to another.

The foreman came to where she sat on the bench and said, 'Do you want to lead us over there, ma'am, to show us where to put things?'

She rose wearily. 'Sure. Let me get my purse and keys. I have to put up the cat.'

On the drive across town, the truck following her, Beth sorrowed over this terrible change. It wasn't that the apartment house she had bought was a bad place to live or not up to her standards. The ground floor apartment she'd chosen for her and Melanie was smaller than her former home, of course, but it was big enough to be comfortable. There was a large living area with a seat set into the bowed front window. The kitchen was small, but who did much cooking anymore? Not the Kapon women, that was for sure. Both of them went in big for frozen dinners, microwavable food, anything easy. It had to be that way once she was working so hard and Melanie in school all day. What they needed, she sometimes half joked to her daughter, was a wife.

The apartment had two small bedrooms, but the closets were generous and the bedrooms themselves light and airy, with floor-to-ceiling windows looking out over the side yard. There someone had planted Indian hawthorn that bloomed pink in the spring and holly bushes that would put out sprays of red berries in the mild Texas winter.

No, it wasn't that their living quarters would be less congenial than the home she had to leave. It was the idea of living with others that would take getting used to. All the other apartments were filled. The renters would all look to her when there were problems. She'd have to keep plumbers, carpenters, handymen, and a pest extermination unit on the ready. Unless she began to feel handy herself and bought some books on how to make her own repairs. That was good for a laugh.

She smiled. She had tried to fix a leaky toilet one time. She'd managed to flood the bathroom before the plumber arrived. So much for her handy, do-it-yourself skills.

And Melanie was right in a way, it could become tiresome to have to deal with neighbors you actually had to speak to, elderly or not. She had lived in her home for nineteen years and probably didn't say more than ten words a year to her neighbors. People in houses kept to themselves. People in an apartment house didn't. They passed one another in the vestibule, on the stairs, going in and out of the house. You couldn't get away with being a private person too busy to talk in that kind of situation. Not in a town like Geneva. She'd run off all her tenants if she did that. Could she be friendly and sociable? Would tenants take advantage of that, neglecting to pay their rent on time, thinking she was lenient? She couldn't afford to wait for the rent. It was all that would keep them from destitution.

On the other hand, her life had been a little sterile, she had to admit it. It wouldn't do her any harm to make a few friends. Everett kept telling her she needed a man. A lover is what he meant. She never told him she had a little crush on one of the English lit professors at the university. If this thing hadn't happened . . .

She sighed, saw the driveway to the apartment house, and pulled into it. She drove around to the back to park, heard the truck shifting down to turn in behind her.

Before she was out of the Jeep someone was standing at the back door, holding open the screen, peering at her as if she were an intruder. She waved at the old woman, noticing that she was not yet dressed for the day. She wore a shabby patchwork night coat and slippers. The woman did not wave back. The screen fell shut, closing the woman into interior darkness.

Beth walked to the drive to wave in the truck. They would have to take her furniture and things in through the front. She hoped the tenants would not get in the way and make this move last longer than it had to.

She had met all the tenants, of course, once she signed the papers buying the house. Why couldn't she remember that old woman's name, the woman who had been at the back door? She was a Russian immigrant and spoke with a heavy accent. Luby? Luyba, that was it. The woman had had to spell it for her.

Oh well, she had plenty of time ahead of her to learn more than enough about them all.

Plenty of time and nothing else to do beyond saving herself from jail.

Melanie spent a little time across the street from the house, thumb in her mouth, watching her mother and the moving men. She had to go to class soon, but it was hard to tear her gaze from the scene of her young life being systematically destroyed.

Finally she left the curb and hurried down the block to her car. Her mother had never even seen her and she was glad of that.

In between two of her classes she sat on the lawn outside one of the university buildings and brought out a spiral notebook. No one yet knew she scrawled poetry across the lined pages and no one *would* know if she could help it. When a friend passed her by and said hello, she carefully bent the cover of the notebook to shield the lines on the page.

Within a few minutes she had written down part of her grief in a poem. She read it over, changing words, moving phrases until she was happy with it. It's not so bad, she thought. Not great, won't win an award, but it's not so bad. She had hoped it might make her feel better to write about it, but she still felt like a piece of shit. She knew she was a romantic and melodramatic and often times she was overly pessimistic, but she couldn't help all that. That's what becoming an adult meant, didn't it, that you just couldn't help it when you found out what you had to work with wasn't pure gold?

She struggled up from the grass, brushing down her long navy skirt, and when she looked up she caught a man staring at her from a passing car. He looked like a creep, one of those farmer-cowboy geek creeps and, anyway, what was he doing staring at her that way? She watched his car roll down the street and turn, leaving the university grounds.

She would be late to class if she didn't hurry. She wished the sun would come out. She wished she didn't have to drive to the apartment house tonight and sleep in her bed in that funny old room with the cabbage rose wallpaper.

God, she just knew she wasn't going to like much of anything now for a long time to come. It was such a bitch when things got so botched up that she couldn't find one single thing to smile about.

Chase drove away from the university smiling at the look he'd seen on the girl's face. She was pretty like her mother, taller, slim as a willow trunk. She had seen him staring and gave him a What's With You look that cracked him up. She wouldn't be so haughty once he got hold of her, no sirree, Bob.

He drove to the girl's house and saw the moving truck just leaving, trailing behind Beth Kapon's Jeep. He followed until the truck turned into the apartment house.

He found a Stop 'n Go in the next block and pulled in. Searching through his pocket he found a quarter and strolled to the outside phone stall. He dialed collect to Dalta's house in Vegas. Denise answered and had him hold until she called her husband. Presently Dalta came on the line. 'What's up?'

'She sold her house and bought an apartment complex. No, an apartment *house*, really. It looks like one of those old homes that have been separated into apartments.' There was a sustained silence. 'Jeff? Did you hear me?'

'I was thinking. It means she's running out of money. She's trying to keep afloat by investing in rental property.'

'That's how it looks to me.'

'Do I have to tell you what to do?'

'Nope.'

'You sound like a cowboy. Picking up the Texas lingo?'

'I guess.'

'How's the woman looking? Worried, upset?'

'Both.'

'What about the charges? Trial been set yet? She's still under suspension?'

'I have to check out the trial date, she could get that postponed for a year or more. She's already had a prelim hearing and the case is being transferred to the grand jury. But yeah, she's not working. And the college let her go, too.'

'Fine! I'm on my way out of the house right now, but you can call back any time, let me know how it's progressing.'

Chase hung up the receiver, stuck a toothpick back into his mouth, and went into the convenience store. He had to have a Twinkie and some Gummi Bears. He was starving to death and dinner time was another couple of hours away.

After paying for his treats, he tipped the brim of his gray felt cowboy hat to the clerk and drawled out a thank you. He had been shopping at the local mall for outfits to wear that would allow him to pass as one of Geneva's natives. He had jeans, cowboy shirts with pearl snaps (which he was becoming fond of), and the hat. He didn't buy a Stetson. Those were expensive and most of the townsmen didn't wear them. Not for daily doings anyway. Maybe they wore their Stetsons for weddings or to church on Sunday morning, how the hell would he know something like that?

When he got the gray felt home he crushed it this way and that with his hands, rubbed a little cigarette ash into spots on the brim. It shouldn't look too new, call attention to itself. He took the Wrangler jeans to an open-air laundromat and washed them three times, at each wash adding in a half cup of Clorox to weather and bleach down the blue of the denim. He could pass now for a Texan. It was so easy to blend in when a person knew how.

He was particularly adept at picking up accents. He had learned that at the movies. He always thought he would have made a good western character actor. He could have fit right in with Hank Fonda and Glenn Ford in *The Rounders*. Or with Clint Eastwood in *The Good, the Bad, and the Ugly*.

103

One abiding trait of the cowboy – not just in Hollywood movies, but in Geneva, Texas – was his unwillingness to speak unless he absolutely had to. He kept his lips sealed, producing a mysterious air about himself. Chase could do that, in fact preferred it that way. What was there to say, most of the time, that hadn't already been said a million jillion times before? Fuck you. That's what he liked to say most often. Fuck you, your priest, and your old mother, man.

He drove slowly past Beth Kapon's new apartment house again before heading to his own garage apartment that afforded him privacy on his comings and goings. The landlord lived in a big, old, run-down, rambling, two-story, clapboard house situated a hundred feet in front of the unused garage and the apartment that sat above it. There was a separate drive shielded by a row of tall cypress that kept anyone at the main house from seeing when he left and returned.

It was cheap too, by Vegas or Chicago standards. Two hundred bucks a month. Of course it was a rat hole, but that's all he wanted. This job wasn't a luxury tour of the state of Texas. It was an undercover, quiet little job where he was supposed to be as invisible as possible, a lizard sunning on a moss-covered rock.

Once at the apartment he showered, shaved for the second time that day, and meant to don fresh clothes before leaving to look for a new café. Somewhere he would find a good cook in this town. Or so he fervently goddamn hoped.

While standing in front of the bathroom sink, face lathered white with lemon-lime scented Barbasol, he thought he heard the creak of footsteps across the bare wood floor in the front room of his apartment. His hand holding the razor halted midway in a swipe down his cheek. He blinked. Felt his heart kick into double-time.

He put aside the razor and crept from the bathroom into the hall, moving toward the front room. He had left his gun in its holster, hanging from a wire hanger in the closet there. That's how it always worked out. Him unarmed.

He came forward to where the hall opened into the room and paused, holding his breath. Nothing there. In the encroaching evening gloom that had invaded the apartment there were shadows shifting with each puff of breeze, moving tree limbs outside the windows, but no one had invaded Chase's apartment. He didn't know now what had made him think otherwise.

Sounds. That shouldn't be there and were. He was *sure* of it.

He turned slowly, head hanging, heartbeat slowing as he returned to the sink and the razor.

If anyone ever found out he was this way, they'd never trust him for jobs again. The Family could never know. No one could know.

It had begun nearly three years ago when he was called upon to take Vinnie Vincenzio out for his last ride. Why, after doing Vinnie, he would begin to imagine someone stalked him and meant him harm, he could not fathom. It wasn't Vinnie stalking him, or Vinnie's friends either. Hell, he never thought of him again once he had put the bullet through his brain and buried him beneath leaf cover in the barrens of New Jersey. Vinnie never should have made noises about taking over some of the Chicago boys' territory.

No, this thing had nothing at all to do with Vinnie except that it began after that job. It was the stupidest thing he had ever heard of and it made him furious at himself, but none of that mattered, it still happened. In fact, it happened at an increasing rate until now he grew frightened and suspicious every few days.

It came out of the blue, when he least expected. He would hear something or *think* he did. He would see someone just from the corner of his eye who was there watching him, then the person just disappeared. Or he *thought* he had seen someone. Cold sweat, clammy and icy, covered his face during these episodes and his pulse quickened.

The thing was, every time it happened he believed it. Until he could check out his fears and lay them aside as imaginary, they held power over him and caused him real alarm.

He supposed it was some form of phobia, a fear of the unknown out there. Not that he knew a phobia from a parking ticket, but that's all it could be. Something deranged in him, something loose in his brain, ricocheting out of consciousness and then back again, bringing sudden and palpable fear.

He did not know how to stop it. He could not tell anyone, therefore it couldn't be talked out and put to rest.

So he lived with it and called himself fool, coward, idiot, and still when he heard footsteps that should not be there or saw an apparition that watched him from corners or doorways or windows or shadows, he jumped, ready to defend himself.

He finished shaving, cleaned his face of the last of the Barbasol, and tried on a grim smile in the mirror.

Once he had eaten, he would cruise past Beth Kapon's new place before turning in for the night. Soon the campaign of terror could commence. The very thought gave him a tingle he could feel down to his fingertips. It was pure pleasure for him, this sort of business.

Highly preferable to being stalked oneself. That was for goddamn sure.

Maybe he ought to kill somebody. It always made him feel better and he stopped being scared for a little while afterwards.

Who could he kill? Not many street kids or homeless people wandering around a place like Geneva.

So he'd have to break into somebody's house, then. Some woman's house. No point in taking out some guy, make the whole affair way too complicated and messy.

That wouldn't be too difficult. Done it plenty of times.

His dick responded to his thoughts, growing and turning like a small trapped animal. If he hurried he could find someone leaving a grocery or a convenience store and follow her home.

Or maybe he could just find a way into the Kapons' new home and hurt the girl. College brat.

He couldn't put it off forever. It was time.

12

Paul stood outside in the cooling night before the front door of the apartment house on Hytell Street. He shifted from one foot to the other in his anxiety. When the door finally opened, an old woman stood before him, her hair done up in a scarf of many colors and designs. She scowled at him. 'What you want? The door is open and you can enter, you don't know?' she asked in a thick foreign accent.

She abruptly turned her back on him and shuffled across the floor to the stairs. He ventured into the shadowed entry and watched her ascend to the first landing and turn a corner for the next stairway to the third floor. He hadn't even been given time to ask her which apartment Mrs Kapon lived in.

He listened then to the sounds filtering throughout the house. He heard voices, televisions, music. None of it very loud, but rather a background of activity that blurred into one constant, low-decibel hum.

He turned around, looking for help. He saw two doors on the first floor, one on his right, one to his left. Behind the stairway a narrow hall led to a back-door exit. On the apartment doors there were simple brass numerals. One. Two. No names. Well, he'd just have to knock and find out, that's all.

He chose apartment one, knocked twice, stood back waiting to find he had chosen wrongly. The door opened to reveal a pretty girl near his age standing there, an exasperated look on her face. 'Oh!'

she said, stepping back. 'I thought it might be one of the old people. Can I help you?'

This must be Beth Kapon's daughter. He knew there was a daughter; he had just never met her or imagined she might be this pretty. Or *bright*. There were streams and rivers of light coming from around her. He had heard she was a student at the university, but he did not share classes with her. He cleared his throat and hoped his voice would not betray his nervousness. 'I'm looking for Mrs Kapon. She was my teacher for Law 107. Is this her apartment?'

Melanie grinned. 'Yeah, this is it all right. But my mother's not here. I'm Melanie. Mom's down at the court house doing some work. Do you want me to tell her anything for you?'

He shook his head slightly. 'Hi, I'm Paul. And, uh, I don't have a message or anything. I . . . is she okay?' He saw the skin around the girl's eyes pucker quizzically. 'I mean, she's not in real trouble, is she? I . . . mean, you know . . . she's so . . .'

'Hey, why don't you come in and have a 7-Up? You like 7-Up?' Melanie reached out and took him by the sleeve, hauling him inside. He was too surprised to protest. Her touch ignited his sleeve so that he glanced there, hoping it would not take fire. Imagine being invited into the home of his revered professor by such an unearthly creature.

He glanced around at the clutter of boxes and wrapping papers, stacked books on the floor. 'You've just moved in,' he said, then wanted to kick himself for stating the obvious.

Melanie swept her arms around at the mess. 'Yeah, just today, actually. Mom's been busy all afternoon and hasn't had time to put things away and I'm always gone, or nearly always. I just got in.' She moved a small empty box from a chair and motioned him into it. 'Sit down, I'll get the 7-Up.'

He sat gingerly on the edge of the chair, taking in all the personal possessions lying about the room. He wanted to get up and check through the stacked books, see what it was Mrs Kapon read or what she kept on hand for research. What glued him to the chair, however, was the girl from the other room, the kitchen, he assumed, talking to him steadily through the open door. He couldn't see or feel her light now and he felt as if he'd been dropped back into a void.

He should have known any daughter of Mrs Kapon would be

beautiful, but not like this, not this lively and full of light that seemed to burst from her gaze to sear him, fly from the pores of her skin, creating a golden aura in her wake as she moved. He could see these things others could not. Mrs Kapon, for instance, was much less intense, her aura blue-violet, the deep color of the woodland flower that hid in shadow beneath trees. Her aura always soothed his troubled mind though he prodded it with his questions, hoping to turn it red, if not in anger, then in frustration, for red would tell him more of the truth than blue ever might.

But gold! He had not met a gold person before, not one, in all his life. It was like walking into a room to stand next to a furnace. A miniature, earthbound sun. Was he exaggerating, he wondered to himself? He was not, not an iota. She truly was exceptional, the aura told him that. He'd never confided to anyone he could see auras. It was New Age-ish and pretty damned whack-o, yeah, but there it was. He saw them. They told him things about people. That's all he knew.

Melanie's golden glow mesmerized him and he knew how dangerous that could be. Look what the aura had caused him to do with Mrs Kapon. How it forced him to hound her and to even find her new home, invading it with his puny, insignificant self.

She had asked him a question. She stood over him holding out a can of 7-Up, smiling crookedly, in a lopsided way, half her mouth up to one side as if she were ready to make fun of him. He could not bear it if that happened so early in getting to know her. Of course later on he would expect it.

'You're not the boy who asks my mom all those weird questions, are you?'

He took the soda can and hoped to turn her half smile into a whole. 'If I am, will you ask me to leave?'

The smile broadened and he knew relief enough to take a sip of the 7-Up. He preferred black coffee, but most kids his age didn't drink coffee, she wouldn't think to offer it, no fault of hers. 'You *are* the one,' she said.

He smiled back. 'I try to keep her life interesting. Your mother is the only brain on the campus worth getting an opinion from.'

'Is she? She's my mom so I guess I sort of overlook how smart she is. Of course, I *do* know she's smart. Having to live up to that can be hell, you know? I'll never be half the brain she is about things like the law.'

'Oh, I bet you have your talents,' he said, offhandedly. She had taken a chair nearby, pushing a folded blanket up behind her back.

'I may,' she admitted. 'So, tell me, you just came by because you're worried about us . . . her?'

He nodded shyly. 'I dropped my class when she was replaced. If she's not going to teach that course, I won't take it.'

'You're pre-law?'

He nodded again. 'You?'

She laughed and her aura shone like melted gold, running all over the outline of the chair, dripping onto the floor around her feet. He almost could not gaze upon her, she was so brilliant.

'Not me,' she said. 'Not law, uh uh. I'm in liberal arts. English major. You know, the major that turns out people with diplomas who have to go to work for fast food franchises.'

'You could teach.'

Her lips turned down in a moué of disgust. 'No, I wouldn't want to teach. That's my mother's gig too. I'm *nothing* like my mother, I already admitted that.'

He took another swallow from the can in his hand. The cold from the aluminum preserved his palm from scorching, but the rest of him exposed to her dazzling aura felt roasted. He thought if he were to look in a mirror at his naked body, he'd see his skin blushing with burn. 'Then you plan to flip burgers after college.'

She did not smile this time. 'One day,' she said, glancing from him to the scattered books on the floor. 'I might write.'

'Oh, then you'll be a novelist. I've never met someone who wanted to be a novelist.'

'I didn't say novelist,' she corrected, gazing at him directly again. 'Maybe, though, I don't know. I might write stories. Poems. Or work in publishing some way, editing . . .'

'Do you write now?'

She stood from the chair and moved like wind to the books. She grabbed up a volume and lofted it into the air at shoulder height, turning with it high, as if it were a gauntlet. '*This* is writing,' she said. 'Keats, Longfellow, Shelley. Compared to this, no, I don't write now.'

Oh she was dramatic, like a stage actress, like one of the greats, though he could not name them for he knew nothing of the arts. But this girl was full of wild seed, bursting with color and vibrancy and overstatement. She would make an impression one day; she would bowl over far greater obstacles than he, knocking them flat to the floor with her unadulterated conceit that the world adored Greatness and Beauty, and that she was to become one with them.

He was in love.

With Mrs Kapon he had been infatuated, granted, but it was her mind he hungered to plunder, not her body or soul. With the daughter he knew instantly, from experiencing her aura, from watching her take up the cherished book of poetry as if it were – no, not a gauntlet – a chalice holding the world's wisdom, that he loved her, loved her, was in love.

He stood, his knees liquid, and went to take the book from her hand. He set down the soda can on a stereo speaker. He opened the cover, riffled the pages, let a line here and there, a phrase, a word, knock at his eyes, enter into his mind. This was a book of classic poets and nothing in it was mediocre or mundane. The book held in abeyance the same gold light that issued from her corporeal being and as he looked down at the pages, he wondered if she had stolen or lifted that light from this place.

He knew why she had chosen it and from the brief meeting with the words there he also knew more about her than she might wish him to know. All the while he read, flipping to this page, flipping to that, the pages burning the tips of his fingers, she watched and wondered at him, but would she understand? Understand that he meant to enter her obsession this way and share it with her for now what she loved, he would also love, what she adored, he would worship.

'You're a funny guy,' she said, breaking through his concentration on the book.

He closed it and handed the volume back. 'I've heard that before. I suppose that it's true. Anything said three times has to be true, don't you think?'

That half-smile again, the tentative one that told him she did not grasp all the underlying meaning he put behind the things he said aloud. She couldn't tell yet when he was making a joke or when he was serious and that was all right. She could grow to know him. There was all that time ahead of them; they were so young. He had never been in any hurry, and now, standing inches from her light, soaking in the radiant energy she projected, he knew he could wait a lifetime, an eternity for her to come to accept his funny ways, his weird questions, his need to own her physically so that he might thrive within that gold she unconsciously and so recklessly projected out into such a uniformly dense, gray world.

God, he was getting as lyrical as the poems in her book. He was glad she couldn't read his thoughts.

'I should be going,' he said, when she could find no response to his question. 'Will you tell your mother I came by and asked about her? Maybe I could drop by again sometime . . .'

She stared at him and said, 'Sure. Anytime. Maybe you and I could break up the monotony of this home for the elderly. It makes me itch to know hundreds of years of living are out there in those apartments. It's . . . oppressive. I think I hate it here.'

He walked to the door and opened it himself. He felt her at his back, felt her golden heat warming him right through flesh and blood to his bones. 'I have questions for old people too,' he said, as he passed out the door into the entryway. 'We shouldn't underestimate those years they own.'

'Own?'

He turned. 'Thanks for the 7-Up. Are you generally around at this time on Wednesdays?'

'Yeah, I don't go out a lot on week nights.'

'Maybe I'll come by again. If that's all right with you.' He moved steadily from her circle of light toward the front door, talking as he went. 'And if your mother wouldn't mind.'

She stood at the apartment's open door watching him until he let himself out. On the walk from the house he tried to breathe and there wasn't enough air. He would hyperventilate soon and he hoped it was when he was far enough away from the apartment house that she would not see him.

She had taken away all the air, all the light, and he walked now head down in an ashen reality. Full dark night.

Melanie was full of talk when Beth came through the door that night. Paul had visited, what a strange boy, what did she think of him, was he half as strange as she thought? But he was intriguing, you had to give him that, she said, prattling like a pre-teen over a first beau.

Beth mentally sagged. So the student she liked least had managed to find her brand new home and trespass while she was away. And the worst of it was it seemed from how her daughter talked about him that he had made an exemplary impression. What she did not need was that boy in their lives. She had no evidence whatever that he was other than a nerdy, Generation-X, nihilist-thinking kid, but maybe that was enough to want him distant. She needed to squash the friendship now, if she could.

'Melanie, Paul was one of my students, but he would be the last one I'd recommend as a friend for you.'

'Why is that?'

Now Melanie had that hard, stubborn tone back in her voice and Beth had to find a way to get around it. Why couldn't she ever reach her daughter on a level playing field without all the wariness of impending battle?

'He really *is* strange, that's why. He asks extremely disturbing questions. He seems more interested in the criminal than in the law enforcement that puts the criminal away.' She was floundering. She really hadn't any certain actions to hold against him. This was going to sound like a form of prejudice against someone Melanie would think she simply misunderstood. 'He often sounds as if he thinks the law is a tool of evil men, that there's nothing good or upright in it.'

'That sounds suspiciously like an unjust personal reaction, Mom.'

'What other kind of reaction could I have, if not personal? And when was my judgment ever "unjust" if I have good reason for that judgment?'

'Oh now she's going to use the logical interrogation technique on me,' Melanie said, turning away to speak to the empty air.

'I'm sorry, Melanie, don't leave the room. Let me try to explain . . .'

'You don't have to. You think because he wears black, he's one of those night-clubbers who like the night and violent music and . . .'

'Melanie. Stop it. You know I'm not basing my opinion on what he wears.'

'Anyone who isn't in a three-piece suit and a pair of polished wingtips is a suspect to you, Mom, admit it. You're so PC, you practically stink of it. If you were a book you'd be called *Saints Preserve Us From Change*.'

Beth suddenly laughed, her face wrinkling and mouth wide. 'Where do you come up with stuff like that?' she asked between laughs. 'What's that title again?' And she laughed some more.

Melanie had halted her stride from the room and her angry huff had turned to sly merriment. Her eyes twinkled as she withheld a smile pulling at her pouty lips. '*Saints Preserve Us From Change*,' she said in a monotone and with a straight face. Then she laughed too. 'Seriously, Mom, you're just too hard on kids. I have lots of friends into black clothing and the music you don't like and with interests in the macabre. You'd be surprised how intelligent they are. Just because they seem strange to you doesn't mean there's anything wrong with them. I told you I thought Paul was strange, but not because of that.

'It's because of how he reacts to things. I showed him a book of poems and for a couple of minutes he seemed lost in the pages, like I wasn't even there anymore. I mean I like poetry, you know that, but it was different for him. He seems to care a lot about you,' she finished lamely. 'He came by just to see if you were okay.'

Beth stooped to the floor over a box containing a pottery vase. She carefully unwrapped it from the drifts of tissue paper covering it. 'I appreciate that,' she said, not looking at Melanie now. 'But I've had him in my classes. I've read his essays. I'm just telling you he's . . . obsessive. He gets on something – or someone – and he won't let it go. I've seen him do it.'

Melanie was silent for a minute and Beth hoped she was thinking it over. They *did not* need the trouble that boy might bring into their lives. 'Well, everybody's obsessive about something or other,' Melanie said, still defending him. 'I know I am. And you are too.'

'Maybe,' Beth said. 'But not in the same way. If you let him hang around long enough, you'll find that out. But by then it'll be too late. He'll be stuck on you for good.'

'Like TarBaby.' Melanie smiled. 'But I wish you'd let me make my own friends,' she said without humor now. She left Beth on the floor, lifting the vase from the box.

'What can I do with her?' Beth asked the vase softly. 'She won't listen to me. Never has.'

'I HEARD THAT,' Melanie yelled from her bedroom.

Beth grinned. No matter how argumentative her daughter might be, she was frightfully good company. She could understand why Paul might be smitten with her if he had spent any time here at all today. And yet it still was not a good thing. It seemed nothing was good just now. There was enough shit going on in her life that maybe one more pile of it wouldn't even be noticed.

After all, he was just a wayward kid. It wasn't as if he was a criminal or con or something. And something worse than that she could not imagine.

It would be all right. Let him latch onto Melanie if she wanted him around all that much. If she tired of him, she'd cut him from her life like severing the carrot top from the carrot. One thing her Melanie could be and that was merciless once she had made up her mind.

That was why she shouldn't even have bothered trying to dissuade her having anything to do with Paul. She had, as usual, wasted her breath. That's what you did with your adult children. You talked to the air and the air didn't answer you, she thought. It was just there, being air.

'Mom, there's nothing in the refrigerator.'

Beth looked over her shoulder. Oh God. She'd forgotten to shop.

'Damn. I'll have to go to the store and get some stuff.'

'Pizza.'

'No. I'll pick up some food. Real food.'

'Kentucky Fried chicken.'

'No!'

'Oh, all right. And don't forget Pope. He needs some new kitty litter and Nine Lives.'

Beth got to her feet and swept back stray strands of hair from her forehead. 'I'll try to remember.'

* * *

Chase sat in the Taurus on the street, watching the apartment house. He meant to find a way into the ground floor apartment on the left where the Kapons lived once it was late enough and the lights were out, indicating they had gone to bed.

His plans changed the moment he saw Beth Kapon leave in her Jeep. That meant the girl was alone. He'd get in and find out how long it would be before she expected her mother back. He'd find out a lot of things.

He left his car, crossing the street in a lope. He went inside the front door, pausing to listen to the noises upstairs before going to the door on the left and pressing his ear to it to listen inside. He didn't hear much. A goddamn cat caterwauling.

He shuddered. Hated cats. Hated fucking hairball-coughing, scratch-ass cats.

He tried the doorknob, found it unlocked – dumb, dumb, dumb – slipped inside, sweeping the room with a quick glance. Empty. She was in another room. He locked the door.

The cat was meowing like something gone wild. It was a hungry meow. Someone ought to kick the little bastard in the head to shut it up.

He padded across the carpet to what looked like a kitchenette with a dining table. Cat was sitting on the floor looking up at the counter. Meowing sack of shit. He glowered at it and saw the hair rise along its back.

He moved into the kitchen and saw a hallway leading to the back of the house. Bedroom back there. He heard faint music coming from that direction. Some kind of new stuff he hated. Wasn't rap, which he hated, too, but something else just as toneless.

He moved down the hall, fully erect now, and went straight into the room without the slightest hesitation. Her back was to him. She fiddled with a compact disk player and didn't feel his presence until he was almost on her.

She turned, gasped. He knocked her to the floor and her hand brushed a cascade of compact disks to the floor with her fall. He must be quick or someone might hear her scream.

He sat on her, held her mouth silent with one hand while he pulled out a handkerchief from his back pocket with the other. He stuffed it into her mouth.

Leaned over her and stared into her eyes.

'What big eyes you have, little girl.'

She bucked beneath him and tried to claw his arms, but he hit her again, this time hard enough to put her out.

Couldn't have the neighbors calling the cops. Uhuh, Charlie. This was important.

Beth knew something was wrong the minute she stepped in the apartment. She was loaded down with grocery bags, both arms full.

The whole place was a tomb. Not a sound.

'Melanie?'

She rushed into the kitchen and dumped the bags on the table. She heard the cat. Muffled. Where was Pope?

'Kitty? Here, Kitty. Melanie, where are you?'

She started for Melanie's bedroom. Or maybe she was in the shower. But no, she didn't hear the water running.

Now she heard the cat again, close by. She stopped at a closet door in the hallway, a closet she'd meant to use for storage of linens. She opened the door and Pope bounded out, squalling madly. He raced off to the kitchen to complain for his supper.

Something was terribly wrong. Melanie would never have put Pope in a closet.

Beth moved now like a flash of light. She was in Melanie's room and on her knees beside the bed, lifting her daughter's head, and she was terrified, so terrified her mouth hung open and she was making odd strangling noises in the back of her throat.

Melanie lay unconscious, her clothes ripped to shreds and hanging from her half-naked body. There was blood. It was on Melanie's arms and one side of her face, blotting one eye socket like splashed paint.

'Melanie!'

Beth leaned down and felt for a pulse, found it, and nearly fainted with relief. But she had to stop this bleeding, it was, it was . . .

He was here.

Beth twisted around to look behind her. She had heard something, someone. He was walking down the hall. Had he been in the closet? With Pope?

Jesus, the son of a bitch was leaving, he was, he was . . .

Beth leaped to her feet and raced after him. All she saw was a man's back, a cowboy hat, and then he was through the shadowed, unlit, cluttered living room and out the door she had left unlocked. She screamed after him, but he was moving fast now, running, getting away.

She chased him, banging her shins on boxes, knocking the back of her hand on the door facing as she stumbled against it, and then she was in the vestibule, at the wide open door, going down the steps . . .

And he was gone.

Just like that. Vanished.

The empty night reverberated with her screams. People came out from houses across the street and behind her tenants banged down the stairwell. She turned, still screaming incomprehensible orders to get help and get it now, hurry, quick, Melanie was hurt, so hurt, call an ambulance, call 911.

She found herself on her knees again without knowing who she had pushed out of her way to enter her apartment. She had Melanie in her arms, trying to drag her from the bedroom and down the hall to the kitchen so she could clean her face.

She had to get the blood off.

Paul knew he shouldn't be coming back to see Melanie Kapon one day after he'd just met her, but he couldn't help himself.

He went in the door this time without knocking. He stood at the apartment door and knocked at first quietly so as not to rouse nosy neighbors and then harder when no one answered him.

He heard a door open upstairs and looked up at the landing. 'They are at the hospital. Not here today,' the foreign lady said in a sad tone of voice.

'Hospital?' His heart locked up.

'The girl was hurt after you left last night. Cut and . . .'

'She cut herself? How bad?'

The woman shook her head and moved her hands in impotent

circles. 'Someone hurt her. Came in when the mother was gone and . . .'

'Oh fuck.' Paul took off, swinging out the door and down the steps. He halted on the sidewalk, the inside of his head bubbling like a cauldron on a fire. Only one hospital, he told himself, you know where to go.

Chase saw the boy leave the apartment house and wondered who he was. One of those freaky kids who looked like vampires the way they dressed all in black; black pants, shoes, shirt, making their skin look pale by comparison. He could have told them the uniform was a stupid rebellion. He had lived through the sixties and the long hair and sloppy clothes and bead necklaces and peace symbols. He knew what he was talking about. You used clothes to make people expect something from you, the way he had adopted the cowboy costumes. If you wanted to *really* rebel, you didn't do it with clothes, you did it with your fists and rocks and with fire, most definitely with fire.

Chase ate the second section of his Almond Joy, chewing slowly to get the full flavor of the coconut and chocolate. He ground the almonds down to fine mush with his big back molars.

Maybe the boy was the girl's boyfriend, although if he was they were certainly mismatched. She was a good looking kid, real good looking, and the boy was . . . well, he was this homely thing with his hair shaved off, head all burry gray like one of those fuzzy kiwis they sold in the grocery fruit department. He wasn't someone to write home about, not in Chase's opinion, and he knew good looking when he saw it. Sharon Stone was good looking. Marilyn Monroe, now she had been good looking, boy, had she. Hollywood had not produced a blonde since like her. Tom Cruise, Al Pacino, even Nicholson, they were good looking. This boy with his hangdog look and fuzzy head, he was not a good looking specimen of the human race, no way, no how.

Not that Chase had any place to call someone else homely, he thought, catching a reflection of himself in the rearview mirror of the rental car he sat in. Harry Dean Stanton, who he resembled, was no one's idea of handsome, inside Hollywood or out. He had character, though, just as Harry Dean did, and that was more than he could say

119

for the weird kid who had been to visit Beth Kapon's house.

What rankled Chase most was that he couldn't match the boy's looks with any actor. He was no River Phoenix. No Cory Haim.

He pulled a brown paper bag across the car seat and reached in for another candy bar. He'd try the Payday next. Or maybe the Clark bar.

While immersed in getting the candy from the bag, a voice spoke so near to Chase's ear at the open car window that he almost shat his pants.

'Hey, you know the people in that house?'

Chase wrenched his neck turning to see who had spoken to him. It was the boy. He thought he had left yet here he was, little dirtbag, he must have circled back to check him out. He felt like grabbing him by the ears and hauling him through the window head first.

'What?' he said instead, grounding himself before trusting his voice not to snap and scream in the kid's face.

'I saw you watching the place. You know someone there? Or do you have any business here at all? Who the hell are you, man?'

Chase looked the boy up and down with a stern look on his face. 'Your mother ever teach you any manners?' he asked. 'Or do you make it a practice to creep up on people and ask them rude questions?'

'It's not rude to wonder what you're doing here. I could call the cops, though, and let them ask you.' The boy backed away from the car and started down the street.

Chase swore, trying to get his seatbelt undone and himself out of the car. He had the door open about to yell for the kid when he heard him say, 'I'm right here,' from the opposite side of the car. He almost jumped out of his skin.

'Hey, what kinda game you playing, kid? Hide and seek? Why don't you get lost?'

'No, I don't think I'll get lost. I think I'll call the cops.'

Again he took off, this time down the sidewalk away from the car.

'Hey, come back here! I'll tell you what I'm doing here.'

Paul turned and eyed him skeptically. He came back to the car and looked across the roof. 'So what are you doing here?'

'Well, it's not supposed to be broadcast to the general public, see, but I've been hired by the prosecution to keep an eye on Elizabeth Kapon.'

'For what?'

'For anything she does. You've heard of a stake-out, haven't you? She's up on charges for felony possession. We think she might try to get some more coke, see, and . . .'

'I'm a law student. I know what kind of raw deal's going on with Mrs Kapon right now. I think you'd better come up with a better story than that. No way the prosecutor, who happens to be Mrs Kapon's friend and former assistant, would hire a fuck like you to watch her.'

Oh God, Chase thought, a sour taste coming into his mouth. He had just burped up some of the Almond Joy and it tasted like coconut boiled in buttermilk.

'Get in the car, kid.' Chase returned to his seat in the driver's side. He reached across and unlocked the passenger door.

After a few seconds, the boy opened the door and looked inside. 'You're up to no good,' he said. 'Tell me what it is or I call the cops.'

'So what if I just take out my gun . . .' Chase took it out from the holster beneath his leather cowboy vest. It was a small automatic and it looked blackly menacing, which was appropriate because it *was* blackly menacing. ' . . . and what if I tell you you're not calling *nobody*?'

He saw the boy's throat work swallowing. A gun always shut them up good and proper. 'How about we go for a ride and we talk?' Chase asked rhetorically. He gestured the boy inside and had him close the door. He placed the gun in his lap and started the car.

The boy sat quietly until they were outside of town. Chase drove until they were on a two-lane country road that led past farms and cattle ranches. He found a dirt road leading to a small creek and turned into it. He parked a few feet from the sluggish brown water and told the boy to get out.

Once he had him standing outside the car he said, 'I don't like kids who wear black and cut off all their hair.'

The boy blinked and looked like an owl.

'I don't like kids who sneak up on me and threaten to call the cops.'

The boy began to say something, but Chase hushed him with a shake of his head that told him to shut up.

121

Chase thought about killing the kid. While he thought about it there was a sudden flurry that sent dry dust and sand into the air. He raised a hand to his eyes. He yelled, 'You little cockbite, I'll blow your fucking brains out.'

He reached forward and the kid had scrambled off. He shot in his direction and that made him stand still.

That's when Chase believed there was someone behind him, watching, about to shoot him in the back. He twirled around, shooting blindly. Dirt kicked up from his shots. There was no one there. He turned back again to the kid. Saw he had moved at least another five feet away.

'You the Kapon girl's boyfriend?' he asked, wanting to know the connection.

'I just met her yesterday.'

'And what are you going to tell her the next time you see her? About me?'

The boy hesitated before he said, sullenly, 'Nothing.'

'Like I believe that, you simple prick,' Chase said, stepping forward before he had finished speaking and striking the boy hard across the head with the butt of his small gun. The boy fell to the ground, crumpling where he had stood. Chase stepped back in time to keep from falling on him. There was blood on the kid's forehead, quite a lot of it. He crouched and put two fingers at the side of his throat to feel the pulse. Okay. Steady enough. Kid was fine. Was going to have a bitch of a headache when he woke up, but he'd live.

'Goddamn,' Chase swore, moving to the driver's door again. He had been right all along. People were spying on him. Someone was onto him. Someone other than this kid; the kid was just a symptom of the larger disease. The danger around this simple operation was growing like fungus on a tree stump, taking it over.

Chase backed from the narrow road to the highway and left the boy lying near the stream.

Now Chase had to change his guise, make himself look different. The kid had made him and would not forget.

This was such a goddamn pain in the ass.

At least he still had the element of surprise on his side. It was something.

He unwrapped the Clark bar with one hand as he drove and began to eat it. He hoped it wouldn't back up on him the way the Almond Joy had. He was really starving to death and he had yet to find a place to eat dinner tonight.

13

Jeff Dalta sat in the cocktail lounge of the Riviera with the showgirl, Jordie. He had received a disturbing call earlier from Chase. It seemed a kid had caught Chase watching the Kapon woman's house and now he had to go to great lengths to disguise himself to get anything done. It might have been best if Chase had taken out the kid, but then that could cause more problems than it solved. Cops came down on kid-killers; the heat would be too much and Chase knew that.

Dalta hated complications. Chase should have been more careful. There was rumor he had a few odd quirks, but Dalta hadn't thought he was stupid enough to let a kid make him.

'What's the matter, sugar? You haven't been yourself all night.' Jordie scooted closer to him in the booth and put her hand over his where it lay on the tablecloth.

'Business,' he said. 'Always business.'

'Is there anything I can do?' Jordie asked, moving her hand from his to rest quietly in his lap.

Damn it, he couldn't concentrate on the girl tonight. He was going to be worthless. He reached down and removed her small hand, placing it back into her own lap.

'It's nothing,' he said. 'I'm just preoccupied.'

'We all have worries,' she said, unperturbed at the rejection of her touch.

He turned to look at her. Her worries were over how to get enough money to buy the pretty expensive toys she wanted. She wouldn't know a real worry if it bludgeoned her over the head. She possessed youth and beauty. She had time on her side. She should never complain.

'You have no worries,' he said. 'You've got me, baby.'

When she frowned slightly he amended what he'd said. He kept forgetting she didn't like to be called 'baby.' 'Jordie. You've got me and you don't need anything – or anyone – else.'

Her face lit up with a smile. Except for the perky hairstyle and the low-cut black sequined dress, she could be the Madonna, pure and untouched by sin or strife.

'You really are good to me,' she said.

Dalta looked out at the patrons in the bar, some drunk, some too weary and broke to get drunk, some cruising, some already set with a partner for the night, and he wondered when he would take over the interest in his own casino, when he could get Tony out of the way so that he could be the boss in Vegas. Then he could be even better to Jordie.

'Can we play the craps table now, Jeff?' she asked, prodding him back to the present. He watched her finish off the whiskey over rocks. She licked her lower lip. It glistened redly in the light from the candle on the table. She smelled of the perfume she liked to wear, White Diamonds. He had bought it for her.

She would want a stake and some winnings before they went upstairs for the real fun and games. This was their routine. Meet for a drink or dinner, play the tables, head for Dalta's suite. He dropped a minimum of a thousand if she played craps – she always went for the pass line – and he sometimes lost more than that if she decided to play seven-card stud. His Jordie wasn't exactly in the league with the high-rollers, but she was a gambler and gamblers were expensive.

'Sure.' He stood, taking money from his wallet for the tab.

On the way into the gaming room, he saw how Jordie commanded the attention of all but the most inveterate gamblers, and he was proud. Her loveliness was like balm to his soul. Unlike the old days on the Strip when most people dressed in gowns and suits to play in the casinos, today the place was overrun with sloppily dressed tourists. Everywhere he looked people were in jeans, shorts, T-shirts, sneakers. What did they think this was, a camping trip? Vegas used to have class. He suspected it had walked out the door when this gambling mecca brought in busloads from LA and the airlines offered cheap, cut-rate packages. It didn't help much that the Strip was trying to turn into a family oriented theme park. The MGM Grand was one gigantic mall inside with its Oz motif and carnival games for youngsters.

It made him sick his City of Sin was being handed over to kids now. On the other hand, that's where the money was.

But with Jordie at his side, dressed to kill from her gold and black spike heels to her dangling, light-reflecting crystal earrings, he felt so much better. She made the bright exotic veneer of the casino pale in comparison. She was like a goddess in his earthly care and it unexpectedly struck him like a wallop between the eyes that she meant more to him now than any of the other show girls ever had. She was too flawless, too breathtakingly perfect for him to lose. Even Denise, on her best days of youth, had never been this gorgeous.

Before Jordie asked, he handed over three one hundred dollar bills so that she might buy chips from the dealer. No doubt she'd lose it and turn her eyes on him in pleading and he'd give her more. The smile she gave him was pay enough, but to think that she would also soon lie beside him in a bed gave him an exquisite thrill of power that traveled down from his throat, where his heart lodged, to his groin where he felt the first stirrings of lust.

Fuck Chase and the problems developing down in Goddamn Geneva, Texas. This was Vegas and he had his baby on his arm.

Dalta had been uncharacteristically short with him. Chase hung up the receiver of the pay phone and stood a moment at the outside booth going over the conversation. Hell, he had only wanted the man to know things were a little different now, know that his maneuvering was more difficult. Dalta shouldn't have raised his voice that way.

The gist of it was Dalta wanted him to get busy now. Stop the fucking around, he had said, wear Kapon down. What was he waiting for, the fucking Fourth of July?

Chase didn't especially like being talked to in that manner. He took it, what could he do, but take it? That didn't mean he had to like it. Dalta and he had been thick before he left Vegas. Now that Dalta was depending on him to handle the Kapon affair, he should have trusted him, but no, he was acting like he was *already* the organization's top man, like his word was all that counted, his wishes were all that mattered. His shit didn't stink.

Well, Chase had a red-hot bulletin for him. He was nothing right now but the leader of some of the boys. He wasn't even in Tony's inner circle. He was a little fish swimming with sharks and he was going to have to depend on Chase to keep him alive.

Or that's what he ought to think. He didn't know this whole operation was orchestrated from behind the scenes by Tony Mace. Served him right, the son of a bitch.

Chase drove home fuming this way, his belly in a knot. Once in the apartment he tore off the faded jeans, the pearl-snap, long-sleeved shirt, the cowboy boots. He threw the hat into a corner of the room where it landed in a puff of dust that had accumulated on the bare floor.

He stood in his jockey shorts and socks in front of the open clothes closet looking at his meager wardrobe. He pulled out a short-sleeved, button-down collar shirt in pale yellow, a pair of cheap double-knit slacks, bent over and found a pair of worn loafers. This is the kind of outfit the out-of-state rubes wore in Vegas. Usually they had their hair slicked back and you knew they carried less than a ten-spot in their wallets.

In Chase's suitcase he riffled through various objects to find a pair of clear, glass spectacles rimmed in silver metal. He tried them on and studied himself in the mirror over the bathroom sink. He needed to grow a beard, maybe a goatee. He would buy hair bleach at the drugstore tomorrow and make his hair yellow as the sun. It would lighten him up considerably. He'd be no Robert Redford, he'd still be a blond, bearded Harry Dean Stanton lookalike, but he couldn't get plastic surgery, for Chrissakes. He wasn't out to kill the President or something.

Would the boy recognize him? Not at a distance. Up close, yeah, maybe. Probably. But if that boy got up close enough to make him a second time Chase was afraid he was going to have to take the kid out. He'd hate to do it, but Dalta was too scary now. And Tony, God, if he screwed up making Tony happy, he might as well leave the country. Chase wasn't about to fail in this job.

Chase turned his mouth down and stared at his reflection. He thought he'd just heard someone walking in the other room, but he was ignoring it. Chances were it was his imagination again.

He had to play the chances and wish for the best. There was too much work to do to be overtaken by the jitters.

He listened hard, heard nothing but the silence booming from the shadowy dark living room.

There was no one there. *No one.*

Hell, he'd better go back out and buy a bottle at the liquor store. Otherwise he wouldn't be able to sleep. Without sleep he'd make mistakes.

He thought he heard a rustling sound and hesitated again, holding still. He had to check. Goddamn it, it was nuts, but he couldn't stand here wondering for another second.

Turning from the sink, he tread carefully down the hall, a replay of what he'd done just days before. He stopped at the opening into the living room and listened. He searched the shadows for a man. When he was confident there was no one there, though this took a full five minutes, he moved to where he'd left the loafers and slipped them on.

All the while he glanced around and over his shoulders, hoping not to be taken from the back. Nothing frightened him more than the idea that he was going to be surprised by death. If he saw it coming, that was one thing, but the thought of it unexpectedly leaping from the shadows gave him the willies.

He needed that bottle bad.

Morning dawned blue and mean, the sky as unforgiving as a block of dry ice. Chase struggled up to the sound of the travel alarm clock ringing, ringing so loud it seemed to be inside his head. The Old Kentucky he had consumed the night before was now working on his brain with an anvil and a ball peen hammer. Ka-BANG! Ka-BANG!

'Oh God.' He groaned and rolled from the bed to his feet. He hurried to the bathroom and pissed a yellow river into the toilet. The hair bleach carton sat on the sink edge. He had to do that. Just as soon as he had one more slug of the whiskey to chase off the last of the heebie jeebies of the night. It wouldn't hurt his headache, might even cause it to disappear, though he wouldn't want to bet on it.

He hurried again to the bed, found the open bottle on the floor. He lifted it to his lips and took a deep swallow. It made him cough and his head pound even harder.

Couldn't help it. Had to get his hair bleached.

He took the whiskey bottle with him to the bathroom and set it on the toilet tank lid. He ripped open the package of hair dye and drew out the two bottles of chemicals he had to mix. The smell was a gag. He took another swig of the whiskey before dumping the bleach preparation onto his head and working it into his hair. He didn't have a head of luxuriant hair growth. It was thinning, though not yet on the march back from his forehead. He was far from bald. He probably didn't need the entire bottle of bleach, but he used it all anyway, working it into a white lather.

It tingled like a million fingers massaging his scalp while he sat on the toilet seat sipping from the whiskey. Within minutes his headache was gone and he felt drunk.

So what was the damn difference? He'd sober up before he did anything seriously stupid. He needed to eat. Something. He couldn't think what; nothing in the world of food was appetizing at the moment. Not even sweets. God, he missed the great steak and eggs they served in Vegas. The steak he'd tried here in Geneva tasted as if the steer had been kept on a diet of corn cobs and packing material.

He tried remembering when he'd finally fallen asleep last night, but couldn't. It might have been one or it might have been four. It was eight now. He might have gotten seven hours sleep or as little as four. Oops, time to get the gook off his hair! If he let it go too long it would burn his scalp. Might even make all his hair fall out.

He dropped onto his knees and turned on the water in the tub. He leaned over and rinsed his hair. Bending over that way made him giddy. He laughed and his laughter rang back at him from the sides of the porcelain tub.

He wasn't used to falling asleep drunk and dead to the world. He couldn't get into the habit, either. He'd seen too many guys end up like bums who did that. His father, for instance. Insomnia? Drink it under. Bills up the kazoo and no money in the bank? Drink it into oblivion. Can't get the old wrinkled pecker up? Drink some more and pretend you're a stud.

If only Chase wouldn't keep hearing someone creeping around his place. If that stopped, he wouldn't *have* to go for whiskey and wake up to get drunk again.

Shit. Some days he wished he could talk to someone about things. He needed someone to reassure him that he was right, it was all in his mind, he was blowing the whole thing out of proportion. He needed someone to say, 'Get hold of yourself, Garduci! Are you a man or are you a little scared boy? Where's the guy who dropped Vinnie, the guy who took out the Scarlotti brothers, Wake Henderson, and all those other goombas back in the old days? Where's Harry Dean Fucking Stanton, man?'

He laughed again and realized he'd had his head down under the tub faucet for a long while. But it felt good. It felt cool and clean and it was noisy down there, he couldn't hear a goddamn thing in the other room.

He finally raised his head and reached for a towel. He got to his feet some way and staggered over to the sink mirror. He unveiled his head, whipping the towel off, and stared at the transformation. He was blond, all right. Luckily he'd interrupted the process before he had gone completely white-headed. There was still yellow there. You couldn't even tell it was a bleach job. His eyebrows were thin and light, his skin shone with an indoor pallor.

He hardly recognized himself and with the glasses on . . . he would look like Harry Dean playing the role of a freaky-looking bookkeeper type. Yeah. How far could you get from cowboy, anyway? This was the real limit.

He laughed again and rubbed at his head with the towel. He didn't think he'd need a beard.

While shaving, he hummed 'Red Sails in the Sunset.' By the time he was finished in the bathroom, he felt nearly sober again.

But he'd keep the bottle for tonight. Just in case.

A flicker at the periphery of his vision caused him to turn around quick to the doorway. He squinted his eyes. He thought he saw . . .

No, he wasn't seeing anything, it was an hallucination.

The thing he didn't think he was seeing moved slightly, as if brushed by a breeze. It swayed, a dark shadow in the shape of a man.

'Who the fuck are you?' he yelled.

The shadow swayed again. It looked like . . . like Jake. Tony's dead kid.

'Jake? That you?' He added, 'Oh shit.'

'Welcome to Hell,' Jake said mildly.

It was Jake's voice. Chase had once watched the kid for Tony when he went on vacation to the Cayman Islands. He'd taken him to a particularly juicy whore palace up in the northern part of the state. The kid was insatiable, screwing three chicks that night. Chase had envied him.

'Jake, is that you?'

'Death's coming, Chase. Death's right around the bend.'

Then he disappeared. Or rather the shadow disappeared and Chase stood in the doorway staring out at empty air. Trembling like a little sad tree in a storm.

'Fuck,' he whispered to himself.

I wish he hadn't said that, he thought. Now I'm seeing ghosts. This shit's gotta stop.

Tony was told Chase was about to make a move. Tony stood from his desk smiling. His wife, who was rarely home anymore, came up the walkway through the rose garden, her long, flowered skirt swishing behind her and between her legs. He opened the French doors and strolled out to meet her.

'This hot wind is constant,' she complained, making an exasperated sound with her lips. She was originally from West Virginia, in the mountains where the climate was much more humid and cool. She had never acclimatized herself to the desert winds sweeping across the plains and down from the nearby mountains.

She halted in the shade of a flowering palm. Tony glanced up at it, marveling at the long dripping creamy white blossoms. 'Where have you been?' he asked.

She eyed him with a frown on her face. He felt it, brought his gaze from the tree to her eyes. 'What's the matter? Shouldn't I ask?'

'I was having lunch with Denise,' she said.

'Ah.'

'I know you don't usually interfere, but she says Jeff's fooling around with the showgirls has run her to the end of her rope. She says he's been seen with a new girl and it might be serious. He's with her two-three times a week.'

'You're right,' Tony said. 'I don't interfere. Love triangles aren't my business.'

'You hate him enough to let his wife leave him?'

Tony studied his wife's unrelenting stare. She was challenging him. Now that he was the head of the Family, she knew if he snapped his fingers, Denise's little problem would disappear. Any showgirl in Vegas could vanish on his say so.

'She leaves him, she leaves him.' He turned to the roses and inspected how the wind had caused new canes to tangle. He reached out to put them to order and his wife touched him on the arm.

'Denise loves him,' she said. 'It's not her fault he's got this weird thing about her weight. She's not repugnant, Tony. She's tried everything to lose the pounds just to please him and he pays her back by openly escorting girls around the casinos. She's . . . she's losing her mind.'

'Family affair,' Tony said, not willing to be brought into it on sentimental grounds. 'It's not in my province to have someone watch Jeff twenty-four hours a day just so he won't go cruising women. Denise will have to handle it on her own. I'm sorry.'

'No, you're not.'

'What?' The vehemence of her response startled him.

'You want her to leave him, don't you? Jeff's your problem so you want Denise to be *his* problem. Would a worthy man who had taken over from your father have left this to be resolved without helping out the poor woman?'

She had never spoken to him so harshly. Never asked him to do something about one of his boys. 'Connie . . .' He drew her into his arms. Ran his hands down from her shoulders to her waist and there drew her even closer to him. 'I can't do what you ask. Not this time. I said I was sorry for Denise and I am, but she'd be better off without him. There are any number of men who would be proud to have her as a wife. Jeff's not one of them. He doesn't deserve her. If he wants showgirls, he'll get them no matter what I do – shy of killing the bastard. And you or Denise don't want that, do you?'

He'd like to kill him. It was better, however, if the Kapon woman did it for him.

She sighed and sagged against him. He loved her breasts, soft and plump, against his chest. They were perfectly matched sexually. In all their years of marriage they had never failed to reach orgasm. Connie was always willing and always good in bed. Which was one reason why showgirls never tempted him at all.

'Denise was just so sad, Tony.' She sighed again. 'It's bad on a woman when she loves a scoundrel.'

Tony chuckled. 'That's a good, old-fashioned name for him.'

'That's because I'm a good, old-fashioned girl.' She nibbled at his earlobe and a thrill went down the back of his neck.

'Don't go anywhere tonight,' he whispered. 'Stay with me.'

'But I have . . .' She stopped and then continued, 'It's not important. If you want me home tonight, I'll be here.'

As she left him with his roses, he marveled at how much he loved his wife. He loved her as much as Jeff evidently despised Denise. Maybe that's what made Jeff such a cruel and devious man. He didn't know how to love a woman, not the woman on the inside, the real woman he was married to. What was the overweight shell when life was done? What was the beautiful woman when she was eighty? It was spirit a man must love, not the flesh so much.

Without Connie he couldn't have lived through Jake's execution in Texas. She was a rock that held him in place on the face of the planet, keeping him from flying off into the burning sun.

It surprised him he could love so deeply and hate so thoroughly. He shrugged, accepting his parallel nature.

The wind continued steady as Tony untangled the rose canes from adjacent bushes and tied them where they should be growing. He began to sweat a little, though usually even in a hundred-degree heat he was rarely affected. The wind was dry and smelled of iron clinging to the rocks on the sides of the volcanic mountains. A bead of sweat trickled down his forehead.

He worked plucking dead or dying blooms from his roses and thought about Chase beginning his work in Geneva, wondering what his first move would be and if it would hurt Elizabeth Kapon to the quick.

She had to pay. She must pay.

Tony's loss demanded it. The hole in his heart would never be filled until the woman's life was changed into dust forever.

That night, Tony was sitting in the study reading a copy of *Time* magazine when his private line buzzed. He picked up the receiver and heard Chase's voice.

'You ought to know I've hurt the girl. The daughter.'

Tony sucked in his breath. 'How bad?'

He heard a grunt and then heard the telephone knock against something as if Chase had banged it against a wall. 'Bad.'

'Then that's good, isn't it? She'll live, right?'

'She'll live.'

'You left a scar for her to remember?'

'Yes.'

'You're my man, Chase.'

Tony replaced the receiver in its cradle and sat back in his chair. Not many people knew Chase Garduci's real obsessions. Not even Dalta knew about it. Chase was a serial rapist and had been all his life. Tony found out everything about his boys and none of them were as fucked up as Chase. That's what made Chase formidable. The black well of his soul was darker than the time before there was a sun.

There was great satisfaction in knowing the Kapon woman's kid had been raped and cut.

It was not enough, not nearly, but it was a start.

14

Chase spent the day in his air-conditioned rental car, air-conditioned stores, and hunting for a breeze between the two to keep him cool. It was a steamy, hot, Southeast Texas day, so humid the air felt too heavy and thick to breathe. How anyone could stand this place during the summer was beyond Chase. They lived in a suffocating inferno.

The natives didn't seem to mind. They went along their mindless way doing the things that made up small, uneventful lives. Driving to work, going to lunch, shopping, visiting the dentist, marching down the drab streets through the palpable heat as if they were a new breed of human incapable of noticing the weather. Or anything else beyond their noses. None of them gave him a second look, but that's what he had wanted, wasn't it, him with his new blond hair and polyester slacks dragging the ground at the heels of his loafers.

After a few hours of mind-numbing people-watching, Chase began to feel invisible and though it was what he had hoped for, it was a trifle unsettling. He was tempted to pinch himself to see if he were real, but that was idiotic, he knew he was real, too real, and burdened these days with a lively imagination that had not ceased making him feel haunted even as he went unnoticed by pedestrians.

As the sun set, Chase purchased a plastic gas container at the local Walmart, and drove to a busy Stop 'n Go to fill it with a gallon of regular unleaded. He also filled the car so that the clerk didn't realize one gallon of the purchase didn't make it into the vehicle.

At eight o'clock Chase, still uneasy and slick with sweat from the heat that rose in invisible waves from the pavement, parked blocks away from Kapon's apartment house. He watched the street for a while and didn't think it was going to have much traffic now that everyone had made it home from work.

At eight-thirty he carefully filled two plastic, liter-sized Coke bottles with gasoline, then screwed on the caps. He cursed when he spilled some over his hands and had to wipe them with a sheaf of napkins from the Burger King.

By eight-forty he was out of the car and walking along the sidewalk with the liter bottles in a brown grocery sack swinging at his side. Just a guy who had made a run to the corner convenience, that's what he appeared to be.

He reached Beth's house at eight-forty-three. Lights blazed in most of the windows. That was good. He didn't want to catch them asleep. Tony said not to kill the woman. Kill her inside, that's what he had to do.

At eight-forty-eight, he had emptied one of the Coke bottles of gas onto a shrub growing at the side of the house. Two minutes later, he emptied the other bottle into the metal trash can at the back of the house. This fire would not ignite the house, it was too distant from the wood framing, but it would send up a good black smoke from the garbage soaked inside the can. Then he set it aflame with matches, hurried to the shrub, made sure it was going to take, then strolled away down the walk back toward his car, again swinging the grocery sack at his side in time with his steps.

He did not stay to see what would happen.

That wasn't part of the job. He'd find out the results tomorrow. Probably on the morning news. If someone died besides Beth, all for the better, but he had experience at these things. It was rare anyone died.

Tonight he thought he might sleep without the whiskey. He had the show on the stage and was dancing as fast as he could.

Paul woke up in the semi-private hospital room just before the sun began its final descent to the horizon. He could go home, the doctor said, just as soon as rounds were made after the dinner meal.

Paul asked him about Melanie. 'She would have come in before I did,' he said. 'I have to find out about her, please!'

Seeing his agitation, the doctor left the room to consult with someone in the admitting department downstairs. He came back in a few minutes, a crease between his eyes. 'Melanie Kapon was seen and released in Emergency last night.'

'What was wrong with her? I heard she'd been attacked and cut.'

The doctor hesitated. 'Please,' Paul said.

'She was sexually assaulted and there were cuts on one of her arms and a slash across one side of her face that required stitches. The police were called in and took her statement and . . . evidence.'

Paul rose straight up in the hospital bed, a horrified expression on his face. 'I have to get out of here. I have to see her.'

'You can dress now. If you want to leave early, just take these papers down to the office.'

Paul dressed, hurrying so much he couldn't get the buttons on his shirt to line up. He had been found, they had told him when he had first regained consciousness, by an old black man who fished the creek where Paul had been assaulted. It had been morning before he had come to himself enough to know he was in the hospital. His mother had been hysterical. She had a policeman waiting just outside his room and went for him as soon as her son woke.

'I'm in the hospital?' Paul had said to the cop who stood over him. He'd turned his head to his mother on the other side of the bed. 'How long have I been asleep?'

All evening and all night, it had turned out. He had suffered concussion and had been unconscious all those hours. No wonder his mother had been frantic. He'd had to reassure her he was fine, he didn't even have a headache. She'd gone to find the doctor anyway, leaving him alone with the cop.

What were the facts? Who had knocked him on the head and why? Paul had done his level best to supply all the details as he knew them. He hadn't forgotten anything. He'd described his assailant down to his resemblance to a movie actor, but he didn't know the name of the actor. He knew some of the movies he'd been in and named those instead.

'Maybe you can find those on video and let us know who it is so we can check it out too. This is a serious offense. You might have been killed or suffered brain damage.'

'My brain is damaged?' Paul had wanted to know, feeling his gut tighten.

'Oh, no, I mean that's what *might* have happened, being hit in the head with a gun. The doc says no permanent damage if you came out of the coma within twenty-four hours. You didn't even get a cracked skull. It was a pretty damn good slam in the head, that's all.'

'Hell, that's a relief.' Paul had laughed just a little and let out his stomach, breathing easy once more.

'So you think this guy was watching the DA's house?'

'Yeah, I'm sure of that. He admitted it to me. I think he's the one who . . . who hurt Melanie.'

The cop had taken his notes and told Paul to keep in touch and call if he remembered anything else or if he saw the man again.

Paul's mother had returned dragging behind her a doctor who looked so tired he should have been in a bed himself, Paul thought. Lights had been shone into his eyes and questions asked of him, testing his memory. Paul had passed all the tests and the doctor had told his mother, 'Not to worry, he has a hard head, he's gonna do fine.'

Now it was check-out time and Paul meant to make it over to Melanie's house just as fast as his legs would carry him. There was a rage inside him against what had been done to her, but he controlled it. Otherwise he might begin breaking things and throwing stuff and the hospital people would think he'd lost his mind when he was knocked on the head and not let him leave.

He rushed downstairs and checked himself out of the hospital. His mother worked as a cashier at HEB grocery and she pulled the night shift. She wouldn't be home until after eleven. He had plenty of time to see Melanie and still be home waiting for his mother when she got off work.

The fire on the side of the house was blazing straight up from the bush and climbing the wall when Paul jogged across the street. He saw it and fear leaped from his brain to his heart and made it pound so hard he thought he might faint.

Fire!

He ran to the front door, stumbled through, and was banging on

Melanie's apartment door, screaming, 'FIRE, FIRE.'

Doors opened behind him and up the stairs and suddenly the lobby area swarmed with the residents, many of them in nightgowns and housecoats, wild eyes wide, all talking at once in dismay and fright.

Mrs Kapon opened the door to him and in a voice louder than all the rest she screamed, 'Get out! Everybody outside!'

Paul looked behind Beth Kapon and realized if Melanie had been home during this commotion, she would have been there. That she wasn't indicated she wasn't in the house. He turned and helped an older woman through the door and out onto the lawn. He heard the fire engine sirens, saw people coming from houses across the street and next door.

He ran around the house to where he'd spotted the fire and saw that it wasn't doing all that much damage, really. It had climbed up several rows of the clapboard, but hadn't yet reached the three-story roof. Jesus, what if he hadn't come over, would Beth Kapon have smelled the smoke or one of the residents seen it before it got out of hand?

His gaze wandered down the wall and he saw smoke billowing from behind the house. He turned, saw the fire truck park at the curb and when the first fireman got to him, he yelled, 'There's another one behind the house.'

By eight-fifty-eight the two small fires were out and Beth stood next to him surveying the smoke-blackened wall. The fire in the back hadn't reached the house at all. It was started in a trash can and was contained. 'It didn't burn through the wall, but that's still going to cost some money to repair,' Beth said. She covered her eyes with one hand and shook her head. 'I can't believe someone would do this. We might have all died.'

'I think someone wants that to happen. This guy's not interested in the other people in this house, though, just you and Melanie.' The old people still hung around on the lawn talking with neighbors and discussing what might have happened if they'd all been asleep in their beds.

'I can see that,' Beth said. 'These weren't exactly accidental.'

Just then the fire marshal asked for Beth to accompany him to the station to help him make a report and discuss the fires, who might have started them. It had already been determined that gasoline had been used in both places, a clear case of arson.

Beth said to Paul, 'Can you stay and tell Melanie where I'm at? She comes home to this and well, I don't want her to get upset again. And she shouldn't be alone.' She glanced back at the wall and shivered.

'Sure, I can hang around a while. Where is she?'

'She stayed at a friend's house today while I ran some errands at the court house. I'm sorry about your head injury,' she said, touching his arm gently. 'It was the same man, wasn't it?'

'Yeah, it was. He's a really scary guy, Mrs Kapon.'

There was a sudden flash in Beth's eyes. 'He's more than that, he's a monster. I'm going to find him and I'm going to . . .'

The fire marshal called to her again and she let her sentence go unfinished.

'You won't have to do anything if I find him first,' Paul said.

She leaned over and kissed him on the check. 'Watch after Melanie for me, okay?'

Paul watched her climb into the fire marshal's car before he went inside. The old woman who wore a head scarf and talked with an accent said from the stairway, 'You do this thing or not you do?'

Paul halted, shocked at the accusation, then he laughed. 'No,' he said. 'I not do this thing. If I hadn't come along, you might not have had a bed to go to tonight.'

'Ah,' she said, satisfied. 'You the hero, yes, the boy super.'

He waited until she had turned the corner on the landing before smiling and entering Melanie's apartment. Could she have meant he was a super boy, like Superman, maybe? Her aura was pale green, like new grass in the spring. He liked her very much.

He could still smell the smoke and the stink of wet scorched wood. It smelled like what he thought despair might smell like if it had an odor.

He sank down into a chair to wait. Now he had a headache. And he'd remembered the actor's name, the one who looked like the man who had abducted him and knocked him fucking silly.

Harry Dean Stanton. That's who the guy looked like. Not identical, but enough to leave an impression on the memory. He hoped that would help the police catch him. It should. Everyone knew what Stanton looked like.

The son of a bitch wasn't just into surveillance, but rape. He needed a long stay in a cell up at Huntsville Correctional. Like for about a hundred and fifty years. Or a good dose of lethal injection would be better.

That's if the state caught up with him. If Beth or Paul got to him first, they wouldn't need the injection.

Chase sat with his legs sprawled out before him. The small black and white television supplied with the furnished apartment flickered gray over the darkened living room. Every few minutes Chase was sure the shadows moved and he jerked his head one way and then the other, trying to catch out the intruder who *might* be lurking there. 'Jake?' he called. 'Is that you, Jake?'

He had heard the sirens in the distance earlier as he drove across town and had smiled at the promptness of the local volunteers. It would have taken them longer in Vegas or Chicago to get to the scene. Half the damned house would have gone up in flame, before they hauled out the hoses.

A rerun of *LA Law* played on the small screen. Chase had always liked the show, except for the blond lawyer who got all the girls, that guy was too slick for his own good, Chase thought. No one got that many women in bed, gimme a break. Even a guy with money, a law degree, and an attitude.

The shadows moved again and Chase tensed. Maybe he should just turn on the lights. Turn on all the lights and dispel the shadows, that should solve the problem of seeing shapes and figures that were not there.

Were not there.

He pulled in his long legs and got to his feet. Within minutes he had every lamp and every overhead bulb burning. He no longer cared about *LA Law* and he also didn't care about the new Kentucky bourbon bottle he'd bought earlier in the day, the one sitting on the sink drain unopened.

He could sleep now that it was bright as noon in the apartment.

In the light there was nowhere for ghosts to hide.

* * *

Chase floated through the next few days like a zombie. He was sleeping little and worrying about someone killing him more.

On the Monday after he set the fires at Kapon's house, he drove by around midnight and shot at the walls.

He was making Geneva headlines. TARGETED, they read, BY A MADMAN.

He laughed at that one. He was about as mad as anyone else, which might say a lot about the general population in this country.

On Tuesday at eleven p.m., he stole around the Kapon house and cut all the phone lines. Then he threw red paint across the back porch steps.

On Wednesday he started to cruise by the house and saw the stakeout. Two cop cars were parked on each side of the street in front of Kapon's place.

He turned the corner and went back to his apartment.

He must lie low just a bit. The cops would get tired of sitting all night out there doing nothing. They'd be pulled off the detail soon and that's when he'd strike again. He'd like to get hold of Beth and cut her a little. Maybe not on the face, like he did the girl. Maybe somewhere no one could see. Somewhere private.

By Thursday of the following week he saw the cops were gone and he did another drive-by shooting. The last time he didn't hit anyone. That was just pure luck. This time he might.

Soon all Kapon's residents would move out, whether anyone was hurt or not.

That's when he would snatch the girl.

She had an appointment with a needle in Las Vegas.

The night Chase shot at the house for the second time, an elderly tenant by the name of Mary Roberson was bringing a cup of coffee to the living room of her apartment for her visiting daughter, Arabel.

The shots struck the house, six of them in rapid succession, and Mary stood petrified, rooted to the spot. She didn't see a bullet enter the window, but she saw the glass smash inwards, spraying everywhere. And she saw Arabel, her middle-aged and unmarried daughter, clutch at her shoulder and keel over in a dead faint to the floor.

Mary Roberson screamed until someone was banging at her door and only then did she drop the coffee cup and saucer and rush to her daughter's aid. The door to her apartment soon opened and people surrounded her, but she didn't speak to them. She was trying too hard to stem the flow of Arabel's rich, red blood.

'They're all moving out. I'm just glad Mrs Roberson's daughter didn't die. If someone had died because of me . . .' Beth stood near the sink washing dishes. Soap bubbles covered her arms to the elbow and steam rose from the rinse sink where she let the hot water run. Pope wound around her ankles, rubbing and purring like a small yellow machine.

'Only three of them are moving, Mom.' Melanie sat at the table with her head on her arms, her face turned toward her mother. She had not said much the past few days. She was like someone deep in the throes of grief. Depressed and angry. Silent.

Paul sat across from her, chewing at his fingernails.

'I don't know why the police didn't stay around,' he said.

Beth shrugged. 'This is a small town. We only have so many cars. Having two or even one sitting in front of the house twenty-four hours a day is impossible. I don't blame them for these attacks.'

'Not everyone will move out,' Melanie said.

'Yes. They will. They've given notice. I didn't tell you.'

Melanie raised her head and looked at Paul. '*Everyone*?' she asked.

Beth rinsed a cup and set it in the sink then plunged her arms into the soapy water again. 'Yes. Everyone. We're going to lose the house. Our savings are gone. We'll have no income. I'll never be able to rent out these apartments now.' She had sat every night on the front lawn in a folding lawn chair, a loaded shotgun across her lap. She slept during the day. It hadn't helped make the renters feel any safer. They nervously twitched aside the curtains at night to watch her, waiting to see if she'd be the next victim of the drive-by shooter. The tension was too much. They were too old to stand it, they told her. They were sorry, but this was life or death. They could not stay.

'But that's not right! Why can't they catch him? The papers even reported what he looked like. Why can't they find him? What does he want? He's already done so many evil things . . .'

Paul reached out and took hold of Melanie's hands to still her shaking.

'I know what he wants,' Beth said, rinsing a plate. 'What I don't know is why. I've been tracking down the whereabouts of all the cons I put away, and one by one I've ruled them out. I can't think who's doing this. But I'm going to search for him myself. This is where I need your help, Paul.'

'Whatever you want, Mrs Kapon.'

'I want you to stay here as much as your mother will let you. When you're here, I'm going to be out driving around. This guy is staying in town. I'll find him sooner or later. He has to eat, he has to shop and do his clothes somewhere, and buy gas for his car. I'm going to find him.'

'Sure, I'll stay around,' Paul said. He almost had Melanie calm again. He'd do anything for her, anything. Her aura since the rape had changed to a somber milky shade of off-white, maybe it was a sickly beige. Her gold was gone. He wondered if she'd ever retrieve it. She was not the same now. She was damaged, perhaps beyond repair.

'You're a good kid, Paul. Maybe I should apologize to you for some things I once said to Melanie. None of it was true. You're a real good kid.' Beth quickly rinsed the rest of the dishes and turned off the faucet. She took paper towels and dried her hands. She turned to the two young people at the table. 'I'm going out now. I'll be back before midnight. You can stay that long?' she asked Paul.

He nodded his head. 'You got it.'

'Just find him, Mom,' Melanie said. 'I hope he . . . I hope he . . .' Tears rolled down her cheeks and she didn't bother to wipe them away. The stitches on her cheek had left the skin puckered and reddened. Plastic surgery might help, they had said. But they couldn't do that until the cut was healed completely.

Beth swooped up Pope and placed him in Melanie's arms. When you were wounded, there was nothing to do but mourn this way. She'd get the bastard who made her daughter look and feel like a broken doll. She wouldn't rest until she did.

* * *

Dalta was happy when told of the situation, but Chase felt himself coming apart more each day. He didn't let Jeff know it, God no, he'd be pulled off the job and never used again, but now he was *sure* he was being stalked and his nerves were jumpy, yo-yoing up and down, driving him insane. He couldn't even pull the trigger on the woman the night he drove past the house and saw her sitting in the lawn chair, a shotgun across her knees. He could have done it, could have hurt her a lot before she ever got her own weapon lifted into position, but he was losing all his nerve now. He felt it dribbling out, leaving him shaky and unable to think about anything but when he was going to take the big one in the back.

'Can I just take the girl and get the hell out of here now?' he asked Dalta.

Chase stood in a pay phone booth outside the Walmart, sun in his eyes, sweat soaking his shirt.

'Man, I'm telling you, this town is too hot for me. They've put out a description of me in the papers, they got cop cars patroling Kapon's place regularly, and I don't see any call to hang in here any longer. I keep this up and they're gonna nab me. Sooner or later, I'm gonna have cuffs on my goddamn wrists.'

Dalta was quiet for a moment and then he said, 'Yeah, you're right. Get the girl and get out of that town. But don't get caught doing it, Chase, do you hear me? I've never heard you sound so wild before. This job must be eating at you and I don't understand why. It's a cakewalk and you know it.'

'Might be,' Chase admitted. 'But this shit town's like a firecracker ready to blow. I can't get near the house now and all her tenants have moved out on her so . . .'

'All right! I said get the girl and get the hell out. Stop that whining, you're giving me a headache. Call me when you get here.'

'Yeah sure,' Chase said to the replaced receiver. 'You asshole.'

Now he sat in the rental car with the vents angled toward his face, waiting for Melanie Kapon to be released from her last class of the day. It was two-thirty. She should stroll out the doors of the building in a couple of minutes. He was parked down the sidewalk, beneath a towering tree, though the shade did nothing to mitigate the terrible

147

summer heat. In the trunk of the car he already had his suitcase stashed.

Time to ride, time to skip this sonofabitching East Texas no-good town. They'd drive west and be in Vegas in a couple of days. He had slept twelve hours straight, thanks to Compoz sleeping tablets, and he was ready for the overnight driving stint. They'd stop for nothing but gas. He'd be so happy to be rid of this job he could hardly think straight.

He saw her coming. Alone, carrying her load of school books on one hip the way mothers carried toddlers. He scooted over to the passenger's side of the seat and had his gun out, pressing against the door. He rolled down the window. When she neared the car he called out, 'Hey, get your ass over here or I drop you where you stand.'

She stopped. She was going to scream. He saw it in her wild eyes.

He raised the gun. It satisfied Chase to watch the hysteria fade as her facial expression changed to one of terror when she saw the weapon. He said, 'Get in the goddamn car. Now.'

For a couple of seconds she didn't move. He said again, quickly and loudly this time, 'Get in the car!'

She came toward him and he opened the door. He slid back toward the driver's side and started the ignition. 'Don't give me any shit, kid.' He thought he sounded like Eastwood in *Dirty Harry*. 'And don't talk to me when I'm driving. We have a long trip ahead of us.'

She began talking immediately, pleading to be set free, just like he knew she would. He tuned her out. He had to get her out of town and get her doped up before she would really shut up. God, this was one of the worst jobs he'd ever been involved in. He ever got this done, he was taking a fucking vacation.

Not far away on the campus a tall man dressed in black watched the abduction from where he lounged near a twenty-foot statue of Sam Houston. He was a foreigner with curly brown hair that threw glints from the sunlight.

He had finished his work on a ranch near Bryan, Texas. Even now the rancher's body cooled where he lay on the Spanish tiled floor of his country-sized kitchen. The man had owned too much land, forty thousand acres. He had made too many enemies, screwed over too many friends. Now he was dead and most of the people who knew him would say good riddance.

Phan Lieu stepped away from the shade thrown by the statue of the man on a rearing horse, and left the area. He looked around him, saw other students moving across the campus, none of them aware of what had just taken place beneath their noses.

Phan knew Chase Garduci. Knew he worked for the Mace family out of Vegas. What's more, he now knew he worked for the man who was Phan's father. The Texas senator had come through with the information.

While Phan was checking on the rancher with his sources in Bryan, it was remarked he wasn't the only game in town. There was other mischief afoot and it wasn't far away – just a few miles, in fact. Phan was filled in on Chase and his involvement with the Kapon family. 'He's in Texas taking revenge on behalf of the Mace family?' he had asked.

'Absolutely. You don't fuck with a Mafia don's son.'

Phan's heart stopped in his chest. When it stuttered into rhythm again he asked, 'What son?'

'You didn't hear about that murder and the trial about five years ago? It was so brutal it made all the national news.'

'I didn't hear. Tell me.'

After Phan hung up the telephone, he stood silently for several minutes. He had not thought a lot about what his father's life had been like after he had left Vietnam. Of course he would have married and had children; he had gone on to live his life as if nothing he ever did in Vietnam mattered. What surprised Phan was that he only had one child, one much younger than Phan, and he'd lost him to lethal injection.

He must have loved him more than anything, Phan thought, to do what he's doing now.

The reason for Chase abducting the girl was pretty obvious then. An eye for an eye, a daughter for a son. That's the kind of man his father was. It was nothing to be proud of, but then look how his sons had turned out. Both murderers. The difference was Phan got away

149

with it. He hadn't been brought up rich and spoiled and impulsive. He did not commit murder because of a petty argument. It was all cold business to him. No emotions involved. That got you killed.

The campus was full of students moving between classes now. Phan hurried to his car. He wouldn't want to be remembered being in the vicinity at the time the girl disappeared.

It was time to head for Vegas. Time to face the man who had made him what he was today.

15

Tony Mace's home stood on one and a quarter acres at the end of a winding road just outside the confines of the Las Vegas city limits. It cost more than half a million dollars and afforded both city and mountain views. The multi-level home of white adobe with a red tile roof had five thousand, four hundred square feet inside. It was large enough for several people to live in without feeling crowded. It tended to lie silent and forbidding and shadowed with just Tony, Connie, the cook, gardener, and driver in residence.

Two Doric columns graced the front entrance that faced a circular drive. On the green front lawn stood one large Joshua tree. Behind the sprawling house were the rose gardens with stone walkways, fountains, scattered garden benches in white wrought iron, and the most beautiful roses grown anywhere in the state of Nevada.

Tony sat now on one of the garden benches having his morning coffee. He had more trouble than he could comfortably cope with and the sight of his roses always helped him control the runaway anxiety that trouble naturally brought with it.

Chase Garduci had taken the girl from Geneva, Texas. The kidnapping was reported in the local paper and picked up by the wires. Every boss on the continent knew Chase belonged to the Macedonia family and many of them were up in arms about what he was doing in the southwest. They suspected Tony was trying to move into the lucrative Texas market. Texas had recently passed a bill for legalized gambling. The Lotto brought in big money. Horse and dog tracks were being built in several locations. Maybe Tony was planning to bring casinos down into the Sunbelt. Did snatching the girl have something to do with twisting a land developer's arm?

Chicago was pissed off. The New York and New Jersey families were paranoid and furious. A south Texas gambling center would undercut their profits in Atlantic City. Even the boys in Houston and Galveston, who hadn't been in on the reason Chase was in Texas, wondered if Tony was out to take over their territory. Was that why one of his soldiers was scouting the state? Why weren't they told? What the fuck was going on? they screamed at him on the phone lines.

Tony had been on the phone for hours talking to the bosses, calming fears, setting up a meeting to reassure them Chase was a renegade on a mission unconnected with his wishes.

There had not been a word forthcoming from Dalta. Chase was his boy, but Dalta hadn't even made a semblance of apology to Tony. Tony told him to ruin Kapon's career. He never told him to take the daughter, though of course he knew Dalta would do something drastic. That was part of the plan. Dalta *thought* this was the way to ruin him. It's exactly what Tony was hoping for. An incident that couldn't be undone, couldn't be fixed, something that brought the Kapon woman gunning for someone.

Now that Melanie Kapon's kidnapping had been splattered all over the nation's newspapers and intrigue was underway, it was a terrible breach of protocol for Dalta to remain silent.

Tony made sure everyone knew it, too. He pretended innocence. He cursed Dalta's name in every conversation he had with his boys. In this final action Dalta was announcing to the entire family that he was a wild card, he was going against all the sanctions, he meant to split from the Mace family.

Tony had yet to explain himself to the other bosses. In a week he was to meet with the eastern leaders at a secluded house in Michigan's upper peninsula. If he didn't still their suspicions, there could be an unprecedented scramble for power. No one was going to let Texas go without a fight. He must assure them this wasn't about taking over their territory. This was a renegade in his camp stirring up trouble. This was personal.

A breeze brought the scent of the roses to Tony's nostrils and he inhaled deeply. It all took so much time. He was sick of waiting.

The breeze rustled the pages of the letter lying in his lap. He set aside his coffee cup and took up the papers. Through vision that slowly blurred with tears he read one of Jake's last letters from Death Row:

I think I'm going crazy in here, Dad. I can talk to other guys in the cells, but I can't see them. What we talk about most of the time is facing the Chamber, that's what we call the place where we'll die. We talk about walking the last walk and bragging that we won't break, we won't let the bastards see us cry. You know I wouldn't do that, I would never cry, I learned enough about crying when they first put me in here and I won't do it anymore.

Once a day they take us out for a little time outdoors and then a shower, but the other twenty-three hours I'm in this cell alone with my thoughts for company. I never knew I could think so many different things. I think up mental games for myself. I think about the past when I was home with you. I think of the Viper and that last ride out of Dallas and how I wish I'd listened to Byron and driven on down to Houston that night. I think about you and Mom. I wonder what it's like at home now without me there. Do you still have the roses?

At this point in the letter Tony could no longer see the small script blurring on the page and he had to turn away his face into the wind. It was true he was no stranger to people he loved spending time in prison, no stranger to the cold, hard fact of death. It was not so long ago the Families had warred.

Although the newspapers didn't follow them as closely as they once did – and he knew this was because there was enough violent crime going on in the country to keep the daily papers full without playing up the Family struggles – that didn't mean there hadn't been bloody and costly wars and takeovers.

So Tony was as familiar with losing people he cared about to jail cells and to death as his father had been before him, but none of those losses came close to giving him the pain he experienced when

153

Jake was marched into the room where he met his death.

Tony shuffled the pages of the letter into order and folded them carefully to slip into the envelope. He replaced the envelope with the others in the metal box he kept locked in his personal vault inside the house. These letters, the last testaments of his son, were the fuel that stoked his rage. He read them over often and they always left him feeling impotent, cold all over and helpless to change the past.

Maybe if he'd tried harder to control Jake. If he'd sent him to a military school or a boarding school outside of the country. If he'd not bought him the Dodge Viper for his birthday and let him drive across country. If he'd not allowed him to carry the gun along for protection.

If he only had Jake back none of these questions of guilt would be necessary. But like the blooms on his rose bushes, life for Jake was one short flash of color and then it browned and died.

Elizabeth Kapon found a way to kill him with the legal system. She could not continue her life as if this had never happened, as if she were not responsible.

Tony hoped Dalta killed the girl Chase stole away. Kapon must feel the same grief Tony felt. She must endure the same torture. If Jeff Dalta was anywhere near as smart as Tony thought him, he'd give orders to do more than kidnap the girl.

'Tony, come inside for breakfast. I have to leave in a few minutes.'

Tony turned at his wife's voice and smiled at her where she stood in the doorway. She wore a pale ivory suit with a gold scarf tied at the neck. He didn't know all the clubs she belonged to, all the charitable institutions. But he didn't have to. He trusted her to help create the cover on his reputation. He was a scion of Vegas. In some places when he walked in the respect shown him was tremendous. And some of those places had little to do with the Family enterprises. They were the mayor's home, the hospital charity balls, the political campaign-raising parties, the policemen's annual benefit barbecue, the circuit judge's chambers. Connie made that happen for the Mace family. She was bright and pretty and her checkbook was always open, ready for her signature.

'I'm coming,' he called, taking up the metal box full of Jake's letters. He held the box close to the front of his chest as he walked toward the house, held it as if it contained inviolate his son's heart and soul.

Beth had faced just one horrible dilemma in her life and that was the early and unfortunate death of her young husband.

Until Beth was caught in the court house hallway with cocaine on her person, she had taken for granted that she had suffered her one great loss and because of that she would not again be picked by fate to suffer such insult again. Now she knew she was wrong. Nothing should be taken for granted. Not goodwill, income, professional honesty and efficiency, or even a roof over her head.

The apartment house was up for sale. Cheap. If she got out from under it with enough to pay off the loan on it that would just be a lucky break coming into play midst all the bad luck. She wouldn't stake her life on it. If she ever won back her license to practice and teach law, it would probably be a miracle. At this point she thought she had more worry and strain in her life than she could handle and stay sane. Therefore, when the police came to her door that late gray afternoon to tell her that her daughter was missing, Beth could do nothing but stare at the two detectives as if they were from another planet.

'Wait a minute.' She licked her lips and blinked stupidly. 'What do you mean Melanie's gone?' She would lay this information out in a simple, straight fashion and then she would understand it. It had taken everything she had to understand what happened the night the man broke into the apartment and raped and mutilated her daughter. Now this. This was too much. Overload, all the circuits breaking.

'We'll find her, Mrs Kapon,' said the taller of the two men. He stepped into the apartment and took her arm to lead her to a chair. 'We have an eyewitness down at the station under interrogation. He knows your daughter. His name is Paul Makovine and he was coming from a building across the street when he saw her getting into a car. He saw the man had a gun, that she was forced.'

'My daughter . . . Melanie . . . she . . .'

'She was abducted, Mrs Kapon. Try not to let this upset you, now; we don't think she's been harmed. The witness said a man forced your daughter into a late model car, then he drove away before the witness could reach them.'

'Upset me?' Beth tried to make sense of the news. She shouldn't be upset. No, of course not. Melanie had been kidnapped and . . .

Beth came to her feet abruptly. Her hands shook and her voice was lost to her for a moment when she tried to speak. A tearing pain ran through her chest, a pain of loss so great it mimicked the overwhelming moments of grief she had suffered the day her husband died.

She swayed on her feet and the detective steadied her. He was mouthing platitudes and reassuring her, something about the car being a white Ford Taurus, about the highway patrol having an APB out. Beth pushed him aside and turned in a circle trying to assimilate all these things at once, but the only thought that stuck in her mind was that Melanie was gone. She was gone. Someone had her, a stranger had taken her. Did the kidnapper show his evil face when he ordered her into the car? Had Melanie seen it? Was she now traveling with that face of evil, terrified and weeping, begging to come home?

'Mrs Kapon, we think you should sit down. When you're feeling better we'd like you to come down to the station and give us a description of your . . .'

Tears did not form in Beth's eyes, not before they welled around her heart and swamped it in such sudden fear and sorrow that she thought she might die from it. She had to act. Must . . . act. Take control. *Do something.*

'Go find my daughter,' she said, grabbing the detective's shirt front like a woman gone mad. 'Find her!'

The two men exchanged unhappy, knowing glances. This was, after all, Elizabeth Kapon, the district attorney under indictment for cocaine possession. She'd sold her house, she had just recently had a fire and drive-by shootings at her apartment building. An intruder had raped her daughter and disfigured her face. It seemed misfortune haunted her every move. Why wouldn't she be hysterical hearing her daughter had been kidnapped?

'Mrs Kapon, we're doing all we . . .'

'Find her.' Beth shouted, letting go of the man's shirt and starting for the open door to the vestibule of the apartment house. 'We have to go after her now. Someone will kill her, someone wants to punish me.'

Luyba, the Russian immigrant tenant from upstairs, stood in the way. She took Beth around the shoulders and clutched her to her bosom, would not free her though she struggled and babbled. 'Shhh,' the older woman said. 'Shhh now, she'll be all right, you'll see, they'll find your girl. I promise you they will. No, no, calm down, and it's going to be all right . . .'

And it wasn't, Beth knew, the thought sifting through her terror. It wasn't going to be all right at all; never again.

16

He did not have time to argue with Melanie Kapon. She was hysterical, predictably, and causing him trouble. He drove as fast as he could, ignoring her tears and pleas, until he found the two-lane highway outside of Geneva that led past the dirt road where he had parked another car. He saw the turn ahead, recognized it by the huge grandfather oak that marked the turnoff. He swerved into the dirt lane, the rear of the Taurus sliding around in an arc as it bumped into the rutted road.

Now they were out of view of the major highway where any time cop cars would be flying past searching for them. He could hear them in the distance, sirens wailing. He hadn't much time.

He jumped from the Taurus and circled the front grill, keeping his eye on the girl in the passenger seat. If she thought of running he was ready for it. He reached her side of the car and swung open the door. 'Get out.'

She hung back a second too long so he reached in and grabbed her arm, hauling her from the seat and to her feet. He marched her to the safe car and deposited her inside. Leaving the door open, he punched the button releasing the pocket compartment just in front of her knees. He brought out a small black leather case and snapped it open. He took out a filled syringe. 'Just a little goodie juice,' he said.

The girl's terror escalated at the sight of it. She was shouting some gibberish that he let pass through his mind and out again, wind screaming through the trees. He took her right arm and shook her until she was still. 'If I miss your vein, it might kill you.' This was not true, but she wouldn't know that. He needed her cooperation to do it right. He never messed with this shit and he really didn't want to kill the kid. She was a good piece of ass. He might want it again and he wouldn't want it dead.

She kept saying no, but he held her and stared down into her eyes until she calmed. He said again, 'If I don't hit the vein, this will kill you. If you let me do it right, you'll just sleep. I'm not going to hurt you. I'm not going to kill or rape you. But if you don't cooperate, and this needle goes into the muscle, you'll never open your eyes again.'

His voice was low and dispassionate; he was still in his Clint Eastwood persona. She seemed to follow his lips as if lip-reading. Then she raised her gaze to his eyes again and he realized she wasn't connected. Her eyes weren't connected to her brain any longer. This was a person who had skipped completely out into the ozone, wahoo.

'Fine,' he said. He leaned over her arm and from the case took a yellow length of rubber tubing. He tied it off and thumped her veins at the crook of her elbow. He gave the injection without any protest from her; she did not move a finger.

She was to be made his physical prisoner and then she was to be made the prisoner of heroin. It was his idea. If Dalta didn't like it, Tony would. He'd get her started on the junk and keep her doped all the way to Vegas. That's exactly what he'd do and, goddamn, would he be glad when this job was over. It wasn't fun anymore. And he had too many things on his mind. He kept thinking of Connie, lusting after her. He kept thinking of seeing Jake in the apartment, welcoming him to hell.

He had even . . .

It was hard to admit it, but it was the truth . . .

He was even beginning to believe in supernatural beings. Not just Jake. But demons and shit. He heard them, sort of. Whispering when it was quiet. And seeing them, in a way. Flitting across his vision like dust devils, there, not there, winking in and out maddeningly.

He loosened the tubing and put everything back into the leather case. He stowed it in the car pocket, shut her door, fetched his case from the other car. By the time he had started the engine, Melanie Kapon was no longer a problem for him. She dozed, her head slack against the window, her arms limp in her lap, palms cupped.

He smiled as he drove from the cover of the trees.

It was a long way to Nevada, but at least they were leaving the state of Texas.

The connections had not been clear to Phan Lieu immediately, a revelation laid out neatly and chronologically. It had taken him months to find all the threads in the tapestry and to understand their relevance. If it hadn't been for the Texas senator who owed him, he didn't know if he would have ever found out anything.

For instance, now he knew Jeff Dalta, on behalf of the Mace family, had sent a man down into the little Texas town in order to create havoc in Elizabeth Kapon's world.

He didn't know exactly how the kidnapping fit in or what they meant to do with Elizabeth's daughter, but he expected they might kill her.

Was he, Phan, afraid of following and interfering with the Mafia?

He was afraid of no one. He knew about the Mafia from having been in a gang of assassins in Vietnam. It was originally the MAFIA. *Morte alla Francia, Italia acclomare.* Death to France, Italy cries out. The word *mafioso* meant keen, spiritual, beautiful. The brutal tactics organized crime had employed over its history did not intimidate him in the least. He had more tricks in his repertoire than any capo or wiseguy ever imagined. He was like don Anastasia – sneaky. Deadly. They called Vincent Mangano, '*il terremoto.*' It meant he was fearsome, like an earthquake. But he came up missing, fearsome notwithstanding. Permanently. And it was suspected Anastasia took him out.

Phan took the travel brochure from the pocket of the passenger seat in front of him and thumbed through the pages. Would this flight never end? He had had to pay extra for the direct flight to Vegas. It was filled with gamblers going on holiday. He could hardly hear himself think the crowd was so noisy in first class. Men laughing, kids bawling, mothers scolding . . . it reminded him of the boat trip over from Nam. Mothers and children the world over were alike. No matter what kind of trip they went on, there was going to be rebellion and reprimand.

He found an article on visiting St Lucia in the West Indies and began to read it. It was one of the places he had never seen. It sounded much more entertaining than Las Vegas. Sea breezes, sunny beaches, and pina coladas on the verandah. He could go for that. Maybe it's where he'd travel for a rest once all this was over.

The girl mumbled and Chase looked over at her. A thin dribble of saliva came from the corner of her mouth and slid down her chin. Disgusting what heroin did to you. It was nothing at all like cocaine. He had read about Hollywood types switching over to heroin for kicks. He had always suspected the people involved in film-making were shy in the brain department. A taste for heroin convinced him. Smack didn't do anything but take you out of the world after turning your brain to so much mush.

They had left the state of Texas behind. It was night, the air filled with a thick fog so that he had to drive more slowly than he wanted. In another hour or so he would need to stop and give the girl a second injection. Addicting her wasn't something accomplished overnight. He gave himself a month, six weeks at least. Dalta was going to approve. Tony might approve even more.

The heroin she got on the trip west was more sedation than anything else, but it was the first step toward destruction.

She was mumbling again, calling in a querulous voice for her mother. 'Mom? Mama?'

Yes, call your mama, he thought sourly. She's the one got you into this, the way mothers always do. He couldn't even remember his own mother. She had been the wife of a wiseguy, a retiring Italian woman who didn't make demands. In fact she made so little fuss that her husband and children hardly knew she was there. And now he couldn't even remember her face. The year he left home, she contracted pneumonia and died. He attended her funeral and he tried to cry, but he couldn't, then felt badly about it. A son should weep for his mother. But how could he when she had been such a phantom in his life?

The fog increased so that he had to slow even more, tapping the brake steadily as tail lights appeared in front of him suddenly, two tiny peering red eyes.

He was going slowly enough to take out the thermos and pour more coffee. He'd add just a bit of Wild Turkey to give it a kick. To drive all night, he would need it. He laughed abruptly, the sound of it startling in the confines of the car's interior. Just think, he thought, two of us strung out on drugs. Booze and smack. The difference being I'm in control and, girl-child, little honey, you're not.

Elizabeth Kapon sat at the kitchen table going over, again, the stacks of case files she had brought from her office. It was the middle of the night, but she wouldn't have been able to sleep anyway with Melanie missing.

Paul sat with her, lounging back in a chair opposite, immersed in reading one of the files, his young face drawn and haunted. His black clothes suited him now. He mourned silently, guiltily. He blamed himself for not reaching Melanie in time before the abduction took place. He had called his own mother and told her he might be gone all night, he was helping the police, he was trying to do something for Melanie's mother.

Beth knew he did not know what he was looking for. He was not really much help, but she couldn't deny him a chance to try. Besides, the house was too lonely without him around. Though they did not speak much, she felt better that he was there across the table, a caring presence. With Melanie gone the rooms echoed with emptiness. She was going to have to get out of them soon. She was leaving the minute she was sure enough that the person behind Melanie's abduction was Jake Mace's father, Anthony.

She picked up her coffee mug and drank from it, grimacing. Cold. She should make a new pot.

She knew she looked haggard. Her hair fell limply over her forehead and into her eyes so that she had to keep sweeping it aside. Her clothes were wrinkled and smelled faintly of cigarette smoke from the hours she had spent in the police station with the chain-smoking detectives. Beneath her eyes were bluish half moons, evidence of a long, hard day, one of the hardest she had lived through in her life.

Pope lay sprawled lengthways across the table. She absentmindedly stroked his belly and felt his purr through the tips of her fingers.

Most of the case files before her had been checked over before. She had been investigating them to find out who might have planted cocaine on her. Now she had separated the files and put them into stacks. In one stack were the men she had put into prison and who remained there. They were not responsible for what had happened in her life. None of them could have orchestrated this sort of complicated plan from a prison cell.

In the second stack were the few men she had convicted and who were now dead for one reason or another. They had died in prison, or been released and died: only Jake Mace had died by the hands of the state.

In the third stack were possibles, men who had been convicted because of her efforts, but who were now out on parole or released after having served time. There were but a few in this stack. She had eliminated several of them by her own investigations. Most had not been serious cases where they spent much time incarcerated. She could not believe those convicts would have returned to ruin her life to this extent. The motive would have been much too weak for the kind of dedicated destruction she had experienced. Also, none of them had the intelligence or wherewithal to have constructed such a labyrinthine plot against her.

Whoever had done all this was nothing if not smart, perhaps even brilliant. This was no regular con.

Also, she had made photocopies of the records from this last stack and handed them over to the Geneva police. They had already been busy tracking down the names, marking them off as they discovered the mens' whereabouts. Alibis were checked. Police in several Texas counties had already eliminated some names, calling in their reports to Geneva.

A stray thought of Melanie wandered to the forefront of Beth's mind. It was a brief flash of Melanie at the front door just before she had left for school earlier in the day. Her arms were full of textbooks. She was in a hurry, her look one of impatience, as she fumbled the door open and called over her shoulder, 'See you later.'

She was the one who insisted she needed to return to classes. The longer she hung around the house feeling sorry for herself, the worse she felt. Beth had tried to talk her out of it, but . . .

Beth forcefully put away the image, that last image she had of her only child. If she thought about Melanie too much, she could not work to find her.

She stood to make fresh coffee. She had turned from the kitchen table, coffee mug in hand, when Paul spoke. She continued on to the counter and began emptying the old grounds and filter from the Bunn coffee maker.

'What about this?' Paul asked. She did not turn to look. He'd tell her what he was talking about. 'This kid you got the death sentence for.'

'The dead don't kidnap people, Paul, but you're right. I've already come to the conclusion this has to do with Jake's father.' She poured water into the Bunn. 'Read on and you'll see Jake's case was on appeal for a while. Public opinion was totally for him being put to death. His crime was hideous. And when he was put to death, his father called me.'

She stared at the glass coffee pot thinking she should one day clean it, try to get out the brown stains from the bottom and around the metal clamp that circled the top. She never kept the house very clean. She wondered if Melanie ever blamed her for those bad housekeeping habits.

'So you think his father is the one who took Mel?'

She noticed Paul had started calling Melanie, Mel. She thought perhaps the boy loved her. 'It's the one thing that makes sense.'

'Well, hell, let's go! Where is he? Let's tell the cops.'

Beth set the pot on the warmer plate and watched the coffee drip through to it. She frowned, thinking. 'I don't think I will.'

'Not tell the cops? Are you nuts?'

She began to think back. Why had the father's words escaped her? It wasn't so much what he had said, she recalled, but how he had said it. At the time she thought he was calling out of a father's grief to blame her, that in some small way she deserved that blame even though it was the young Jake Mace who had pulled the trigger and killed two innocent people. And it was the state who had taken his life. She, personally, had not done it. But she knew and Jake's

165

father knew that if she had not been the district prosecuting attorney, Jake's attorneys might have made a deal, plea bargained him down to life, maybe even with the possibility of parole one day.

So she had, essentially, killed him. That was a fact she couldn't get around by blaming the state executioner.

'Beth?'

She turned slowly to the table, the fragrant scent of the fresh coffee in her nostrils. 'Does it say in the records what Jake Mace's father did for a living? It was a rich family, they brought in the best lawyers money could buy, but I never knew what kind of business the Mace family was in. Some kind of retail . . . ?'

Paul bent his head to the file and searched through it, flipping aside pages and pages. Finally he said, ''Don't see it here. Guess 'cause this is on the kid, not on the father.'

'He was no kid . . .'

'Well, yeah, I know, I mean when he committed the murders. He was a teenager, right?'

She almost wanted to argue whether or not an eighteen-year-old boy was a kid or not, whether he was an adult who knew what he was doing or a spoiled brat, immature, hotheaded, and pointlessly, evilly cruel. But arguing the case again wasn't her concern at the moment.

'I need to know more about the family,' she said, tiredly. 'And it's too late tonight to find out anything. I'll do it first thing in the morning.'

'What about calling the cops? Shouldn't we do that?'

'No. I want to handle this. By tomorrow morning I'll know where I should go to look for her.'

'You don't think the cops can get her back, do you?'

'No, I don't.'

'Can you?' he asked. 'Can you get her back?'

'I'll die trying if I have to.'

He came to her and hugged her shyly.

Beth lay her palms lightly against the material of his black T-shirt at his ribs and briefly let her cheek touch his. He was a fine boy, one she might have at one time wished were her own. He was gawky and not very handsome; he was strange and persistent and immovable, but he was one of the few assets she had left, a real trouper, a loyal ally.

166

She repressed a gasp of pain that tried to come up her throat. She swallowed hard. Tried to smile, weakly patting the boy on his shoulder now that he had stepped back to leave. 'Thanks, Paul. I'll see you in the morning.'

He grabbed a knapsack from the floor and hoisted it over one shoulder. 'Try to sleep, Beth. It won't help her if you wear yourself down.'

She watched him leave the kitchen and as he made his way down the short hall to the living room and the door there. 'Come lock this,' he called.

She did as he said, but without any spirit. No one was going to break in. No one would shoot at the house anymore or throw paint on it or set fire to it or break into it to steal a girl's young soul. Those scare tactics had been done by the man who took Melanie from the campus. She was pretty sure of that. She didn't know why or who the man was, but she just knew she was in no physical danger now.

She wiped down her face with her hands, and moved toward the lighted kitchen and the coffee waiting for her there.

She would go over Jake Mace's records again herself. Paul was right, the greatest damage had been done to the Mace family. Since she could not find any leads on any of her other convictions, it must be Jake's father who had done all this.

And if it was, God help him.

Morning dawned bright, sultry, hot as steam from a cooker.

'Everett, can you come by the house for a few minutes? I need to talk to you.'

Beth had seen Everett at the police station after Melanie was abducted. He had acted as her friend, supporting her during the storm of emotion that had left her hardly capable of standing on her feet, much less answering questions such as: When was the last time you saw your daughter, Mrs Kapon? Does she have any enemies? Had she mentioned to you seeing anyone suspicious hanging around the campus? Does she usually take rides with strangers?

When she saw Everett turn into her driveway, Beth went to the front door of the apartment house lobby and waited for him. He glanced at her as he came up the walk and she knew he noticed her high color, her agitation. 'Are you all right, Beth?' he asked before he reached her.

'Not yet, Everett, but I will be. Come inside.'

She led him to her apartment and firmly closed the door. The only tenant she had left in the house was Luyba, the Russian immigrant, and the old dear had a habit of wandering into Beth's front room to check on her if the door stood open.

'Will you have coffee?' she asked Everett.

'Coffee is fine. What's this all about?'

'Sit down at the table and I'll tell you.' Beth busied herself getting them coffee. She might as well not delay what she had to say. 'You remember the Jake Mace case I prosecuted?'

'How could anyone forget it? That was a vile boy.'

'Well, I think it's his father who has done all this to me. He must be the one responsible for taking Melanie.'

Everett accepted the mug of coffee before replying. He sipped and then lowered the cup to the table. 'You have any proof of that?'

Beth made an exaggerated hand gesture. 'We're not in a court of law, Everett.'

'That's not what I meant, take it easy.'

'I'm sorry, it's just that I've been up most of the night and my nerves are shot. Here's what I have . . .' She drew a folder across the table toward her and opened it. 'I've gone through all my cases from the beginning, from when I first took the office of district attorney. The police have helped me. I've eliminated all the people I've prosecuted except for the Mace case. I never told you this, but the night Jake was executed, Jake's father called me. It wasn't an out and out threat, but there was menace behind his words.

'And if you'll look at what's happened to us, you'll understand that someone hates me, someone is passionately determined to destroy my entire life. Taking Melanie was the last step in this string of occurrences. Anthony Mace, that's Jake's father, had his only son taken from him. Now I've had my only daughter taken. You do see the similarity in that, don't you?'

Everett took off his glasses and rubbed at his eyes. He looked weary and ill, a man with the weight of years dragging him down. Beth wondered if his health was failing. She had heard a rumor that his heart disease was worsening. For a long time he had had to be careful and stay on a strict diet. Could he have had a stroke and not told anyone? 'Beth . . .'

She waited. She needed to talk this over with someone not emotionally embroiled in the situation. She needed an objective outside source to tell her she was not running in the wrong direction.

'Beth, that's no evidence at all. It's a presumption. Whoever did this might not be connected at all to the other things that have happened to you. In fact, none of it might be connected – the cocaine bust, the break-in, the drive-bys, the fire, and now Melanie's disappearance. You considered that, didn't you?'

'It's connected, Everett. Even the police believe it's all a concerted effort. This morning I did some checking on the Mace family. I had Cienci make some calls for me. You remember Cienci, an investigator we used for the DA's office about five years ago?

'The Maces, they're in Las Vegas, you know. They own casinos and all kinds of other businesses there. And their original name isn't Mace. It's Macedonia. Does the name ring a bell? Remember the headlines not long ago about the big funeral held in Vegas for Macedonia? The crime boss?'

Everett's eyes behind his glasses now took on a glittering spark of interest. 'That's the Mace kid's father? The Mafia kingpin who just died?'

'The funeral was for his grandfather.'

Everett whistled. 'Oh my.'

'You see now, don't you? Anthony Macedonia is the head of a crime syndicate. His son is put to death in the state of Texas. The father calls me the night of the boy's death with vague threats. Not long afterward everything I touched turned to shit. And now he has Melanie, I know it's him. Of course I don't have any *proof*. I couldn't bring the authorities in to help me; they wouldn't run with anything so vague as a feeling, but it's him, I know it is.'

'Why wasn't his connection to crime mentioned in the papers during the boy's trial?'

'His father didn't show up in the courtroom until the end, remember? Until the verdict was announced. And the Vegas people aren't well-known to our reporters here. Jake's name was Mace.

That was his legal name. No one connected it to *Macedonia* and the family he came from in Vegas. If we'd gotten any coverage from the Houston or Dallas newspapers, they would have ferreted it out, but this trial was kept pretty local. All any of us saw was that the family had money. They were able to hire expensive out-of-state attorneys. They appealed the case as far as they could go with it and they didn't win.'

She paused, took a swallow of coffee. 'Everett, I know it's Mace. He's paying me back for calling for the death penalty. He's taken Melanie to Vegas.'

'Would he kill her?'

Beth drew in her breath slowly. 'I can't think that way. If I do, there's nothing left for me in the world. She's all I have, Everett. I think . . . I think Anthony Mace wants to see me suffer. It's an act of irrational revenge. I don't think he'd just spirit away my daughter and kill her. He could have had her killed anytime. Or maybe he doesn't want to kill her until . . . until he makes sure I'm close to getting her back so it will hurt me more. Maybe – I know this is crazy, but I've been thinking all night – maybe he wants me to know all about it so that when she does die, I'll know the moment I lose her, the way he knew when he lost Jake. He'd want me to know about it and not be able to stop it.'

'My God. Beth, you need to call in the FBI. If they've taken her across state lines, you can get help in this.'

Beth shook her head. 'I have no proof of that. The highway patrol completely lost the car. The FBI won't do anything with suspicions.

'I'm going to Vegas, Everett. I need your help. I need some money, fast, a loan, and I don't have anything left and no way to get any money. I don't have time to go to a bank for a loan and I have very little jewelry I could sell. I'd need a few thousand because I don't know how long this will take.'

'Well, of course, I'll loan you money, but . . .'

'Don't try to talk me out of it. I'm going. I'm going right to Anthony Macedonia to ask him what he wants. At this point, I'll do anything to get Melanie back. If I call in the FBI, and if they *did* believe there was merit in the case of a kidnapping across state lines, there wouldn't be a chance to talk to Mace first. If the authorities get close, I think he'll kill her and no one will ever know; they may not ever find her.' The horror of what she'd just said seeped in once she'd spoken the words aloud. It was unbearable to think that way. The only possible way she could take action was to don the cloak of her attorney self and approach the solution intellectually, above all emotion.

'Do you think you can do any good, Beth?' He reached and took one of her hands in his. 'How are you going to bargain with the head of the mob? What do you have to offer?'

Beth had but one thing, the only thing Mace might be interested in. Her own life. She meant to swap it for Melanie's release if she had to. But she couldn't tell Everett that or he wouldn't help her. He'd call in the federal help before he left her house.

'I just have to see him,' she said, sidestepping his question. 'I want to let him know that I know now it's him and that he's won. I want him to know he's ruined my life and that's punishment enough. I'm going to beg him. I wouldn't do that for anything except my child. I'll beg him for mercy. If that doesn't work, I'll kill the son of a bitch.'

Everett shook his head and frowned. 'Oh Beth . . .'

'Will you loan me enough money to find out? I want to get a flight by tonight.'

He sighed, giving in. 'All right. If you're determined and I can't talk you out of it. I'll go by the bank when I leave here. Drop by my office anytime after noon and I'll have a few thousand dollars for you. Will five be enough?'

Beth smiled for the first time, though it was a slow, sad smile and her eyes still looked worried. 'You're the best, Everett. If my credit cards weren't maxed out, I wouldn't ask this, you know that.' She stood with him and gave him a kiss on the cheek. 'I think you should get more rest. You look peaked.'

He laughed half-heartedly. Ran a hand over his gray cheeks. 'No rest for this wicked fool.' He turned to the hall and made his way to the door. Beth realized how old he was, something she hadn't noticed before. He walked like an old man, his shoulders slumped, his hands dangling by his sides. He was a tired old man, with failing health. Soon she might lose him, too.

The thought propelled her forward and she stepped in front of him as he opened the front door. She looked him in the eyes a moment as if a look could let him know that she loved him. Then she hugged him until he barked out a little laugh and pushed her away.

'Let me go, I have to get to the bank.'

'See you later,' she said, stepping aside and letting him pass into the lobby. He let himself out and the click of the door latch made her come to herself.

She had too many things to consider, a dozen things to do, she couldn't dawdle here at the door, staring off into the middle distance lost in thought.

Melanie might be in Vegas, fighting for her life.

She couldn't know that until she flew there and found out. If someone else had taken Melanie, she'd find that out too. Some way she'd make Anthony Macedonia tell the truth. If he wanted revenge for Jake, he must take her, not her daughter. What kind of life could she live if she lost her only child? This couldn't happen. It *wouldn't*.

17

Chase took a room at one of the strip motels on Boulder Highway leading from Vegas to Hoover Dam. When he drew back the dingy, olive-green curtains at the front window, handling the material with two fingers, he could see the highway, the traffic, and, across from the motel, a car pawn outfit. Some people got so desperate and broke while visiting Vegas they pawned their cars.

It looked as if the place was doing a thriving business; the lot was full. Those abandoned cars represented one not very interesting story: obsession. Gambling took the wheels from their owners and left them destitute. Chase knew there were even pawn shops for houses, that a person could hand over a deed and borrow money on it. If there was any value in eyeteeth, there would probably be an Eyetooth Pawn where the counters overflowed with teeth wrenched from bloody gums.

People were nuts. Certified assholes. He didn't begrudge them their passions, he had one or two of his own, but gambling away everything you owned seemed to be one of those addictions that could be controlled simply by walking away.

Perhaps it wasn't. He could be wrong. There were dark urges inside people that were more complex than they appeared on the surface. He could understand wanting to win. He had always wanted to win and most people did. That had to be why gambling was such a hot pastime. But pawn a car or a house?

He let the curtain drop into place. Gloom returned to the shabby room. He sat down in the turquoise vinyl chair and took up the television's remote control. Flipping channels. Surfing. Spending time the only way he could.

Dalta had told him to hold the girl and not to move around. Stay some place people wouldn't find them. This rat-hole motel was anonymous and unremarkable. It fitted the bill.

The girl lay on the double bed in her underwear. A beige silky bra and panties. She had a nice shape, her skin smooth and white as bone. He would have to walk her into the bath today sometime and stand her beneath the shower. She was beginning to smell. He also needed to get her to eat a little something, soup maybe. All she had taken on the trip were Dr Peppers and one donut.

Occasionally she groaned in delirium, strange counterpoint to the squawking voices from the television. Now and then she was able to pose a slurred question. They were repetitive ones. What do you want with me? Why are you doing this? He never answered. He tried to think of her as no more than an object, like the hard plastic chair he sat in or the grungy carpet at his feet. If he got the urge, he might cut her again.

He loved the wound on her cheek. It announced: CHASE WAS HERE.

Or he might do something more than cut her.

He shook a Winston from the pack on the table and lit it with a gold lighter. He blew out the smoke into the already smoky gray room. He turned the cigarette around and contemplated the burning end. Lost in meditation, he heard those smacking noises from the demons that flitted in and out of his line of vision. They were hungry, he assumed. They *liked* roasted female.

He took a drag. Smoking was new to him. Speaking of bad habits, he seemed to be taking them on rather rapidly. Drinking. Smoking. It was all the hours he spent waiting.

Over the years he had devised ways to live through the empty hours, little mind games, games of observation, even the tying of knots from grass shafts and toothpicks and threads he pulled from cloth. A few months ago at a stakeout, he had found a half pack of cigarettes with a cardboard holder of matches stuffed down between the pack and the cellophane. It lay on the ground not a foot from him

174

and out of idle curiosity and boredom he shook a cigarette out into his hand. He lit it. Inhaled, coughed, grimaced. Like a gambler hooked on a slot machine, he shook out another and smoked that one too. He proceeded this way to smoke the entire half pack at one sitting. By the time he'd reached the last cigarette in the pack, he no longer coughed or gagged. He knew he liked it, the taste of the tobacco, the sensuous feel of the smoke filling his lungs and flowing out again. He would smoke now.

Ah well, he thought, blowing out a perfect circle of smoke. Ah well, this is the modern world and these are the chains we choose to wear, Jack.

In a little while he would cruise down the Old Strip and find a likely-looking dealer to sell him more heroin for the girl. While out, he had to remember to buy a carton of Winstons and a new bottle of Wild Turkey. He and the girl had habits to feed, chains to cinch in place.

He didn't see how else he could sit in this rundown, fly-shit motel room watching the flickering images from TV hour after hour, day after day.

Chase frowned and drew deeply on the cigarette. He hated his life. Maybe that was why he kept having the paranoia attacks where he believed someone was watching him and coming after him. The reason why he thought he saw demons, horned and fanged and loathsome.

He had always hated his life.

Jeff Dalta lay spent upon the silk sheets. He could hear Jordie in the shower, singing. Sex endowed her with increased energy. He screwed her and she popped right out of bed afterwards, bathing, powdering, putting on her make-up, doing her hair. She was a ball of fire, his girl.

He sighed and rolled onto his side, pulling the sheets between his thighs. The drapes were open on the neon-painted night beyond. He could see from where he lay the unfinished Bally Tower standing in the center of Vegas like an obscene phallic symbol pointing to heaven. The damn thing was costing too much and they'd run into trouble with all the other casino owners who didn't like the idea of the tallest building in the world standing in the middle of Vegas – mainly because they didn't own it. Suit was brought against Bally's and had halted the building process for the moment.

The tower would naturally draw crowds once it was finished and crowds translated to money. After the millions invested in pyramids and jungles and white tigers and all the other exotic façades and features, naturally no one wanted a casino that easily dwarfed all those expensive investments.

Jeff didn't like the tower a bit. For one thing, it didn't belong to him. If he had had an interest in it, that would have been another thing.

Jordie tripped into the room bare-ass, a towel wrapped around her head. She was searching for something in the large dancer's bag she carried. 'I thought you'd be sleeping,' she said, glancing over to the bed at him.

'Can't,' he said, 'I have to get home soon.'

'Well, if you leave before I do, say goodbye, okay?' She turned for the bath again, a cosmetic bag in her hands.

What a wholesome looking woman she was, he thought. Tennessee raised good horse flesh and excellent woman flesh. It was too bad Vegas was going to ruin it. For it would. Vegas night life ruined everything that touched it from the gamblers to the owners to the showgirls.

And *that's* not my problem right now, he thought.

He rolled onto his back and stared at the ceiling.

Chase had brought the girl from Geneva, Texas. He was busy shooting her up with heroin. Maybe he, Jeff, ought to just go give her an overdose, get it over with. But Beth Kapon wasn't in town yet. It was too early to take out the girl.

Tony knew they had the girl. All along he had known what was going on. Why did that surprise Jeff? It pissed him off royally, of course, that he couldn't do anything without Tony Mace knowing about it. He guessed he was a goddamn idiot thinking he could in the first place. Someone, maybe even Chase, reported in to Tony on every move. If Jeff ever found out who, he'd strangle the prick.

Ever since Chase had hit town, Jeff had been nervous. He had not obeyed Mace's orders. He had gone *beyond* what he had been asked to do. Now it was in the open that he was working against Mace, not for him. He'd have to keep on his toes, be careful.

Out in the hall he had a bodyguard on duty, just in case. There was no telling what Mace might do since he'd been crossed. He must understand what Jeff was up to – trying to lead the Kapon woman to Mace's front door.

It was a wonder Jeff was able to make it with Jordie tonight, he had been so nervous. He'd had his doubts right up to the minute she had taken him into her mouth, but then he forgot the world and there was nothing in it except the woman swaying over him, her long hair brushing like bands of silk against his belly.

He flopped onto his stomach and buried his face down into the pillow, his hands over his head. Sex. Not sex, he thought, that's behind me. What's before me? Will Mace try to have me killed now?

He rolled to his side and squinted through the wide hotel windows at the top of Bally's tower with the giant machinery attached like a praying mantis to its unfinished top. The millions of lights below rose through the sky, lighting it up from beneath with fire.

Goddamn it, no! It was all going to work perfectly. The Kapon woman would go after Mace; she'd wade through hell and high water to reach him and when she did, Mace and his henchmen would come tumbling down.

Jordie came back into the room naked just as Jeff finished dressing. He was slipping on his shoes and bending to tie them. 'Leaving, Sugar?' She gave him a peck on the cheek.

He grunted, stood, took up his coat jacket. 'You need any money?'

Her eyes darkened. 'You don't give me money, Jeff. Remember? We play the tables before we come up here, but you don't give me money after we make love. I guess you've mistaken me for one of your bitches.' She turned to stomp away and he caught her arm.

'I'm preoccupied. I'm sorry. I don't know what I was thinking. I just thought you might want some spending money, buy yourself a pretty dress or something.'

'Fuck you,' she said, twisting her arm free and heading for the bathroom door.

'Jordie, don't be that way. Don't use that language on me. I said I was sorry.'

She halted, but did not turn around to face him. 'You mean it? You're sure you're sorry?'

'Yes, I really mean it.' He said it in a contrite voice, saddened at all the mistakes he made with women when his mind was on other matters. He couldn't lose this woman. 'Please forgive me.'

She looked over her shoulder at him. With her lashes lowered that way she was a siren, a bold and vampy goddess. 'All right. This time. Don't do it again, Jeff. I'm no whore. I want that clear with you. You ever treat me that way again, I'm outta your life for good.'

'I won't do it again.'

She tossed her head and disappeared into the bath. He winced when she slammed shut the door. Beauty had a price tag. It came packed with dynamite.

He slipped into his coat and let himself out. He had to call people, surround himself with some of the boys. What did Emily Dickinson say about things working out, about hope? Hope 'is the thing with feathers/That perches in the soul/And sings the tunes without the words/And never stops – at all.'

18

Melanie lifted the lids of her eyes with the kind of determined effort that required coordination from both the gut and the mind. *I'll see,* she thought, *what there is to see. At least I could try to do that, if nothing else.* Her flesh felt made of heavy steel. She might be paralyzed for all the use her limbs were to her. If it were such a chore to open her eyes, she could not imagine how much exertion it might take to lift an arm or clench tight the fingers of her hand.

She knew very little of her situation except that it was precarious. The man who possessed her and made her into a helpless ragdoll did it by keeping her drugged out of her mind – at least she knew that much. She knew so little beyond that. She didn't know if it was day or night; she had no idea where she was, what bed she lay on. It was as if she had been dropped down the rabbit hole, like Alice, and nothing from that time forward made sense.

Thirsty! She moved her tongue around a bit in her dry mouth and finally settled on sucking her bottom teeth to produce saliva. If she could say something, she might find relief. She could hazily see her captor not more than four feet away. He had slid down in the chair until only the bottom of his spine stopped him from slipping to the floor. His legs disappeared beneath the edge of the mattress that cut off her field of vision. He had his fingers templed and touching the end of his nose. He was not looking at her, but at the far wall where a television droned. She could not see the TV, but heard it buzzing with voices and saw the blue flicker from the images.

179

She wanted desperately to beg the stranger to release her from this horrible fog. She formed the words in her head all in a row, lined up neatly and in order, but before she could slip her tongue and lips around the first word – '*Please . . .*' – she lost consciousness and swam away from the dim, smoky room.

When she came back to the room, her eyes were open, magically this time, without effort, but she didn't know how long she had dreamed. Not long, she believed. The man still sat in the same position, hands templed, gaze trained on the television. The light in the room looked the same. Those were the only elements of reality she had to judge by. The light. His position in the chair.

The world was a narrow place now. Her perceptions restricted to an area comprising not more than a few square feet. She could not even turn her head. She tried to force the muscles of her neck to the task.

It was no use. She blinked and almost drifted away again. She mentally shouted WAKE UP, trying to keep herself in the present and feeling something, anything.

Who was he? The skin of his face was rough, rugged, careworn. If she were to touch his face she thought the sensation might be like stroking wrinkled tinfoil. His profile was sharp and angular – pointed nose, jutting chin, high hard cheekbones. He wasn't ugly, she decided. Just craggy, like a down and out character in a movie. She thought she smelled whiskey and concentrated on that smell, identifying it from the smoke scent that overlaid the air in the room. Yes, whiskey. He might be a lush. A drunk holding her prisoner with injections of . . .

She did not know what he injected into her veins. She was not conversant with drugs and their effects. Whatever it was there was power enough in it to turn off the world and take her traveling through mysterious landscapes she couldn't even begin to understand.

The edges of the room began to waver, the man's shape and the chair he sat in blinked in and out of sight. No, no, not yet, she thought, not now, let me stay a while . . .

Just as a radio signal might weaken, her thoughts scattered slowly, first encountering static that broke up all the patterns, and then fading out into a vast white noise that filled her head.

Her eyelids drooped; a tiny sigh whispered from her lips. She felt the potent tug of a new, tantalizing dream just beyond the land of white noise. 'Come,' it said, 'and dream with me.'

Melanie finally gave in to it, slipping from the room, leaving all worry and fear behind, riding a magic carpet into the high, downy clouds of phantasm.

The evening flight from Houston Intercontinental to Las Vegas was packed with tourists. Texans with gambling fever. In the triple seats in front of Beth Kapon were three middle-aged women who wanted to turn the flight into a party. They bought drinks from the flight attendants, asked for extra packs of peanuts, and told jokes to one another that kept up a cacophony of laughter.

They were driving Beth crazy. Didn't those women know that there were serious matters going on in the lives of some of those around them? Had they no command over the actions that made them look like buffoons?

Beth shrank against the window and stared down into the darkness beyond the wing lights. An elderly woman sitting next to Beth said, 'They probably make this pilgrimage to Vegas several times a year to blow off steam.'

Beth turned to look at her seat companion. The man on the other side of her, on the aisle, was asleep, his head cushioned by a small white pillow. 'I just wish they'd be quiet for a while,' Beth said.

'You're not going to gamble, are you?'

Beth eyed her, wondering if she was one of those people who pried, who made it a habit to interrogate strangers. 'No,' she said, 'I'm not going to gamble. Not in the way it's usually meant, anyway.'

'Well, I go gamble in Vegas every three months. The money I win supplements my income. My name's Kate Corgie. I used to be a school teacher for HISD, the elementary grades. I'm retired now, of course, and Vegas is my one big vice in life.'

'It sounds like you make your vice pay for itself.' Beth turned to the window again and blinked back sudden tears. The thought of Melanie alone and helpless somewhere came out of nowhere to remind her of her quest. Her hands trembled and her shoulders began to shake. She felt Kate lay her hand across her own two to steady her.

'Is something the matter?'

The three women hooted and laughed, causing other passengers to turn their heads toward them. When they quieted, Beth said, 'Family problems. I'd rather not talk about it, I'm sorry.'

'I see,' Kate said. 'Then indeed you have a weighty matter on your hands. I'm truly sorry to hear that. I shouldn't have intruded.' She took her hand from Beth's hands and sighed tiredly. 'When women discuss problems, it helps them to find a way to solve them. But sometimes you can't even talk about it. Sometimes you're stuck with doing it yourself.'

One of the male flight attendants stopped in the aisle next to the three raucous women passengers and began a conversation with them, smiling, nodding his head, interested in their jokes.

During the rest of the flight Beth blocked out the noisy entourage in front of her bobbing around in their seats and stared out into the deep darkness of the night beyond the jet's window.

If she had known the woman named Kate better she might have told her that what she was doing was unheard of. Mothers did not go to crime bosses and try to work out deals. Attorneys didn't negotiate hostage situations concerning their children. It was a lunatic move and it might not work, ultimately.

But she had to try.

If Anthony Mace had spirited away Melanie, he was the only one she could appeal to. She would speak to him as a mother to a father, not as an attorney to a Mafia don. He must be impressed with the fact she had not called in the FBI and pointed them in his direction for kidnapping charges. If nothing else, he must understand they could settle this as a personal matter, and not bring in the authorities unless there was no other alternative.

She didn't know yet what plea she might enter that could cause Mace to relent and release Melanie, but it would come to her spontaneously, the way many of her more brilliant closing arguments came to her when she stood before a jury seeking a conviction. She must rely on reaching Anthony Mace on some level other than a planned, superficial one. He wanted revenge. She understood that. But couldn't he see it would not bring his son back? And couldn't he realize that if he took Melanie and kept her or harmed her, he only added more grief to the world? She must make him understand.

If she couldn't, she was prepared to talk of an exchange. Her life for Melanie's.

What about Mace's wife, Jake's mother? Couldn't she appeal to another mother to help her in this crisis?

Then if nothing worked at all, she was prepared to commit murder. She didn't know before that she had it in her, but she did. She knew it for certain now. The night she found Melanie unconscious on her bedroom floor covered in blood she knew it.

She fervently hoped not to have to do that.

A glow on the land below alerted Beth that the plane was descending to earth and the city of Las Vegas, Nevada. The pilot had been speaking for some time over the intercom system and she hadn't heard him. She now buckled her seat belt, turned to Kate and smiled a little. 'We're here,' she said.

'Almost. And it's been a long flight, hasn't it?' She meant the clattering women and she meant the worry Beth carried.

'Everything ends,' Beth said cryptically. 'One way or the other.'

'I certainly hope it all works out for you and your family.'

'I hope so, too. Thanks.'

The city beyond the window spread out to the edge of a ridge of mountains. As they descended, Beth could make out some of the famous casinos and could even see the Strip with its long neon necklace of lights.

She hoped Melanie was somewhere down there. If she wasn't, if this was a wild-goose chase and she had made a mistake, if the Mace family wasn't involved, then she didn't know where to turn. It was just possible Melanie had been taken by someone unconnected to Beth's other troubles. But that would be too coincidental and life had proven to Beth there were reasons behind most occurrences. Even the patterns of the universe did not appear to be coincidental.

She clenched her hands and breathed deeply as the plane landed on the runway, the tires squealing from braking. Ahead of her lay the city and possibility. Behind her in Texas waited arid grief and scalding loss. She could only move in one direction.

Forward.

* * *

Phan Lieu stood in the shadow of a crape myrtle which shimmered in the breeze right on the new Strip, buying drugs from a fifteen-year-old. It boggled his mind to see he could get anything he wanted right next to a tree planted two feet from the sidewalk streaming with tourists. It further disconcerted him to be getting them from a kid.

The boy was short and skinny, wearing a baggy, green army jacket in a hundred-three night heat. He was a kid of few words, all business.

'You live out here?' Phan realized the kid reminded him of himself at that age. He had been scrambling on the streets of Haiphong when he was fifteen, and selling something more serious than drugs. Would this kid make a good assassin? He probably would.

'Naw, I live at home.' He counted the money Phan had paid him, counted it carefully, squinting in the near darkness at the numbers on the bills.

'You live at home and do this as a sideline, for spending money?'

The kid glanced up from his counting and his face aged. He might have been a forty-year-old man. 'I sell to buy stuff for myself, if it's any of your business.'

'Crack?' Most of them were hooked on it.

The boy nodded and went back to counting. 'I recommend it over what you're getting, man. Don't gimme no high and mighty shit, okay?'

Phan could have refuted him. The difference between a cocaine habit and crack cocaine was like the difference between boiling and freezing. He could quit the coke if he wanted. He knew the kid and all the others like him strung out across the country couldn't kick crack even when you put them in therapy programs, locked them up, or threatened them with death. Crack was taking out a whole generation.

'Coke like this isn't addicting.'

'Bullshit and camel turds.' The boy folded the money and put it in an inside pocket in the army jacket.

'You don't know what you're talking about, kid.'

The boy looked him square in the eyes. 'Don't I? Mister, you livin' in some kinda fantasy if you don't think that stuff will get you just as bad as when it's made down into rock.'

'You don't know everything.' Phan turned on his heel and joined the crowd on the sidewalk. The kid didn't know anything. It reminded him of a poster he'd seen once in a little café that read: 'Teenagers! Tired of being hassled by your stupid parents? Act now! Move out, get a job, pay your own bills, while you still know everything.'

The warm night smelled of dry desert, hot food, and desperation. Too many of the faces that passed him had a confused, crestfallen look. They were the suckers, the tourists who brought too much money to Vegas and lost it all. They were the fodder that fueled the casinos and bankrolled them. It wasn't the high-stakes gamblers who made Vegas into a gambling mecca. It was the little man with his paycheck and his small savings or his vacation money.

But then none of this surprised Phan. From a tender age he had known the secret about humankind. *They were all suckers.* They wouldn't be such easy targets for assassination or for gambling dens if they weren't.

A craving hit him for the drug in his pocket and Phan stumbled a step or two along the sidewalk just as if he were suddenly drunk. Damn! For a few minutes he had almost forgotten his need and now it had come back twice as hard, hitting him in all his nerve endings like a jolt from heaven. He must get someplace private to snort a little of what he'd bought from the kid.

Then what the kid had said to him returned and he almost halted in the middle of the stream of tourists.

The kid couldn't be right.

He couldn't.

Phan Lieu was no junkie for the stuff. It was a lie.

But that's not what his body was signaling to him, turning him into a jittery, frantic mess of misfiring neurons. What his body had just told him was: *I got you, baby. You're mine.*

He took a handkerchief from his coat pocket and wiped away the new perspiration that had spread over his forehead.

No matter what reasoning processes his mind was going through, he still had to get off this street and open the coke vial. His nose was running and his hands shook.

Maybe . . . maybe he *was* a junkie. All the signs pointed to the

185

fact. He shrugged and went on down the street to find where he'd parked the car. It didn't matter whether he denied or accepted his responsibility for the drug use. What mattered was getting somewhere private he could get his fix.

19

Melanie had been drifting in and out of consciousness the way waves wash to and fro on the shore. With a soft rushing hiss the white noise receded and she felt the mattress beneath her body, felt the dryness at the back of her throat, smelled her own rank body odor. Her eyes opened a slit and she couldn't see anyone in the room. But she heard someone at the door.

This was a motel room.

She hadn't known that until now. A cheap motel room with bagging curtains at the window and a doorknob that took a key. Someone was manipulating the doorknob and then there were scritching sounds coming from it. Did the key not fit? It might be the maids. Might they come in and find her lying here, unable to help herself? She could find her voice if she had to and beg them to go for . . .

The door opened and two men came into the room. Neither of them was the man who had taken her from the college campus. One was small and wiry, his hair iron-gray. The other was large, bald, and extremely ugly. His nose was crooked, as if it had been broken and never set, and his cheeks were volcanic with pockmarks.

They looked at her a moment, looked around the room, the small, older man checking the bath. Then the ugly one came to the bed and said, his voice coming to her from a far distance, 'We're getting you outta here. You know where your clothes are?'

She tried to shake her head, but only managed to move it to the left, to the right, and that was all. It was enough. The two men began to search the room and she heard the small man call from the bath, 'She's got jeans and stuff in here.'

'Bring them along. I'll just wrap her in the sheet to get her to the car.'

They would not dress her then.

Her heart beat quickly and she licked her lips in preparation to speak. The ugly man was winding the sheet she lay on around her body like a shroud; she was being tumbled onto her side and back again. She was about to ask what they wanted when the white noise charged from the back of her head, filling her mind, sweeping her away to oblivion.

She did not know when they lifted her from the bed and trod from the room, her body, limp as the dead, hanging over one side of the big man's shoulder.

Chase unlocked the door to the motel room and the second before he stepped inside knew the gig had gone sour. He felt it along the hairs of his arm, the hairs at the back of his neck. He had a gun from an inside jacket pocket before the door was fully open and he saw the bare mattress.

Gone. Vanished.

He stepped inside quickly, shut the door, and stood casing the room for clues. The door to the bathroom was ajar. Someone had been in there, looking for her clothes, he assumed.

She had not walked out. She was in no state to escape on her own. And if she had in some way found the strength and presence of mind, she wouldn't have taken the sheet and carried her clothes along in her arms. Her slippers sat on the floor where he had put them, just beneath the window air conditioner unit.

The phone rang and the jangling made him flinch. He lifted the receiver. Dalta said, 'They tell me you were out drinking tonight and you left the girl alone.'

'Oh Jesus, then it was you. I got back here and find her gone, I thought . . . well, I didn't know what to think.'

'What I think is you're worn out from your trip to Texas,' Dalta said. 'I had Hunter pick the girl up. He's kept an eye on you since you hit town. He says this wasn't the first time you went out and left her in the room for hours.'

'I ain't drunk, Jeff.'

'Well, you're certainly the fuck not sober either.'

'Aw, c'mon, everybody has a drink now and then. I don't sleep so good. I go out for a nightcap and . . .'

'Don't give me excuses, Chase. I'm having Hunter take over now. You've done a good job over the past weeks. We can't let anything go wrong.'

Chase burped behind his hand and hoped Dalta didn't hear it. 'Okay, all right. You're not mad at me, are you? I mean, I got the girl here and she's still okay.'

After a pause Dalta said, 'I'm not mad. Take a vacation, get out of town again. I had the boys leave you some money on the dresser.'

When the line went dead, Chase mumbled, 'Ungrateful bastard,' and dropped the receiver into the cradle. He fumbled for the desk lamp, got it on, and found a wad of bills held together with a rubberband. He dropped it on the desk again and picked up the phone. He dialed Tony's private number.

'I'm outta it,' he said.

'What happened?'

'Aw, I went out for a bottle and Jeff had me cased. They came and took the girl before I got back.'

'You hurt her again?'

Chase thought of the cigarette burns, just two, he put as brands on the inside of each white thigh. 'Not much.'

'You kept her on the smack?'

'Oh yeah.'

'Okay, don't worry about it. I got word her mother's in town. It's all coming together now. You've been most helpful, Chase.'

Chase put down the phone and took up the money again. He had the band off and was counting it when the door opened and the nightmare he had been plagued with for so many weeks walked through the door. He was tall, dark, faintly foreign-looking, and he had a gun in his hand.

'Who are you?'

'This is nothing personal. I thought you should know.'

'What do you want? You want this money?' Chase held out the roll of bills. Chase was already making a move. One hand held out the roll of money while his other hand slid around under his arm to reach for his gun.

'You work for Anthony Macedonia?'

'No, I . . .'

The stranger fired the Ruger Mark II .22-caliber twice in rapid succession. Two little *pffftt-ing* sounds, that's all it made.

'You shouldn't lie,' the man said, watching solemnly as Chase fell across the desk and then to the floor.

I knew he was coming, Chase thought. *It was a premonition. I knew I wasn't losing my mind. There was always someone coming for me. I wasn't fucking crazy.*

Beth Kapon marveled at the slot machines dotting the Vegas airport lobby. Departing and arriving passengers played them, using the beginnings of their money or the leavings.

She found a cab outside and asked about an inexpensive hotel in the city. There was no point in pretending she knew her way around a city she'd never been to before.

'Most of them are inexpensive,' the cabby said, grinning. 'That's if you get one in a casino. I'd recommend the Sahara.'

'The Sahara's reasonable and near the Strip?'

'Sure it is. On the new Strip you've got the Frontier, Silver City, Westward Ho, and Stardust, lots of 'em.'

'The Sahara will be fine.' She settled back in the seat, gripping her hand bag. She couldn't squander the money borrowed from Everett. She had to make it last until she had found Melanie.

The billboards were a neon lure as they left the airport and headed into the city. She caught herself craning her neck to see some of them, unable to control her curiosity. The cabby kept up a patter about where to play the slots, what casino had the best poker tables, where the midnight steak dinners were cheapest, but she let the information roll over her. This was not a pleasure outing. She gambled for one thing only, for life, and it wouldn't be won at the tables or the slot machines.

Even though it was a little after ten p.m., there was a line of people waiting to register at the Sahara. Young yuppie couples in shorts and sandals, old people with frizzed hair and impatience in their eyes, even children with their families, dancing nervously around the mound of luggage beyond the wine-colored ropes separating the registering guests from the main lobby.

The monotonous clanging of coins and ringing bells of the winners at the nearby slots filled Beth's ears. While she waited, she studied the gamblers. They were dressed, surprisingly, in attire ranging from casual to sloppy. The one feature they had in common was the look on their faces, intense and turned inward. The lobby exuded the deep odor of cigarette smoke. Although she couldn't see it, she expected it was in all the fibers of the maroon carpet, maybe even in the walls.

By the time she had secured a room in one of the hotel towers, shown the guard her room pass so she could reach the elevators, and found her room, she was so tired she couldn't stop yawning.

She would shower and get some sleep. Early tomorrow she would visit Anthony Mace and make her plea for clemency. He and his wife would be the toughest jury she'd ever faced.

She had to win this one.

Either that or someone was going to die.

Dalta left Jordie at the Riviera Hotel and had a valet bring him his car. Earlier Hunter and Claude had called with the news. They had moved the Kapon girl and everything was under control. It was obvious to Dalta that Chase couldn't be trusted any longer. He had picked up a drinking habit and left the girl in the room alone too long at a time. She might have managed to leave if she had stayed with Chase.

His Cadillac rolled smoothly along Rancho Drive toward the Lone Mountain section of Vegas where Dalta kept a safe house. It was an unassuming little tract house sitting on a desert parcel of land outside the city limits on Lone Mountain Road. He had picked it up from an old, batty miner who still irrationally believed there were fortunes to be found in the hills. Luckily when offered real money, he jumped for it, deserting the place in one weekend.

The lights of the city dimmed behind Dalta as he moved from the main arteries of the city out toward Lone Mountain. The wind, if he'd rolled down his windows, would have been sharper here, no tall buildings to provide a break for it.

He wanted to see the girl. Had Chase been giving her the correct dosages of smack? You could kill the kid if you gave her too much in one injection. He didn't want her to die, not yet. That was another reason to take her out of Chase's hands. Fortunately, Hunter had worked once as a nurse in Chicago before coming to Vegas. He knew what to do.

The dark out here was impenetrable. A glow from the city in his rearview mirror was all that reminded Dalta he wasn't lost out in the desert. He couldn't see many stars yet. He'd have to get farther out of Vegas for that.

Habitation along Lone Mountain dwindled to a small ranch house here and there as he drove. He was beyond the subdivisions, the convenience stores, the gas stations. He found it eerie every time he left the city limits. He was so used to the twenty-four-hour lights that turned night into day that true, deep darkness made him apprehensive. It was a little like being lost in an unlit hallway in a big house and feeling for the light switch.

His headlights picked up the rundown tract house set back from the road. He turned into the long dirt drive, recognizing the old model blue Ford. Before he had the car door open, Hunter's big form stood in the doorway, silhouetted from behind by the light in the house.

They greeted one another and Hunter stepped aside to let him into the front room. Claude Ganley lay on a swaybacked sofa watching an old black-and-white gangster movie on TV. He waved and Dalta nodded in his direction. Real wiseguys got a kick out of the movies about Legs Diamond and Capone and Bugsy, especially Bugsy.

'She's in here,' Hunter said, moving past Dalta towards a bedroom at the back.

The girl wore underwear and was covered to the waist with a blue pastel sheet. She breathed with her mouth open, her breasts rising perceptibly as she did so. She was asleep.

Dalta was struck first by her beauty and then by the stench in the room. He turned to Hunter, disgusted and showing it. 'You need to bathe her.'

'Okay.'

He turned back and walked near the bed, looking down at her.

'Pretty, ain't she? Except for that cut on her face. Chase did that,' Hunter said.

Dalta stood quietly over the girl wishing the most incredible thing. That she was his daughter. That she could take the place of his overweight, poor little girl. Why did everyone have beautiful daughters, but him?

Infuriated by both his envy and disloyalty to his own flesh and blood, he turned away and hurried from the room. Hunter caught up with him at the door.

'You know where to find me. I want daily reports,' Dalta said. 'Get her cleaned up and make sure she eats something. Keep some fluids in her. But don't let up on the injections.'

As he drove back toward the radiance that was Vegas, he grieved over what he was doing. Taking physical beauty and ruining it. Destroying it. Soon she would be rail-thin and haggard. The healthy intelligence in her eyes would turn to a foxy and furtive gleam. Her arms were already marred with track marks. Her hair had already lost its sheen.

Why couldn't she have been a repulsive-looking girl, or at least homely? Why did she have to have a heart-shaped face – still lovely despite the stitches – unblemished, beautifully proportioned arms and legs, a small waist and flat tummy? Why did she have to have the lips of a Greek goddess and the long, tapering fingers of an artist?

Dalta swallowed hard to get the lump from his throat. Nothing could get to him like a beautiful woman. He had no sympathy for anyone but the most comely. It was like Beckett said. 'Beauty is one of the rare things that do not lead to doubt of God.'

In what he was doing, Dalta was about to efface a rare instance of that beauty. Chase had started it and he was finishing up. Goddamn him. Goddamn him for falling so low.

He shook himself mentally and gripped the wheel hard with both hands.

It could not be helped. If he wanted power, Tony's power, even beauty would be laid upon the altar for sacrifice. In fact, throughout

193

history, that's what happened. A man gave up either love or beauty in order to be a leader of men. He almost wished that this time it had been love.

20

Dalta had removed his tie, jacket, and shoes. He had just finished reading over more of Emily Dickinson's poems to calm his nerves and had closed the book. Time for bed. The house was quiet except for the ticking of the mantel clock. Denise and Lydia were asleep in their bedrooms. They never expected him home for dinner these days and so ate alone and went to bed before he returned.

Weeks ago Denise had come to him crying after he came into the house from a late night with Jordie. Her face was puffy and red; she wrung her hands. His heart lurched in his chest, thinking something had happened to Lydia.

'What's wrong?' He hurried to her and grabbed her by the shoulders. 'What's happened? Where's Lydia?'

'She's in bed, she's all right.'

'Oh, Jesus, don't meet me in the middle of the night like this, you almost gave me a heart attack.'

'Jeff, I want a divorce.'

The pronouncement made him blink, made him wonder if he'd had too much to drink. She had said this once before and he had thought he'd never hear it again. 'What craziness is this?'

'I can't live this way anymore.'

'Now Denise . . .'

'You're never home with us. You stay out with your women every night. Lydia might as well not have a father. And it's been years since I had a husband.'

It was that old story again. She had come to him this way once before, when he had first started staying away from home, and he'd told her then as he'd tell her now – *there would be no divorce*.

He turned from her, sickened by how awful the crying made her look, like a fat circus clown with a face painted red. He entered his study, hoping against hope she wouldn't follow him. But she did. He heard her weeping behind him. He poured himself a drink, his back to her. 'Don't you get tired of repeating this scene?'

'Jeff, I mean it. You can have the house and half the investments. Lydia and I will move out.'

He turned, sloshing some of the whiskey over his knuckles, furious that she would put him through the wringer again. 'You're not getting Lydia. If you want to go, go. But you'll leave her with me.'

'No judge would rule in your favor, Jeff. I can take her if I want to.'

'*No, you can't take her if you want to.* I told you last time that was out of the question. She's my daughter and she lives with me.'

'Why, Jeff? You don't even love her. You treat her like a poor relative, a poor, dumb relative. Don't you know how you are with her?'

'I love Lydia.'

'You love the *idea* of Lydia. The idea of a child of your own you think you can change. If you truly loved her, you'd let us go.'

'You're not going anywhere.' He strolled to the leather sofa and sat down, still not looking at her.

'Jeff . . . ?'

'Go to bed, Denise.'

'Jeff, why don't you love me anymore? You know I've tried everything to lose weight. What do you want from me? Do I have to stop eating altogether, is that what you want?'

'It wouldn't hurt you any.' He winced after the words left his mouth. He shouldn't have said that. She was in a dangerous mood. If he hurt her too much more, she might really go to court and fight him for custody. Not that she'd win. She'd *never* win.

'You've made me hate you,' she said. 'I don't want to, but I hate you, Jeff.'

He turned his head and looked at her to see how much damage

he'd done this time. 'We do all right, Denise. Just let me live my life and I'll let you live yours. Lydia needs both of us; she needs a father and a mother. You know what happens to kids when their parents break up. Lydia needs us both here, in the same house. You have to control yourself and not make these kinds of scenes. How do you know she's not awake upstairs, listening?'

Denise wiped her eyes and cheeks with her hands. 'Do you think she doesn't know? We sleep in separate rooms. You stay out every night. You look at her like she's a . . . a . . . pig. You think she misses any of that? How stupid do you think she is? She's not a baby anymore, Jeff. She's ten years old.'

'I love my daughter! If you loved her, you wouldn't be acting this way. You'd make things smooth between us. Now will you go back to bed? And no more talk about a divorce. You know I can get to any judge in the county. You try to take Lydia away from me and I'll make sure you'll never see her again. Is that clear?' His voice had hardened. She must not misconstrue his intentions.

He heard her leave the room, heard the rustle of her gown and housecoat, heard her tread on the stairs. The scent of a delicate flowery perfume followed her out.

He hadn't wanted to be so harsh or to threaten her that way, but she left him no other recourse. She knew he spoke the truth. If she filed for divorce and custody, he'd find a way to bring the verdict around in his favor. Lydia was his. She might be fat, yes, she was fat, and she was not pretty, but she was only ten, that might change. It was probably still baby fat. Could any daughter of his not inherit at least a little of his good looks? Kids changed as they grew up. She might yet surprise him and be a knockout. Then he'd buy her the most beautiful gowns, take her to the best hairdressers and make-up artists. He'd take her around to show all his friends. He would say, 'Have you met my daughter, Lydia?'

When he was boss and Tony Mace was out of the way, the entire Family would hope for a son to court his Lydia.

Denise wouldn't take that chance away from him. Everything he'd done had been their future. One day everyone would respect the Daltas and no one, *no one*, would dare make fun of his wife and daughter. Even if they both grew into obese cows, no one would whisper a word about it, not to Don Dalta, not even behind his back.

He frowned as he stood to put the poetry book back in the shelf. He didn't like to think about Lydia's weight problem. It was the Kapon girl who had caused it. Lying on that bed with the blue sheet outlining her slim body, the drift of hair across the pillow, the soft curve of her cheekbones and the translucence of her skin. He wished Chase hadn't sliced open her cheek. He should have told him not to do anything like that. Chase was too ready with the knife.

A sound from the front of the house interrupted his thoughts. He moved from the study toward the front hallway. It was too shadowy. He should turn on the lights and see what . . .

As he stepped past the study threshold an arm came around his neck. A whisper at his ear said, 'Let's go back inside.'

He was propelled back across the carpet to the sofa and pushed down onto it. His heart thundered with panic. Then he saw the intruder and was even more confused. He didn't recognize him. He didn't think Mace had a man working for him who was part Asian. And who but Tony would send someone to him?

'That's right, you don't know me,' the man said, pointing a deadly .22 automatic at Dalta. He took a seat in a chair opposite the sofa. 'But I know you. And Chase Garduci. I know him. But he's dead now.'

'Chase is dead?' Dalta licked his lips. His glance flicked to the end table next to the chair where the Asian had taken a seat.

'Oh, you keep a weapon handy?' Phan Lieu reached over, feeling along the front of the end table for the drawer pull. He never took his eyes from Dalta, never let the gun waver. He got the drawer open and brought out a .357 Magnum. 'Nice,' he said, looking at it a moment before slipping it into his pocket. 'You like big guns.'

'Did you kill Chase? Why?'

'Let's not talk about him. Why don't you tell me the names of the rest of your men and where they're staying? I won't even need to write it down; I have a good memory.'

Dalta laughed, but his eyes bored into the stranger. 'Who the hell do you think you are breaking into my house in the middle of the night and threatening me? Are you going to kill me if I don't give

198

you names and addresses? Who do you work for? Whoever it is he's made a fatal mistake.'

'I work for myself. And no, I won't kill you. But I think you'll tell me what I want to know.' He reached into another pocket and brought out a small black remote control. 'Know what this is?'

Dalta shook his head although he actually did know what it was.

'It's a radio transmitter. Know what it's for?'

Again Dalta shook his head, but he now felt a fear that slithered from the back of his mind to the front, causing his heart rate to rise again. If he laid a hand over his chest he would feel it pumping hard.

'It detonates a radio fuse on a small hidden bomb in your house. Unless you tell me those names, I won't tell you where the bomb is. And if you don't tell me the truth, if I'm sent on a wild-goose chase, I take this with me and I push this button.' He held up the transmitter and showed Dalta the tiny red square.

He had been in the house for some time, Dalta knew now. There was no chance he was lying. A man who carried himself like this man, a man who favored the Ruger automatic, was a man who knew very well how to install and ignite a radio-controlled bomb.

Dalta said, 'I don't understand what you're doing. You'd kill my little girl?'

'Your girl won't be here with the bomb.'

'Why not?' Now Jeff felt true fear grip him. *Lydia.*

'Because I'm taking her with me when I leave. I wouldn't want you calling your men after I go and letting them know I'm coming.'

'You can't take my kid.'

'I'm taking her. I take her or she's going to be fatherless when she wakes up. It's up to you. If you don't give me any trouble, I'll leave her unharmed somewhere you can find her tomorrow. If there's trouble . . .' The man shrugged. 'I've killed far more people for less good reason.' He stared, his gaze unyielding, black and steady as that of a viper.

'I've got two men in a house out on Lone Mountain Road.' Dalta couldn't dick around. He saw no way to out-maneuver the Asian. 'Some of the boys have an all night poker game tonight in a back room at Birdy's Casino downtown.'

'Go on.'

199

'That's all.'

'I hate liars. Chase lied and I killed him.' Phan shifted the gun and blew a hole in the sofa just to the right of Dalta's shoulder. The noise probably wouldn't have carried upstairs to alert Denise. The Ruger's muzzle velocity was so high it produced nothing like the blast from a regular automatic. It was a preferred weapon for terrorists since there was no silencer needed. This fuck knew all the moves.

Dalta wet his lips. 'All right,' he said. He named the rest of his men and where they might be found. There were more than half a dozen altogether, who he thought of as his boys, the men Mace had let him handle and be captain of.

'You've been most cooperative,' the Asian said. He waved the small, black item in his hand. 'You can find and remove the bomb upstairs if you're fast.' He paused. When he continued, his voice had dropped even lower and was more menacing. 'If I look for these men and discover they've left – and you don't know where I'll go first so don't try calling anyone – but if they're not there, you lose Precious. Would you like to make some calls just to be sure your men are where you say they are? We wouldn't want you to make any mistakes.'

Dalta immediately reached for the phone. He dialed the number at the safe house. It rang five times before anyone picked up. 'Hunter, it's me. I was just checking. Everything okay?'

The Asian smiled.

For the next ten minutes Dalta made phone calls, verifying the whereabouts of his boys.

Finally he hung up the phone. He couldn't look at the smiling man for fear he might start shaking.

'When I get through with them, I may be coming back for *you*.'

Dalta believed him. 'Are you doing this for Tony?'

'I work for myself, I told you that. Now if you'll excuse me, it's going to be a long night.' He stood and gestured Dalta to rise. He followed him up the stairs and down a hallway to a closed bedroom door.

Dalta stood helpless while the stranger lifted Lydia onto one shoulder while keeping the Ruger trained on Dalta's chest. Lydia was not light. The man, however, seemed unbothered by her weight.

Lydia awakened and said sleepily, 'Daddy?'

'Go with this man, baby. He's a friend of Daddy's and you'll be safe. Do what he says, okay?'

The girl murmured something as the man headed out of the door with her, but Dalta didn't know what she'd said. His heart was racing too loudly, filling his ears. He stood at the bottom of the stairs and watched the door shut and as soon as it did he was turning, running up the stairs.

He had to wake Denise, get her out of the house. My God, what was he going to tell her about Lydia? How could he admit he had allowed someone to take her away? What kind of a father would do that?

Outside it was dark despite the street lamp. It had to be past midnight. Phan admired Dalta's remarkable calm even after he had told him, 'You can search for the bomb or even move out of the house when I leave, but before you do, I have to tell you something,' he had said.

'What's that?'

'The bomb might be on one of your cars rather than in the house. Or it might be in the garage. Or it might even be in your wife's handbag. It *might* be anywhere.'

He left by the front door, moving rapidly away from the house to where he'd parked the car down the street. The girl was heavy, but she had automatically clasped her legs around his waist and that made it easier to carry her. He grinned when he turned and saw all the lights in Dalta's house coming on. Whether Dalta began a search or just woke his sleeping wife and called for someone to pick them up, it would take time.

Time enough to take care of Dalta's nest of punk guerrillas.

Epstein, Dalta's attorney, had Denise in his car when the bomb exploded, taking out the top floor of the Dalta house. Jeff had just left the front entrance of the house, hurrying down the steps, and was caught in the falling debris. He threw up his arms, screaming. Smoking timbers and chunks of roof shingles rained on top of Epstein's car, dents from their weight popping like firecrackers going off in a clatter above their heads.

Epstein threw open the driver's door and ran around the car to see about Dalta. He found him on the ground, knocked out cold. There was a gash on his forehead, but otherwise he didn't seem to be hurt. Trust Dalta to be lucky.

Flames burst from the top of the house and the noise in the structure roared like a freight train crashing through. Epstein lifted Dalta to his feet and dragged him over to the car to get him inside.

The Asian wasn't kidding around, the attorney thought.

He'd kill anybody, the motherfucker. And he didn't keep his promises either. He had said he wouldn't detonate the bomb if he had time to find the men. Well, he'd had plenty of time. It was almost daylight; it had been hours since he'd left and there were reports coming in from everywhere about the systematic murders. It was a wholesale slaughter, the killing of more than seven men in various places in and around Vegas.

When Mace found out, he was going to go ballistic. Despite their differences, Dalta's men were technically under Mace. He'd put a hit out for this if Dalta didn't beat him to it. You didn't muscle in on the Macedonia family. Good grief.

Phan taped the little girl's mouth with wide gray tape and then tied her to an iron post standing at the back of a deserted and closed service station. Someone would come along and find her when morning came. She was in view of the sidewalk and the street once the sun rose. She had been a brave kid, not too many tears, and he suspected she knew more about what kind of business her father was in than her parents imagined. It was as if she had expected to be taken from her bed one night and tied up alone in a dark part of Vegas. That or something equally as unnerving. He assured her she would be fine. Someone would see her as soon as there was light.

He did not apologize. Sometimes kids got hurt because of who their parents were. He knew that truth more than most. At least she had not had to live her childhood on the street in Haiphong, riddled with hunger and foreboding.

He had saved the killing of the men in the house on Lone Mountain for last. They were the farthest from the city and it would take too much time to get there and back. He took care of the others first. It hadn't been easy, it hadn't been clean, especially in the private back room of the casino where he had more men to take out than was comfortable to handle, but he had not lost the knack. He was fast, efficient, cold, going in with the gun in his hand and shooting the man closest to him. He used the Ruger, sparing just one shot for each victim until he had them down and then he checked to see who needed a second. He'd had to hurry. Security guards from inside had come through the door just as he left through the rear.

It was five a.m. and the sky to the east was beginning to lighten from coal black to a muted, dull gray. There were still a few stars out and the sky was barren of cloud cover. Phan had never seen so many clear days in succession as he had in the town of Las Vegas. Of course it sat in a desert, but still you'd think they'd get a sprinkle of rain sometime.

He turned into the drive and shut his lights off. The best way to handle this was to knock on the front door and walk in. That's what he had done when he went after Dalta's men who were at home in bed. The men, rather than their wives, had answered the door. Two shots, *bang-bang* to the heart, and it was all finished.

He stood now at the front door, knocking. In his right hand was the Ruger held at about the level of a man's chest.

The door opened with a man talking, grumbling about the late hour, who the hell wanted in? He was a small, skinny man wearing solid blue pajamas. Phan did not speak or hesitate. He shot him twice, stepped over his body, and moved into the house. He saw a light come on toward the back and headed in that direction.

The second man, large, wearing striped boxer shorts and a sleeveless T-shirt, came toward him with a revolver in his hand. Phan raised the Ruger. He thought he squeezed off a shot. The next instant he found himself thrown against the doorjamb and sliding to the floor.

He whispered a curse in Vietnamese. He blacked out, came to again, felt the fiery pain in his side.

The man who had shot him sat hunched in front of him, taking the Ruger from his limp hand. He had the ugliest face Phan had seen in years. He could be a monster with a face like that.

'Who the fuck are you?'

203

Phan got his tongue around some words, but they were in Vietnamese. He had to speak English. God help him, he had fucked up, that never happened.

The other man grunted, getting to his feet. He lumbered to a phone sitting on the arm of a sofa and called someone. He swore, hung up and called another number.

'Tony? We got a situation here.' He proceeded to explain Phan's intrusion and the murder of Ganley. When he hung up, he came back to Phan and slapped him, twice, across the face.

'Had yourself a hot night taking out our boys, haven't you? If it wasn't for Tony, I'd cut your balls off right now, man.'

Phan hadn't any doubt he meant it. 'Tony Mace is my . . .'

'SHUT UP.'

This time he hit Phan in the face with his revolver and the world died in a collision of stars.

Tony had been up all night. The reports coming in from all over Vegas were bad. When the phone rang again he expected more bad news. He was surprised to hear from Hunter.

'Hey, Tony, I got a guy here just killed Ganley, tried to kill me.'

'Is he Asian?'

'That's the fuck, you know him? I tried to call Dalta, but his line's dead.'

'Dalta's house was bombed.'

'Well, shit. What's going on?'

Tony filled him in on the murders of seven other men within the past few hours. Then he told him what to do with both the girl and the assassin, assuring him first that he was not in any trouble for following Dalta's orders to this point.

Now Tony sat drinking orange juice and waiting to hear from Dalta. Surely he'd call him now. He couldn't be stupid enough not to.

Phan woke to consciousness with a groan. He hurt like he hadn't hurt since he was a kid and the American soldier, Red, had found him lying asleep next to the well on the outskirts of Haiphong. Red had grabbed him, taking him like a bitch dog, from behind. If he ever found Red . . .

204

He heard wet slapping sounds and turned his head carefully toward them. Must orient himself. Must know what had happened

He saw walls of dirt, smoky timbers, and lantern light illuminating the coupling. He remembered now. The man on top of the young girl not ten feet from him was the big ugly guy who had shot him.

They were in an old miner's dig, that's where they were now, had to be. There were broken rail tracks in the center of the tunnel. A rotting wooden cart lying on its side on the other side of the tracks. It smelled of damp and musky sex and earth in here.

He turned his face away from the view he had of the heavy man's backside methodically pumping up and down. The girl just lay there as if dead to the world. She was either really dead or knocked completely out.

Yeah, Phan thought, disgusted. That's what you do, fuck 'em when they don't have a chance to save themselves or fight back. Fucking coward. He was no better than Red.

Phan tried to get loose from his bonds. The asshole on the girl might try to fuck him next and that wasn't going to happen. He'd die first.

The ropes looped around his wrists behind his back and then down to his ankles. He lay on his side, cramped into a fetal position. He'd gotten out of worse before. No manacle or shackle had been able to hold him. Although that was when he was younger, and he still knew the tricks.

He squirmed, careful not to make too much noise. Not that the coward would hear him, the way he was involved.

It took about five minutes of real effort. Phan's face turned red from holding his breath. His side had been hastily bandaged and now that bandage broke loose, spilling new blood that slid down the front of his belly, soaking his shirt.

He got one hand free. Then the other. Feet next.

By the time the ugly man was finished with the girl and had rolled onto his back on the spread blanket, Phan was on his knees, on his feet, moving like a wraith in the flickering lantern light.

He was on the other man before he knew what was happening, squeezing two thumbs into the eye sockets while the body surged beneath him to buck him off. The eyes popped. The victim screamed so loud dirt shook loose from the ceiling between the timbers and drifted down to cover them both.

Phan reared back and brought down the heel of his hand on the man's nose, ramming the bone and cartilage into the brain.

Sudden silence filled the tunnel.

Phan leaped off the dead man and went on his hands and knees to the girl. Elizabeth Kapon's daughter. He recognized her from the day she was abducted by Chase from the Geneva college campus. Poor goddamn kid. He looked at her a moment before gently reaching down to pull up her dirtied jeans over her hips.

'We're getting out of here,' he said. 'No one's going to hurt you again.'

Her head hung from his arm as he scooped her up from the blanket. He staggered with her, following the track lines to the mine exit. The day outside blinded him and the girl groaned low, almost a growl. He carried her to the car parked to the side of the mine. Inside he lay her on the back seat, tucking her legs in. He found his Ruger on the front seat and the keys in the ignition.

He glanced down at his wounded side and pressed a hand there, grimacing.

Must take care of it. Soon.

He still had the vial in his pocket. There might be enough left in it to get him back to Vegas.

21

Beth woke from a nightmare, yelling her head off. She halted in mid-shout, realizing all at once that she had been dreaming, she was in a room in the Sahara in Las Vegas, and she had to find Melanie.

She turned on the bedside lamp and checked her watch. It was not quite five o'clock. She'd go ahead and shower and dress, eat something, or try to, and then drive to Mace's house. She had found approximately where it was located on the city map she'd bought in the airport. She could be there by eight, before he left for whatever business he had to do for the day.

She had a quick shower, put on one of her better suits that she usually wore in court – a navy blue silk skirt, a big loose jacket, and a cream blouse. For good luck she slipped a chain around her neck with a locket on it. Inside the locket was a picture of Melanie taken when she was fourteen.

Downstairs inside the casino Beth saw that the gamblers were still at it. They filled the poker and twenty-one tables. Weary arms pulled down the handles on the slot machines and bells clanged out news of the winners. They had either been up all night or had risen this early to play the games.

In the restaurant she ordered eggs and toast and coffee. Next to her table sat a fat man in a brown suit. He sat with a pretty, raven-haired companion, enjoying breakfast. The man looked like he'd just stepped out of *The Godfather*. He wore three gold rings on each pudgy hand. His hair was black and sparse, his shiny brown pate showing through. Hadn't guys in organized crime cleaned up their image yet? It could be that this man gobbling down hunks of ham dripping with egg yolk was just a tacky used car salesman trying to pass himself off as a wiseguy.

Beth had no idea. She had never prosecuted anyone involved with the Mafia – except Jake Mace. She didn't know if they really looked like the fictional Corleones in the movies or not. The photos she'd seen in the newspapers of recent crime bosses going to trial, though, looked nothing like the fat man sitting next to her table. The bosses in the newspaper accounts today looked more like successful attorneys, it seemed to her, than some street hoodlum with too much money and not enough taste.

She dawdled over coffee, having a second and a third cup. Her hands trembled when she raised the mug. She hoped she wouldn't be this way when she showed up at the Macedonia's house. She must be the picture of concerned motherhood, not nervous, not afraid, willing to make a fair truce, and then willing to be threatening if she had to.

The man in the brown suit stood and left money on the table for his bill. He took the pretty woman around the waist and guided her toward the casino. Beth watched him go, wondering who he really was, wondering if he was who he was telling the world he was. She noticed people moved out of his way as he passed. Whether he was a salesman or a wiseguy, his presence cleared his way. She guessed it didn't hurt to look like a movie gangster. People were trained by the movies.

She straightened up and took a deep breath. It was almost seven. She too should be on her way.

One more sip of coffee. Then she'd be fortified. The breakfast wasn't sitting too well on her stomach. But if she hadn't eaten, she would have been more nervous than she already was.

She waved over the waitress and asked for her ticket.

It was time to go. It was time to settle affairs and find a way to return to her real life again.

22

Tony Mace was sitting over coffee and breakfast rolls at a glass-topped table on his patio when he was told there was a woman to see him. He wiped his mouth with a napkin and went to the front entrance hall of the house, wondering who could be calling so early in the morning. It was probably someone needing his help in a family matter. One of the wives of the men the Asian had murdered during the night.

He knew her immediately. Struck dumb that she stood in his foyer, he simply stood there, gaping.

'You know who I am, Mr Macedonia. I've come all this way from Texas to talk with you and your wife. I think you know what it's about, too. Is your wife at home?'

Tony stepped through a doorway and called to his butler, 'Tell Mrs Macedonia to come down. We have a visitor. We'll be on the patio.'

He moved back to where Beth Kapon stood waiting and said, 'She'll be down in a minute. Would you like coffee?' He had found his voice and controlled his amazement, but behind his bland and courteous exterior seethed a great abiding hatred for the woman he led through the den and the dining room to the French doors opening onto the patio. His hands itched to reach for her throat. His mind rebelled at her presence, screaming for him to do something, to push her against the wall and tear off her face.

That wouldn't do. She had to be sent to Dalta. One of them

would die when she met him and the other would soon follow.

He gestured she take a seat at the patio table. He took his place and lifted the napkin to spread on his lap. 'Have you had breakfast? I could have our cook bring you something.'

'I've eaten, thank you.'

He poured coffee and moved the cup and saucer across the table toward her. He thought if she accidentally touched his hand, he'd recoil as if burned. Yet he couldn't let her know his revulsion. He must keep the mask in place.

He knew why she was here. She had discovered her troubles were caused by him and the family. Or at least she strongly suspected it. He'd known eventually she would come to him; it's what he had counted on. But now that she was suddenly here, he had to regroup and marshal all his wit and intelligence to convince her he was not the enemy, never had been, that the entire plan to discredit her, take away her livelihood and kidnap her daughter was not his doing. It was a set-up, a power play engineered by an enemy in his own camp.

Connie appeared in a mauve dressing gown, her hair tied back with wide white ribbon. She did not know Elizabeth Kapon on sight; he hadn't let her attend the trial.

Connie smiled tentatively. 'Hello,' she said, taking a chair at the table.

'Connie, this is Elizabeth Kapon. She was the prosecuting attorney at Jake's trial. Mrs Kapon, this is my wife, Connie.'

Connie sat unmoving for a moment, the realization sinking in. 'You were the *prosecutor*?'

'Yes, I was, Mrs Macedonia. That's part of what I've come here to talk to you both about.'

Connie looked away, a pained expression marring her tan, elegant face. 'What is there to talk about now that Jake's gone?'

'Please hear me out. I'm here as a mother, pleading a mother's case. You've lost your child, you know the heartache involved. I don't want to lose mine. I know you have my daughter.'

Connie flinched and faced Beth. Tony held up two fingers together asking to interrupt. He said, 'That's where you're wrong. We don't have your daughter, Mrs Kapon. I know who does, though. I couldn't stop him from taking her, even though I tried.'

210

'Tony?' Connie, confused, blinked in incomprehension at her husband.

Tony reached out and touched her hand to quiet her. 'Mrs Kapon, you know what position I hold. We need not pretend I'm a normal businessman. You know I'm not and there's no point in denying my affiliations with organized crime, as the press calls us. What you don't know is that for a few years I have had a man who is nominally associated with me who has grown into a jealous rival. He wants my position as head of the family, do you understand?'

Beth was silent, listening. She nodded her head for him to go on.

'This man has done all those terrible things to you. He was the one who set you up on the cocaine charges.'

'She was set up? Tony, what's been going on?'

'Please, Connie, just listen.' Tony patted her hand. 'Both of you will understand everything in just a few minutes.

'When I found out, I went to him and said I knew what he was planning. He wanted you to do just what you're doing this minute. He wanted you to come to me and believe it was all something I ordered to get revenge for Jake's . . . for his sentencing.

'But I assure you, as God is my witness, that it isn't me, Mrs Kapon. I could not control this man. He sent a man by the name of Chase Garduci to your hometown and had him harass you. And *he's* the one who has stolen away your child. I wouldn't do that. I would *never* do that.'

'Let me understand . . .' Beth brushed the hair from her forehead and frowned in concentration. 'Someone who wanted to implicate you and bring you down so he could take your place did all this to me? And he now has Melanie?'

'That's correct. That's exactly it. As soon as I heard of the kidnapping, I knew he'd gone too far. I knew one day soon you'd decide I was the only one who had a motive to harm you and you'd show up here. I didn't know it would be this soon, but I've expected you to come to me. That's what he wanted. Have you called in the FBI? Should I expect a visit from them later today?'

'Oh, God, the FBI,' Connie said, her voice alarmed.

'I haven't called them yet. I was hoping that by coming to you and pleading for my daughter's return, I could settle it without the authorities getting involved. And I was afraid if I called them, you might . . . you might do something . . . drastic.'

'I swear it's not me, Mrs Kapon. I lost my son, but I'm not bitter against you.' The lie rolled easily off his lips, but his mind screamed at him for saying it. He had to add more. 'Jake did something inconceivable. He wasn't brought up to murder, whether you believe that or not. *I* have never murdered anyone. These are not the days of Tommy-guns and bootlegged liquor. We're not *monsters*. I would never take a woman's child from her. I hope you believe me.' She must. She must believe him.

Connie turned to Beth. 'He wouldn't, you have to believe that. He loved Jake, we all loved Jake, and we're hurt and we'll always grieve for him, but it wasn't your fault. It was an awful mistake. What happened was . . .' Tears clouded her eyes and she turned away to wipe her face. She couldn't finish speaking.

'Who is this man?' Beth asked, leaning forward, so intense she seemed coiled to spring.

Tony saw her hands were clenched on the tabletop and in her eyes was the fierce look of a jungle animal seeking its prey. He almost smiled. He had convinced her. He hadn't known it would be this easy. Connie had helped him, of course, with her completely sincere backing of his story. She knew nothing about his plan or anything about what Dalta had been up to. She played right into the scene and gave it an aura of authenticity.

'His name's Jeffrey Dalta. He is a dangerous man, Mrs Kapon.'

'Why couldn't you stop him? If you're the head of the family, why didn't he listen to you? Don't you have ways of influencing the men beneath you? Do you know what they've done to my daughter? She was raped! The man you called Chase, the one who came to Texas to set me up – he broke into my house, he cut Melanie's arm and her face, he . . .'

She had risen from the table and was punctuating her words with her fist, banging the glass tabletop. She shouted, her face livid with despair and rage.

Tony rose, too, but he did not move to her. Connie had sat back from the table, her face limned with shock.

'Please, Mrs Kapon . . .'

'Please? Please?! You didn't stop them. You let this happen, didn't you? Whether you had a hand in it or not, you don't care what happened to my life and my daughter. Where is she? Where do you have her?'

She stepped quickly around the table to Tony and raised both her fists. He caught them before she was able to strike him. He wanted to break her arms. He called back the control he was about to lose.

'Stop it,' he commanded. 'I told you I don't have her. Go to Dalta. He knows where she is. He's the one, Mrs Kapon. He did all this, not me. I told you, I'd have stopped him if I could have.'

'So I'm supposed to take care of this by myself?' Beth asked, still shouting.

'Go to him, Mrs Kapon. Tell him you know what he's done. He thinks his maneuvers were covert and that you'd send the authorities after me. He never thought, I suppose, that you'd come to me and ask for a talk first.'

'He'll give me Melanie if I ask him? I warn you, if I don't have her back within twenty-four hours, I'm going to turn you all in, every goddamn one of you. Now where can I find him?'

Tony gave her directions to Dalta's house. He stood as she left, listening to her retreat through the house to the front door.

Connie looked up at him. 'Is all this true? You didn't have anything to do with it? Jeff's been terrorizing that woman? Someone raped and kidnapped her daughter?'

'That's right. That's what he's been up to for months. I didn't do anything.'

And technically he hadn't.

His phone began ringing before he could pour more coffee.

'What?' he said, astonished at the news he was hearing. 'Hunter's dead?'

Connie saw he was conducting family business and excused herself from the table.

Tony held the phone, listening, and his fury did not peak until he was told the Kapon girl had been taken. 'Find him, whoever he is. Find him and get back the girl!'

He hung up the phone with a shaking hand. Even the sight of his rose garden could not still his wrath.

* * *

Phan Lieu drove past Sam's Town Casino on Boulder Highway, passed the motel where he had kept a room, and headed out of Vegas toward the small bedroom community of Henderson, Nevada. Not far from the Clark County Museum he found a sleepy little motor lodge and, pulling a jacket over his bloody shirt, took a room at the end of a long row of forest green doors. He didn't think Mace would find him here.

He had found the heroin and syringes in the dead man's car before he ditched it for his own back at the house along Lone Mountain Road. At the rate the girl had been given the drug, she'd be hooked on it in another few days or a week, if she wasn't already. He took a chance she'd go into withdrawal and stopped the injections abruptly. He thought she might wake up feeling so bad it would seem like death was preferable.

He signed into the motel as Mr and Mrs Tom Lingham. The elderly man running the desk glanced past him to the car and saw Melanie apparently sleeping, her head against the window. 'Been driving all night?'

'Been losing our money in Vegas all night,' Phan said.

The old man nodded sagely. 'We get a lot of gamblers burned outta that city and on their way to the Dam or Lake Mead. You going to see Hoover Dam down at the state line?'

'Oh, we might. My wife's going to need some rest first. Let me take the room for a week. All the sights are within driving distance, aren't they?'

'You betcha. Here's yer key and I hope you and the Missus have a nice stay.'

Phan thanked him and returned to the car. It was mid-morning and he was tired from the all-night ordeal. Not just tired. Fatigued and weak from blood loss.

The day was already hot, too bright, the sun scorching his back. Melanie moaned as he drove through the parking lot toward their room. 'It won't be long now,' he said to her. 'You'll have what you need in just a few minutes – sleep. We'll *both* have what we need.'

Once he had the girl in bed, he thought he might sleep for a century. But first he had to clean the wound. The bullet had gone through his side, which was fortunate for him, but he didn't know what it might have hit or how much damage it had done.

He stood beneath the shower, head against the wall, gritting his teeth as the lukewarm water sluiced over his body, washing blood down the drain.

He slept just under six hours, dreaming of his life in Haiphong. He was young again, laughing with the other boys in the underground home they called their own. He hadn't been used in an assassination for more than a month and it was easy to forget that's what he did to earn his keep. For a while the boys all forgot and were simply children again. They played games and told stories, drank weak beer lifted from the Americans and held feasts where the food was spread out to the very edges of a plywood table.

These were the happiest times of his life. Nothing since had ever rivaled them. He was a part of something greater than himself. He enjoyed the camaraderie and the security of having friends willing to defend him, if necessary, friends who would bribe him out of jail, care for him when he had a fever or an upset stomach, be there when he was lonely and feeling depressed.

He had told a few of them about his mother and how he had watched her die. He was able to speak of the soldier they called Red and that night when he was caught sleeping by the well. He laughed about old Nuea, the aged woman who had taken him in for a while, and how there at the last she must have wanted him as a substitute for her lost sons the way she began to surprise him with small gifts.

In the dream he had been sleeping in one of the Army cots and was awakened roughly, someone rocking the cot as if it were a cradle. When he opened his eyes, he expected to see his friends playing a trick on him, laughing, their teeth flashing white in their soft brown faces, but instead he saw a girl crawling to the edge of a bed.

He sat straight up, pushing sleep away from him, reaching for the day in this new world, this present time where he had no friends and there was no laughter. A single streak of hotwire pain ran down his side then subsided. 'Where are you going?' he asked.

'I want to go home.'

'Well, you'll be going home soon. Right now you need to rest.' He reached for her arm and hauled her toward him. She fell back onto the pillow.

'I feel sick. I'm going to throw up.'

He didn't doubt it. She looked pale and she clutched at her stomach.

He hurriedly moved from the bed and helped her to her feet. She staggered in his arms toward the open doorway to the bath. He hoped she'd hold it down until he could get her to the toilet. He didn't want the room stinking of vomit.

She dropped to the floor and put her hands on the toilet rim, gagging. He turned his back, leaving her there, and found his suitcase to get fresh clothes for them both. Maybe today she could bathe herself. Feed herself. If she could keep something down.

He heard water running in the sink and returned to her. She looked up at him, face dripping water. Her eyes were haunted. Accusing him of a sin he had not committed.

He smiled at her. 'Ready to have a shower?'

'Who are you?'

'I'm Phan Lieu.'

'Phan? Who are you?'

'I'm your world, Melanie. That's all you need to know. And I'm not going to hurt you. I won't let *anybody* hurt you from now on.'

Beth couldn't reach the house at the address Tony Mace had written down for her. The circular drive was blocked with fire engines and cars. She parked back from the crowd and walked along the street until she came to the opening between a column of conifers. Black smoke still curled lazily into the pure blue sky. The top half of the once beautiful home had been gutted by fire. She saw firemen removing rubble so that the fire trucks could follow the drive out when they were through.

Neighbors stood around talking together in hushed tones. Melanie asked a man in plaid shorts what had happened.

'They say it was a bomb or something. It blew up the whole top floor. That's what started the fire.'

'Was anyone hurt?'

'We don't know. I don't think anyone was home, though. The

ambulance came, but it left a little while ago and there wasn't nobody in it.'

Beth shielded her eyes from the sun as she stared at the ruined house. 'This is where the Dalta family lives, isn't it?'

'Yeah,' the neighbor said. 'Guy owns a lot of property in Vegas.'

'Where would they be if they weren't at home?'

'Hell if I know. Maybe they have other houses and they were away. Sure gonna be surprised when they come back. Maybe it was a gas leak or something.'

It looked like more than a gas leak to her. It looked like a fighter jet had flown down into the subdivision and dropped a bomb. 'Do you know where he works?'

'Who, Dalta? Hell, I couldn't tell you that. You from the paper or something?'

'No, I was just wondering.'

She moved away from the group and headed for the car. She needed to find a phone, call Tony Mace. She must find where Dalta had gone.

Epstein dropped Denise off at her mother's house and drove from there directly to Dalta's office in the casino. The streets of Vegas were packed with cars, bumper to bumper traffic moving snail-like past the Mirage and Treasure Island. At a stoplight he glanced over at a playful water fountain, spurts of water leaping as if by magic from one fountain to another, glittering in the sunlight. A girl in a black halter top lounged on the concrete wall of the fountain, dipping water in a cupped palm. When the sun hit the falling drops, they sparkled like a spray of diamonds.

Dalta sat in the backseat, cleaning his forehead with a wet towel Denise had brought to him from her mother's house.

'I want you to find him.'

'You know I can't do that, Jeff. That's not my job. I couldn't find my ass in the dark.'

'Then call . . . call . . .'

'There's no one to call. They're all dead.'

'I'll find him myself then!'

'Sure, okay, take it easy.'

Epstein saw a couple of bums sleeping on a grassy incline, jackets thrown over their faces. Kids danced along behind strolling parents, couples held hands, and the casino entrances coursed with patrons going in and out. If it hadn't been for Dalta's house going up in flames, he might have tried his luck on the roulette today.

But there'd be no time for gambling for a while. The Asian had started a firestorm. He might have killed Dalta's little girl.

'If we knew the guy's name, we could maybe get some information on him,' Epstein said, glancing in the rearview mirror at his boss. That was what he was good at, paperwork.

'I don't need to know who he is. At this point, I don't give a fuck who he is or what he's up to. All I need to know is *where* he is. Nobody takes my daughter like that and leaves her chained up like a dog. Nobody!'

Epstein turned into the casino's drive and stopped in valet parking to let Dalta out. Dalta exited the backseat without saying a word, not goodbye, kiss my ass, or thank you for saving my life.

Man, Epstein thought, putting the car into gear and driving away. I've never seen him this way. I wouldn't be the Asian for any amount of money right now. No ma'am.

Tony sat in the den talking on the speaker-telephone while arranging a vase of roses on his desk. 'They got out all right?'

Epstein told him about how close it had been, with Jeff just moving down the steps when the bomb blew.

'Our friend is quite clever, isn't he? He plants a bomb, says he won't blow it, then blows it. Takes a kid, leaves her where she can be found come morning. Where's Dalta now?'

'The casino. He's going hunting for the guy soon, though.'

'All right, keep in touch. I want to know every step you make. I want to know every single move Dalta makes. Right now we've lost the Kapon girl and the Asian both. I want them back.'

'You betcha.'

Epstein hung up the pay phone and smiled at two pretty girls coming down the sidewalk toward him. 'Morning, ladies.'

They smiled back, causing him to think of a roll in the hay with one or the other, maybe both, and then they moved on past. He watched their hips sway in the short shorts until other people closed in behind them, blocking his view. He sighed as he walked to his car parked at the curb. Why couldn't he be young again, have a full head of hair instead of the balding pate? Then he wouldn't have to daydream about pretty girls like that, he'd have one of his own.

And why in the hell did he have to be mixed up between Tony and Jeff this way? Fence-sitting was always the most dangerous position.

He just hoped the Asian didn't know about him. Oh, good grief, he sure hoped not.

Maybe he ought to just buy a ticket to South America and stay away for a couple of years. By the time he returned, the Family turmoil would have been concluded.

The more he thought about that as he drove, the more it appealed to him.

There were some real pretty girls down in Peru.

23

The day melted into dread night. Automatic sprinkler systems sprayed gallons of water every few hours, dousing the tropical vegetation growing around the casinos and lawns.

Beth thought her home in Texas was hotter, but there was a sameness about the temperature and dryness of Vegas that made her feel lost in a Dali clockwork dream.

She was also scared and depressed, though that had nothing to do with the town of Vegas. She had tried for two days to find Jeff Dalta without success. The twenty-four hours she had given Mace was long past and she was still hunting, but she wouldn't wait much longer. If she didn't find him tonight, tomorrow she was going after Anthony Macedonia. She had followed all the leads he had given her, checking out different casinos, but she was stonewalled. Managers pretended never to have heard of the man, bartenders shook their heads, waitresses couldn't be bribed to whisper his name. The one lead Beth found came from a restaurant maitre d' in Caesar's Palace.

'He's come in here before.'

'Have you seen him lately?'

'Not in a few weeks. You might try the Four Kings, I think he's got a girlfriend who works there, a dancer. He's brought her in here with him before.'

'Where's the Four Kings?'

'Down at the end of the Strip.'

So she had gone in search of a dancer who might in turn lead her to Dalta. The Four Kings wasn't as razz-ma-tazzy as the newer casinos, but it wasn't as old as the Stardust or the Sahara, either. Its only outstanding feature proved to be the year-round presentation of a stage show featuring a chorus line of long-legged girls.

The manager wouldn't allow Beth into the dressing room area so she waited until he was busy elsewhere and went through a door marked *Private*, down a hall, and found the dressing room on her own. What could they do, throw her out? Big deal. She was too desperate now to care.

She still believed she could find Melanie on her own. Mace had implied Dalta wouldn't harm her daughter more than he already had. He was holding her so that Beth would turn on Mace. Dalta, she was reassured, had little left to gain by doing anything radical.

In the dressing room Beth wasted no time. Did they know Jeff Dalta? Had they seen him? Wasn't someone dating him?

While she asked her questions, the girls avoiding answering with any real information, a woman with a southern accent spoke from behind. 'Why are you asking about Jeff?'

Beth turned to face her. 'Do you know him?'

'I might. It depends on who's asking and why.'

'Look, I could pay you . . .' Beth fished in her purse for bills, brought up a twenty.

'I don't want your money. Tell me what this is about.'

Beth took the woman by one arm and guided her to a peach-colored satin sofa against the wall where they would have more privacy. 'I'm looking for my missing daughter.'

'You think Jeff has something to do with a runaway? Lady, you must be crazy.' The young woman laughed and tossed her head. Blonde hair cascaded around her shoulders and down her back, a flurry of long curls.

'She didn't run away. It's too complicated to explain, but I think your friend might know where she's staying. I need his help.'

'Why don't you call him up and ask him, then?'

'I can't find him. His house was . . . in a fire. I don't know where he went. No one seems to know. You've got to help me, please.'

The woman's face changed, softened. Her accent thickened. 'It's pretty important to you, huh?

'My daughter is the only thing I have left. I've lost my job, my home, everything. I have to find her; she's in terrible jeopardy.'

'Well, I don't guess it would hurt to tell you Jeff should be by tonight after the show. He'll be out there at one of the tables in front waiting for me. You could meet him there.'

A wave of relief swept over Beth with such force that she thought she might collapse into the other woman's arms. She wanted to hug her, leap up and shout. The search for the elusive Jeffrey Dalta had taken her into every casino on the street. She had been asking people about him for hours on end and coming up empty.

'I don't know how to thank you.'

'Well, honey, this doesn't mean Jeff can be any help to you locating your daughter, but I guess you'll find that out for yourself tonight when you meet him. I'm sure he'll do what he can.'

It was evident the young woman cared a great deal about Dalta. What would she think if Beth accused him of sending someone to rape and kidnap an innocent girl? Did she even know he was a Mafia wiseguy hoping to usurp a mob boss? Did she know he had a wife and child?

It didn't matter what the girlfriend thought of Dalta. Beth was just grateful she had reached the end of her long, frantic search. She thanked the woman and left the dressing room quietly, blessing her stars that a stroke of luck had finally come her way. Who said there were no winners in Vegas? She would find Dalta and then she would find Melanie. She didn't know how she was going to get through the next few hours, but at least the nightmare was nearly at an end.

She stepped out into the direct sunlight and pawed through her purse for a pair of sunglasses. She needed them for the glare, but she also needed them to keep strangers from seeing there were tears in her eyes.

It was time to buy a gun. She found the rental car and drove through town, looking for a gun shop.

Dalta followed the Asian's every move once he discovered his whereabouts. It appeared the man had been on the run, taking the girl with him to a little motel near Henderson. Dalta told no one he had found the Asian or that he had tailed him. This had turned into a private affair and he would work his own private justice. The bomb that had ruined his house might have killed his wife, and the thought of his little girl tied up next to a broken-windowed, graffiti-covered service station all night long in the dark, her mouth taped shut, and what might have happened if some screwy bastard had found her helpless like that, made him want to cram a fist down the Asian's throat and make him choke on it. He wasn't getting away with this shit. Not in this lifetime. He was going to die for it.

In less than an hour.

It was after midnight and Dalta had just relaxed with his head turned to the side on the headrest in the car when he saw the door to the motel room open and his prey appear outlined by the light inside. He was a tall guy, couldn't be full-blooded Asian built that way, and certainly not with that shock of curly dark hair. He had a parent or grandparent who originated in the West. It annoyed Dalta they hadn't been able to find out anything about him – where he came from, what he was doing in Vegas, why he wanted control of the Kapon girl. No one in the entire network of Families had a clue who the guy might be. He wasn't connected. He was some kind of lone wolf, a killer, professional and utterly unpredictable.

Now where was he going? The past two nights he had stayed inside and hadn't left the room until mid-morning each day to pick up food.

Dalta thought fortune was smiling his way. He had just been working out a way to get to the Asian inside the room, but it would be so much easier in the night, in the dark.

He waited until the man started his car and drove onto the street before starting his own car. He stayed a long way behind to keep from being spotted.

On Boulder Highway he saw they were headed for Vegas. Did the bastard have friends there? Was he reporting in to someone, maybe one of Mace's rivals who had come in from the East Coast?

It surprised Dalta when the Asian parked right on Las Vegas Boulevard in the center of the casino district. He parked two blocks ahead of the Asian's vehicle and sat still, waiting to see what he was up to.

A couple of minutes later he watched him cross the busy street and move down the sidewalk. Dalta exited his car then and crossed over too. He hated to have to kill the guy in the open this way, with so many people around. He meant to use a gun and once gunfire was heard, there'd be a panic on the street.

Well, shit, he would get out of any trouble if a cop snatched him for this. What was he worried about? Still, he'd better take his chance while he had it. He couldn't put it off any longer. The whole Family was in an uproar. News of the feud had spread, whispers circulating all through the family, and Mace was having a hard time keeping everybody calm. A lot of the boys wanted to drop Dalta, get him out of the way, and Mace wasn't going to be able to stop some hothead from doing it if this thing wasn't straightened out soon.

Dalta had pleaded stupidity and begged for Tony's forgiveness. He hadn't meant to go so far, he told him. He hadn't meant real harm. He didn't know if Tony believed him or not, you couldn't tell from what he said to your face – or rather over the telephone.

The Asian had stopped, climbing from the sidewalk up onto the grass where there were a few trees planted, their leaves ruffling in the easy breeze. He was talking to some kid in an army jacket. He was buying some shit, of course, that's what he was doing. He was hopped up on something. That's how he'd managed to take on all those men in one night. Either that or he was a type of professional even the Family rarely employed.

Dalta moved with the flow of pedestrians until he neared the place. He strolled right up the embankment and came up behind the Asian without a pause. He had the gun in his jacket pocket. He lifted it, put pressure on the trigger, and was mentally steeling himself against the gunshot blast when suddenly the Asian was turning around.

Dalta's gun went off, tearing a hole through his pocket, deafening his ears, but it was all wrong, he didn't know if he'd hit the Asian, and now the man's face was right before him, the eyes dark and fierce, the teeth flashing, a knife flashing, a knife whipping past like a bat darting between them.

Dalta's hand loosened on his gun, his knees unlocked so that he could turn and run, his shoulders swiveled and he took a step backward. People on the sidewalk had screamed when they first heard the gunshot and now they were scattering away in both directions and even into the street. It was strange how they moved, like liquid, all blurred around their edges, in slow motion.

Dalta didn't know he'd been killed until he glanced down at his chest and saw the pearl-handled stiletto protruding from it. His eyes saw it, but his mind wouldn't admit the meaning of it. He wouldn't have been stabbed, it had all happened too quickly, no one could move that fast. The Asian couldn't have known he was coming, he had approached so rapidly from the crowd. How could he have heard him or known he was marked? How could he have buried the knife so fast Dalta never even knew it?

'Goddamn,' he muttered, staggering down the incline. He felt it all go at once. His knees, his legs, even the muscles in his arms. He had meant to reach up and pull out the knife – it burned him now, deep in his chest – but he realized it would have made no difference. He realized that where the knife was buried meant it had gone straight for his heart. If it had pierced it, he'd already be dead, but it was close enough to drain all the strength from his body. He said again, 'Goddamn,' and grimaced in a swift spasm of pain that took his breath away.

He involuntarily dropped to the ground before he ever reached the sidewalk. He lay on his back on the grass, gazing up at the open sky above the bright, neon lights of the casinos, the knife still embedded in his chest. There was beauty up there, in the sky, beauty unmarred and eternal.

His hearing left him. It was quiet though he knew the Asian was saying something to him for he saw him bending over and saw his lips moving.

All Dalta could think was: *Leave me alone, move out of the way. I want to see the sky. I never get to see the stars.*

Then he thought: *I hope my baby remembers me.*

'Lydia,' he whispered. His last word.

Phan lurched across the street holding his right side where his makeshift bandage had torn loose when he'd moved so quickly. He drove away just as patrol cars slammed to a halt at the opposite curb.

He had known he was being watched and followed. He had expected the hit, watched, waited for it. At least he'd been able to buy the drugs off the kid before it happened. And he had been able to tell Dalta how stupid he'd been to follow so closely. 'If you'd stayed clear of me this wouldn't have happened,' he had said to the dying man. 'Not that I don't think you ought to die, you piece of shit.'

Blood dripped from between Phan's fingers where he pressed his hand to his side. He was bleeding all over the front seat. The top of his slacks were wet with blood and his shirt was soaking all the way up to his armpit. His clothes were sticky and cold, clinging to him. The car smelled like a slaughterhouse.

He had to hurry back to the motel and get the bleeding stopped again. He had been beaten and stabbed before, but never shot. It felt like a hole had been punched in his flesh and gasoline poured in every time the wound reopened. He didn't know he was grinding his teeth against the ache in his side or grunting into the dark of the car as he drove away, but then he listened carefully and heard the sounds he was making. '*Uh-uh-uh-uh.*'

Even with Phan's kind and patient encouragement, Melanie couldn't come back all the way. She was halfway in the world and halfway out of it. She straddled a spot between reality and a landscape reserved only for the insane.

Time, for instance, was unknown. She hadn't any idea of its passing, could not determine night from day. She knew she sat and stared, that she knew. She found herself doing it. Propped up in bed, staring at the wall across the room. On the wall hung a badly-framed cardboard picture of a barn sitting beside a country road. She watched the picture, waiting for it to come alive, for a horse and buggy to go trotting past it, kicking up dust from the dry, brown ruts. Then her mind would wander and be . . . elsewhere.

Attending to healing, Phan said. Working at survival.

Once when she came to to find her vision filled with the far wall and the country picture, she felt a buzzing on the inside of her thighs and she reached down and threw off the sheet. It felt like bees were burying their stingers in her. She spread her legs and saw the twin burns, no bigger than her pinky nail, on each inner thigh, high up, near the panty line.

She immediately drew the sheet over herself again and looked at the wall. Better the barn and the empty road. The skeletal autumn trees.

Once she went to the toilet to relieve herself and she was bleeding. She didn't want to tell Phan. She didn't think it was her period. It was redder blood, fresh. She blotted it away and folded toilet paper to use as a pad.

Another time she was in the bathroom, bathing again, the tub full to the rim. She scrubbed and scrubbed until her flesh all over was pink and raw. When she got out to dry herself she caught sight of her face in the medicine cabinet mirror.

'Not me,' she mumbled.

The face was bad. It had a terrible cross-stitched wound running across one cheek all the way from the top of the cheek bone down to the chin. And the eyes had blue moons beneath them. And the pupils of those eyes were as empty as her heart.

She turned her back and waited until she stopped shaking before trying to dress.

Phan talked to her for hours on end. He said some things she remembered and many she did not. He assured her there was a way out of this labyrinthine jungle that was her sullied and broken mind. He admitted his own wounds, his fragile hold on the world at times, and then he touched her face, gently, until she shut her eyes, shutting him away.

She dreamed. Of home, her childhood home in Geneva. Of classes and friends and good times. She also suffered nightmares that were so violent that once she fell off the bed to the floor, screaming.

Phan got the Geneva phone number out of her and called, but reported no one answered. There was a machine.

Melanie did not know where her mother might be. She might be dead. It was possible. So possible that she stopped thinking about it.

She was going home anyway. Phan promised he would send her on a plane, just as soon as he finished up some last business he had in Vegas.

She did not like or dislike Phan. She understood he had rescued her from not only a naked enslavement to men and heroin but perhaps from an ignoble death. Yet she could not find it in her to like, dislike, or care, really, about anything.

She was out of it too much. She stared at the wall and waited for this phase or attitude or misery or whatever it was to leave her. She was sure she would like Phan then. She would be able to live again then.

One time she woke and Phan lay in his clothes on top of the covers, sleeping. She turned into his arms and cried, 'I want to die.'

'No, you don't. You don't want to die.'

'Then I want to kill someone.'

'You don't want to do that either. You won't have to. I will.'

She didn't know who he should kill. She didn't understand it when he told her about some men who had kidnapped her. She couldn't remember their names and who was responsible for what.

Phan told her not to worry about it, she didn't have to remember just yet. 'You're a survivor,' he told her. 'Believe me, it's true.'

She sat now in the bed, studying the picture on the wall opposite the bed. She heard a sound at the door and turned her head in that direction.

As soon as he cleared the door she wished she could scoot down in the bed, cover her head, and go to sleep. She had never seen so much blood.

'You're hurt again.'

He slumped into a chair and said, 'Could you bring a wet towel and some clean dry ones?'

'What happened?' She moved lethargically though she knew she should try to move faster. She stacked towels in her arms, then remembered he wanted one wet. She ran water in the sink and almost was hypnotized by the swirl of the water going down the drain. She shook herself, dropped in a towel, watched it soak and turn pale gray.

When she reached him, she saw he was opening a small vial and snorting white powder from it.

'Dope,' she said tonelessly. Her nerves jumped just below one eye. She wanted some of it. She couldn't have it, but she wanted it. That's what had been done to her. She had been given the evil gift of longing, such utter hungry needfulness.

She dreamily unbuttoned Phan's shirt and pulled it loose from his waist. He shrugged out of it. Now they could both see the damage.

'Doctor.' Melanie didn't want to touch it. The torn flesh made her stomach lurch. She covered her eyes.

'Here, let me do it.' He took the wet towel from her hands and began to dab at the wound. As he did so he made a soft groaning noise.

'Need a doctor.'

'I can't do that. This is a gunshot wound. They'd have to report it.'

'Why's it bleeding?' She remembered this being an old wound. Or was it new? No, she remembered he was hurt before this.

'The man who ordered your kidnapping came for me.'

She fought back a sudden urge to throw open the motel door and run for her life.

Phan finished cleaning the wound. 'Get my aftershave lotion. Please.'

She had to pull herself up again. It was so much trouble. All she wanted to do was to lie down and sleep, lovely sleep.

She managed to find the bottle in the bathroom and bring it to him. She watched while he poured it over his side. He yelped once, then bit down on the pain, his face turning hard and stony. 'Hand me the clean towels now.'

He took the folded towels and pressed two of them against his side. 'This isn't as bad as it looks,' he said. 'It's just blood.'

The room smelled of the astringent lime aftershave and caused Melanie to recall a time during those missing days when she had smelled something similar. Limes. Someone had limes. Cut, halved or quartered, squeezed into a drink. Who was that and where had she been?

'Can you tear some long strips off the bed sheet that I could use for a new bandage? We used up all the gauze I bought.'

She sat down on the side of the bed and pulled the top sheet into her lap. 'Is he coming here?' she asked.

'Who? Oh, you mean the man who did this tonight. No, he's not coming. He's dead.'

She paused, the half-torn sheet in her hands, and stared at him. 'Good,' she said finally. And it was. It was good, that's all she knew.

She finished tearing strips, some too small and these she discarded on the floor. She handed the others to him, then crawled into the

230

center of the bed and cushioned her head in the center of the pillow. She was very tired. So tired. She wanted to sleep. Just sleep.

Beth sat at a front table for the show in the Four Kings until the dance numbers ended, but no one joined her at the table. She kept looking around, trying to determine if one of the men in the room might be Jeff Dalta. Once she frowned up at the dancer who had told her to come and then looked around the room, hoping the girl would stare in some direction where Dalta was sitting, but she didn't. Maybe she couldn't see out into the audience through the spotlights on the stage.

Once the show ended, Beth sat dejectedly drinking a Virgin Mary. The dancer joined her within minutes, having changed into a stunning red gown. She came directly to Beth's table and said, 'He's not here. I don't know where he is. He hasn't even called.'

'Well, when he does will you have him call me? I'm in 2046 at the Sahara.'

'Yeah, I'll tell him.'

Beth left and took the rental car to her hotel. She had a message from Everett waiting for her at the desk. She decided to return his call since it was earlier in the night in Texas. He picked up on the first ring.

'Beth? Are you all right? Have you found Melanie?'

'I'm all right, Everett. I'm close to Melanie, I think, but I haven't found her yet. And it's killing me.'

'I think it's time you called the police on this Mace character, Beth.'

'Mace said he didn't do it. He blames one of his men.'

'You believe him?'

Beth closed her eyes and lay her head back on the chair. 'I don't have much choice. But I've spent days trying to find the man and I haven't been able to do it. I'm beginning to wonder if it was the truth, after all.'

'Beth, call someone. You're an attorney, not a detective. You need help.'

'Yes,' Beth admitted. 'I'm beginning to think you're right. I keep winding up in blind alleys and at dead ends.'

231

'There's no telling what's happening to Melanie. You can't let this drag on. She's been in danger all this time.'

'I know. I'll do something tomorrow. It'll end tomorrow.'

'Good. I've been worried.'

'I'll call you as soon as I find out anything, Everett. I'm sorry I didn't let you hear from me before now. I've just been . . . I've been busy. Is Pope all right?'

'Your cat? Sure, he's fine. Eats a lot.'

When they said goodbye and hung up, Beth wandered over to the window and leaned her forehead against the glass. Below her the city sparkled and shone, a river of car lights streaming below the towering neon signs. The streets were more alive at night than during the daylight hours. Somewhere out in that city was her daughter.

She looked at her wristwatch to see the time. Almost midnight. It was too late to go to Anthony Macedonia tonight. She'd go first thing in the morning. Either he would turn over Melanie to her or she would show him what she carried in her purse.

24

Phan ached so much he couldn't help the periodic wince that transfigured his face. It felt as if a maniac had thrown a punch to his side and was still there, punching. He breathed shallowly every little while, sipping in small bits of air. When he breathed deeply it was as if his ribs might rip right through the hole in his side.

In the passenger seat the girl was out. She went into sleeps that mimicked comas. He'd called up and reserved a flight for her. She would be leaving for Houston at five that evening. He hoped she could travel alone. She wasn't herself yet, and he had his doubts she ever would be. He had seen the bruises on her body, the cigarette burns on her legs. She'd been tortured the way he'd seen crazy kids in Vietnam torture little lizards, pulling their legs off, breaking their tails, poking out their eyes.

He was an assassin, yes. He killed. But even murder was preferable to systematic torture that scarred the mind and left it desperately lost on a barren, twisted stage.

Phan did not care much for people, most of whom were capable of doing what had been done to Melanie. He'd never grown attached to anyone during his lifetime, though he still had a fondness for the boys in Vietnam. But for anyone else the percentages in it were too low. In his business, he couldn't trust anyone.

He wasn't attached to the girl either, but she was probably the first person in his life he'd made any effort to help. It surprised him what a sense of warmth it gave him to have been instrumental in her rescue. Not that he'd make a habit of such heroics. He wasn't altogether happy with how complicated it became once you were responsible for another person's well-being.

Melanie Kapon reminded him of a much younger person, probably because she was just a college kid from that hick Texas town and didn't know a thing about the world. She still didn't understand how closely she had come to either dying of an accidental overdose or becoming firmly addicted to heroin. She hardly remembered any of the time she'd been drugged, and seemed to make a concerted effort *not* to remember any of those lost days. She was afraid, he thought, of remembering all the events she didn't want to know, couldn't bear knowing. Too many men had taken advantage of her unconscious state. Too many vile, despicable men who were more animal than man.

He, too, possessed animal instincts, but he controlled them and only let them loose when stalking and murdering a victim. This did not make him a better human being, he knew; it just made him less a monster than some others.

He looked over at the girl, her mouth slack in sleep, her pitifully thin arms spotted with yellow-gray bruises. Those would go away. Not so the bruises to her soul.

It was ten in the morning and they were driving to Mace's house. He'd order the girl to stay in the car. He wouldn't want her to witness what he was about to do. She had seen enough of horror to last her lifetime and more.

Beth finished a glass of orange juice and paid her check at the register of the Sahara's café. She was annoyed she had overslept. She must have been more tired and dispirited than she had known. The sun had been up for hours by the time she rolled over and opened her eyes.

Just before she left the room she received an enigmatic phone call from the dancer at the Four Kings.

'Did Jeff ever call you?'

'No, why?'

'I left several messages at his office and I haven't heard from him yet. I mentioned you and your room number. I just thought he might have . . .'

'No, I haven't had any calls.'

'It's not like him to stand me up. Or not call me back when I leave him a message.'

Beth heard the sulky tone in the other woman's voice. She waited. Who the hell, besides his girlfriend, cared where Dalta was now? Beth had begun to believe that had been a misdirection on Anthony Macedonia's part. He *must* have lied to her. He knew where Melanie was. He really *was* the one who had the motive to hurt her. He'd just thrown her off his trail by claiming someone else had arranged for Melanie to be kidnapped from Geneva.

Well, today she would not plead, she would not be polite, she would not be reasonable. Today she would find Melanie. They would give her daughter back. *Today*.

As she drove up the winding street leading out from the city limits of Vegas to Macedonia's house, she felt the fury she had kept under control for so long now simmering near the surface. She gripped the steering wheel and drove faster than she should. If Macedonia thought losing his son to the death chamber was bad, just wait until she got through with him. He'd have no life left worth living once he was locked up for most of the rest of his days in a Texas penitentiary. They'd send him to Three Points for the federal offense of kidnapping and transporting a person across state lines. Not many people ever got out of Three Points Federal. It was like being sent to the bottom of the earth.

The son of a bitch could learn how to make four concrete walls his home for what he had done.

Or if he refused to hand over her daughter, even after threats, she had the gun. She knew how to use it.

And she would not hesitate, for she had nothing left worth losing.

'You stay in the car.' Phan opened his car door and stepped out slowly, nursing his throbbing side. He smelled the sweetly overpowering scent of roses and, glancing about, saw a garden of them.

Melanie made sounds in her sleep as if someone were prodding her in a painful place on her person.

'Hey.' He leaned in the window on his side of the car and shook her arm. 'Hey, I want you to stay out here in the car. Promise me.'

The lids of her eyes flew open wide and she looked startled. She cringed from his touch. 'Where am I?'

'You're safe as long as you stay in the car. I don't want you leaving it, do you understand?'

She nodded, licked her lips, pulled herself up in the seat straight. 'I want to go home.'

'Soon. Soon.'

He had taken the drive around the side of the estate to the back of the house to park just outside a four-car garage. He hadn't wanted neighbors seeing the car if they happened to hear anything. Mace's house was away from the street and his neighbors were sparse, but it just wasn't good business to leave the girl sitting in a strange car in front of the house.

He approached the house across a brick patio. He came to closed, double French doors and tried the brass handle, found it unlocked. A man like Mace shouldn't leave doors unlocked. In fact, he should have had a personal bodyguard watching the place. *Arrogant*, Phan thought. *A real arrogant fuck.*

He stepped inside what appeared to be a study with a wide, polished mahogany desk and a wall of books. There was no one in the room, but surely they had heard the car in the drive.

Just as he was thinking he would need to move through the house to find someone, a Hispanic maid came into the room. She gasped in fright that was replaced by a scowl of hostility. 'Who are you?'

'Tell your employer I've come to see him. *Now.*'

She lost all trace of her first irritation at finding him in the room and dropped back into her role of servitude. She turned in the door and left him alone.

Phan braced himself for laying his eyes for the first time in his life on the man who was his father. He knew Mace would not look like the young man in the boot camp photo taken so many years ago, the one given to Phan's mother.

While the seconds ticked past, Phan studied the room and the furnishings. He might have had this. His mother had deserved a rich life. She had given birth to the firstborn, to the heir. Phan's brother

236

had enjoyed a life of comfort and privilege – at least as long as he had lived.

Mace entered the room, startling Phan. He frowned, having evidently been told by the maid a young man had been found unexpectedly in his house. He didn't appear to be armed. He must not have any fear at all.

Phan felt his heart thumping too hard and he drew in a long breath to control his emotions. He was out of control. After all these years and a thousand nights of fantasies about how this would happen, he now stood across the room from the man who had fathered him. It was a moment of epiphany, one so great he felt slightly dizzy and had to put his hand on the massive desk to steady himself.

He stared at the other man, noticed they were approximately the same height and build, they even stood the same way, feet slightly apart as if ready for any sort of emergency. He stared harder. Nothing about his father's face looked like his own. But his hair! He had a mop of curly hair, still thick and coarse and black as coal. It made him look younger than his years. Made him look rakish, a swashbuckling Don Juan. No wonder Phan's mother had fallen in love with him and was so destroyed when discarded.

'What do you mean breaking into my house this way? If you don't get out this minute, I'll call the police.'

Phan still could not speak. But now rage came bubbling up, rage he had carried inside him since he was a child cursing this man's name, though he had no name for him and called him, in his thoughts, *father, cursed father.*

'You won't want to call the police,' he said finally. His voice was cold and unemotional, betraying nothing. He had played this drama over in his mind for years. He would not falter now, he swore that on his mother's grave.

'Yes? Why wouldn't I? What do you want?'

'You are Tony Mace? Anthony Macedonia?' He paused a moment. 'In 1964 and 1965 you were in the army infantry in Vietnam.'

Mace's frown deepened. He looked impatient. Phan took the time to assess how he was dressed – casually in tan slacks and a snow-white sport shirt open at the collar. His eyes were unfaded brown, like an old walnut shell, and he possessed an expressive face that shifted perceptibly from moment to moment with his thoughts.

'I'm Anthony Macedonia. I was in Vietnam. What's this about? I warn you, I'm at the end of my patience. Strangers don't just walk into my house and ask me questions. I know who you are. You're the one who killed Dalta's boys. The one we've been calling the Asian. And you killed Dalta last night, didn't you? I'd like to know why.'

'You're not afraid of me.'

'That's correct. I am *not* afraid of you. If you had wanted to kill me I don't think we'd be having this conversation.'

Phan moved around the desk until he stood in front of it. They were still several feet apart. Mace had not moved far into the room, as if he wanted to make sure it was safe to do so before coming closer. He professed no fear, but there was a little there, hiding behind his unblinking stare, behind the pressed line of his lips.

'In the summer of 1964 you met a young Vietnamese girl. You got her pregnant. She told you and after that, you disappeared from her life.'

Mace said nothing, but he looked behind him to be sure the hall was empty and then he closed the door. 'How do you know all that?'

'Your wife doesn't know, does she?'

'That's none of your business. My life is none of your business. Why have you gone back that far in my life and dug all this up?'

'Why did you desert my mother?'

That's all he wanted to know before he killed the man. He hadn't known he'd blurt it out so quickly, simply, but it was the one question he needed answering most.

Mace didn't blink, didn't move. After a few shocked seconds while understanding dawned, he said, 'You're her son.'

'I'm *your* son. I'm your first son, your firstborn, the son you deserted. My mother died when I was five. You didn't know that because after you found out you had gotten her pregnant, you stopped caring what happened to her, didn't you? I guess you thought she'd raise some little bastard child and no one would ever blame you for leaving them both behind. After all, thousands of GIs did it. Not one in five hundred took a Vietnamese girl home to mom and pop.'

Mace moved to the wall at his left. He went to a painting and took it down from the wall, standing it on the floor. Phan saw the combination safe.

'How much do you want?' Mace asked.

The doorbell rang and both of them recoiled and waited.

Beth rang the doorbell. When the Hispanic woman opened the door Beth said, 'I want to see Mr Mace.'

'I'm sorry, Mr Mace is busy, ma'am.'

'I don't care if he's busy, I want to see him.'

'I'm sorry, that's just not possible.'

Beth hadn't known she'd be denied entrance. She stood rooted to the spot, staring at the closed door. She raised her hand and punched the doorbell button and held it. She could hear the bell going off inside endlessly. Finally when the door did not open again, she yelled, 'Let me in!'

When the door still did not open, she went down the steps and began to circle the house. There had to be another way in.

She'd not be stopped, by God, not now.

Melanie felt a sticky wetness in the seat and looked down at herself. She might be sitting in a spilled drink or . . .

She gasped on seeing the blood. It was red as flame and it was everywhere. Her jeans were soaked at the crotch and down the thighs. The seat was wet, and her hands, she saw, raising them before her face, were covered.

She began to keen low in her throat, frightened at the amount of blood coming from her. She felt it now, seeping from between her legs. Gushing.

She was dying. Hemorrhage. That's what it was called. She was hurt somewhere, up inside, deep where they had . . .

Her keening grew in volume and her heart thudded in her chest.

Not her period, that blood which had been slowly flowing from her the past days. She was going to die from this. Now the blood raged from her.

She rocked back and forth in the seat, staring around wildly, unable to find a solution. She hadn't any napkins. She needed a blanket to sop all this blood up with. She needed to find Phan to help her. She . . .

   . . . was going away.

   . . . to where it was peaceful.

   . . . where it was safe.

Phan had the Ruger automatic out instantly. He was across the room and standing within arm's length of the man who was his father. 'You think I've come to blackmail you for money?'

'What else could you want? Now put away that gun. All that happened years ago. I was just a kid, really. What was I supposed to do? Let me ask you that. What was I supposed to do? Take your mother as a wife, go through all that redtape to get her sent to the States? Why do you think so few soldiers tried it? My commanding officer never would have let me do it. I was non-com at the time, I wasn't some big colonel or general who could do as he damned well pleased just because some girl got herself knocked up.'

Phan reached out with his free hand and slapped Mace soundly across the face. Mace's head snapped around and a red mark bloomed on his cheek. He brought up a hand to his face and his gaze changed from calculating to a stare as lifeless as igneous rock.

'My mother loved you. She kept your picture. She tried to take care of me even when her whole family turned their backs on us because I was an outcast. She worked the lowliest jobs because she was a fallen woman, an outcast herself who had gotten entangled with an American and produced a baby no one wanted. Then she *died*, died from overwork and undernourishment. Died lonely and broken, just a young woman. Have you no thought to what you've *done*, to how much *misery* you put us through?'

Phan let the words tumble out. They weren't rehearsed; he had never thought what he might say to this man once he told him who he was.

'I can give you money or I can call the law,' Mace said.

'And I can kill you fast or kill you slowly.'

Mace ignored him and turned to the safe. He twitched the combination dial, carefully lining up the numbers. He took the handle and pulled open the door.

'Do you know what I am?' Phan asked.

'I don't really care,' Mace said. 'I just want you out of my house and off my property.'

'I grew up on the streets of Haiphong and in order to live, I joined a band of child assassins. That is what I am. That is what I have come to do today. All the training I ever had was for this one day in my life. I've wanted to kill you since I was old enough to understand what you did.'

Mace reached into the wall safe. 'I have two hundred thousand dollars in cash here. I can get you more . . .'

Phan choked on the rage now. He couldn't swallow, couldn't breathe, couldn't stand to look on this man another moment or he thought he would burst like a Roman candle going off in the sky.

Mace did not bring out money from the safe. He brought out a small tin box and opened the lid. Inside Phan saw letters with canceled stamps.

'*This* was my son,' Mace said, lifting the letters and letting them fall to the floor between them. 'I lost him. My son is dead. I have no other son.'

Beth completely circled the house and saw a car sitting outside a four-car garage. Someone was in it. She'd demand that person let her into the house.

She walked quickly across the paved drive, but her steps slowed as she neared the vehicle.

Melanie.

She ran, flinging herself at the car door to rip it open. All the while crying Melanie's name.

Once she had the door open and was leaning in, her arms reaching for her daughter, she smelled it.

Blood.

Then she saw it.

Everywhere.

'Oh, Melanie, baby. Oh my baby.'

From the waist down Melanie was soaked with blood. She sat stiffly, a mannequin, staring straight ahead. She had not yielded to her mother's embrace or responded to her voice. Her face was closed and her eyes empty, so empty.

Beth jerked back and the entire world darkened as if someone had dimmed the sun.

She turned and set off for the house, running, flying, screaming.

She came to a set of French doors and hit them at full-tilt, bursting through into a room. She saw . . .

Anthony Mace reaching into a wall safe.

An Asian man, young, his gaze following the falling letters to the floor.

She looked at Mace again and she saw . . .

One of his hands reaching into the safe at the same time he dropped the letters. He brought out a gun. He was going to kill the younger man.

Both of them turned at her entrance. She had stopped screaming the moment she came through the door, but now she screamed again, 'SHE'S BLEEDING TO DEATH, CALL SOMEONE, CALL FOR HELP.'

Beth didn't know how it all happened so fast after that one swift look her way. Her heart was in her throat, seeing Mace turning, his gun hand sweeping the air as it pivoted toward her. She would be shot now, she would die, she was at the wrong place, at the wrong time. And if she died, who was to save Melanie?

Then there was a short burst of high-pitched sound and she thought she had been gunned down, exactly the way she had been in her old nightmare, but she felt no pain, felt nothing but a paralyzing numbness. She hadn't been able to change anything in the dream and she could not change a single thing now.

As she watched in amazement Mace jerked and fell against the wall. He dropped his gun.

The Asian man stooped, picked it up.

Beth broke from her frozen stance and rushed across the room. 'Give me the gun, give it to me.'

She took the Ruger from the younger man's hand and turned to the still-standing Mace. He bled from the wound to his arm. Blood dripped to the floor off his fingers and the sight of this blood combining with her daughter's blood out in the car caused her to back away two steps, raise the Ruger and say, 'I'm going to hurt you like you hurt me.'

'I don't know what you're talking ab . . .'

She fired and missed. She spread her feet a little, aimed low, holding her wrist steady with her other hand, the way she had been taught in gun safety classes. She fired again.

Mace leaped and screamed. The door to the room banged open and the maid and Connie rushed into the room out of breath.

Beth swiveled, the gun held out toward them. She said, 'Don't move or you'll go with him.'

She swiveled back again, aimed, fired.

The first shot to hit him went into the top of his shoe, probably blasting apart his toes. This shot went into his leg just above the bloody foot. It took him down to his knees. He stared up at her, his lips white and face pale as snow. 'I didn't do it,' he protested.

'Kill him,' whispered Phan.

'You did do it,' Beth said. 'You're the one. You set it all up. You wanted to take her from me the way your son was taken from you. And you've almost done it.'

Again Beth swiveled from the waist, pointing the Ruger at the two women in the room. 'Get out. One of you go call for an ambulance. *Now.*'

The Hispanic maid jumped, fleeing the room.

'Kill him or I will,' Phan said.

She switched back to cover Mace. She aimed, pulled the trigger slowly, squeezing it so her aim would hold steady.

Mace screamed, the bullet entering the thigh of his undamaged leg. Now there was real blood. The floor was pooling with it all around where he kneeled, rocking and swaying and uncontrollably moaning.

Behind her, Beth heard Mace's wife pleading and begging, but it was too late for that. It had been too late the minute she had flung open the doors and stepped into the room. She couldn't see anything but Melanie in the car covered with blood, her eyes empty as the dead. She saw Anthony Mace overlain on the vision of her daughter. He had to bleed.

He had to bleed just as much.

She aimed the gun for his shoulder and pulled off a shot. He was thrown onto his back, one leg beneath him. He was saying something to her, but she couldn't hear it. She couldn't hear anything anymore but a rushing of wind through her ears and the sound of her daughter's low-pitched keening.

She fired once more, aiming for his gut. His body jerked halfway around on the floor until he was facing them now, his face contorted with pain and shock.

Beth dropped the gun. Phan picked it up.

'I'm taking my daughter to the hospital,' she said lifelessly. 'I can't wait for an ambulance.'

She ran from the room the way she had come into it, swinging around the open French doors, and disappearing into the sunshine.

Phan stared at the dying man. He said to the woman, without turning, 'Leave the room. Leave us alone.'

He listened until he heard the door close. Mace's wife must have loved him enough to leave him to the privacy of his final moments.

Phan sat near his father's body. 'Shall I end it?' he asked. 'You're dying.'

Mace looked into his face, focusing on him. He twitched from the several sites of pain burning all over his body. 'Do it,' he said between gritted teeth. 'If you're my son, for Godsakes, have some fucking grit and fucking do it.'

Phan brought the Ruger up to his father's temple and quickly squeezed off the shot that would take him into eternity.

'I'm your son,' he said.

Mace had not lied. There was a great deal of cash bundled inside the safe. Phan took it out and stacked it in the crook of his arm. He didn't need it, but the girl's mother had possibly saved his life. He'd give it to her. He hadn't thought Mace would have a weapon in the safe and he might not have been able to avert being killed by it. Mace knew he'd be so hurt by the words he'd spoken about his son who had died by execution that he would be distracted, an easy target.

It was good he was dead. It was right he was dead.

He paused before walking away from the body on the floor. Scarlet blood covered the carpet. The scattered letters were soaking up stains, the envelope edges spiked with ruby. Phan leaned down and took a couple of the letters written by his brother, ones that had not been touched by the blood. He slipped them into his pocket.

Keepsakes. Like the old boot camp photograph. Just keepsakes he needed to remind him of what he had lost.

Now, Phan thought, it is over.

It is finally over between us.

25

Everett drove them from the airport. Beth sat next to him in the front seat and Melanie sat in the back, but she would not put on the seat belt. She perched on the edge of the back seat, her arms aligned along the top of the front seat, watching the road. Beth thought her daughter had been given a new chance, but it would still take time before she would use it. They had kept her in the hospital for four days before releasing her to come home. She had hemorrhaged nearly to death, but they had been able to staunch the flow. It was her mind they worried about, not the physical injuries.

Beth prayed for normalcy to return. Melanie already seemed a little better.

Everett had a perpetual smile stuck on his face. He nodded a lot and even laughed a little, nervous and not knowing what to say. He had already told Beth the good news when he met them at the airport. He had convinced the judge to review the circumstances of her court case due to the events of the last few weeks. She would be cleared, Everett assured her. She would be reinstated with the Bar Association, get her teaching position back, and if she wanted to, she could ask the voters for her county district attorney seat. He thought she had a good chance of regaining it.

At least, Beth thought, she did not have to worry about money for a while; she and Melanie would be all right now. Phan had made her take what his father had offered to pay him. He had said, standing in the hospital room beside Melanie's bed, 'It's mine. Call it my inheritance. Mace never did anything for me or my mother so I think this is my money. I don't need it, take it.'

'I don't know if I want mob money,' she protested.

'Take it,' Phan had said. He moved to Melanie's side and squeezed her slack hand. 'Goodbye, kid. Watch your back.'

So Beth had a lot of money in the traveling bag sitting next to her on the seat. And she was sure, along with Everett, that she would be exonerated of the drug charges.

But getting Melanie back alive was enough reward.

As Everett took the off-ramp from the freeway for Geneva, Beth thought about Jake Mace and how he must have taken this same exit. That one decision more than five years ago had meant the loss of life for so many. At least it had not included her daughter's life.

Paul Makovine was waiting for them at the house. When he hugged her, he hugged her hard, and she wondered how she could have ever disliked the boy. Funny how you can change your mind about people, she thought. Funny how some people walk into your life and everything is changed forever.

He hugged Melanie then, gently, the way you hug a very ill person. Melanie stared at his face the longest time. Then she said, 'Paul.'

The grin Paul gave her was so brilliant Beth could almost see an aura of gold surrounding his shaved head.

Luyba stood in the door calling out, 'I've made a thing to eat. Come in, come in, the bugs are flying.'

Everett walked with a bounce in his step and behind him Beth trailed, her daughter and Paul at her back.

Pope met them at the door. Melanie paused and bent over to retrieve the kitten. 'Hey,' she said. 'I know you . . .'

Everyone was silent, watching the interchange between girl and cat. When Melanie smiled and said, 'Pope,' Beth took a good deep breath and ushered them all into the apartment.

Home at last.